WICKED

MAGGIE GILES

RISING ACTION

Text copyright © 2024 by Maggie Giles.

All rights reserved. For information regarding reproduction in total or in part, contact Rising Action Publishing Co. at http://www.risingactionpublishingco.com

Cover Illustration © Nat Mack
Distributed by Simon & Schuster

ISBN: 978-1-998076-65-9
Ebook: 978-1-998076-67-3

FIC031010 FICTION / Thrillers / Crime
FIC030000 FICTION / Thrillers / Suspense
FIC031000 FICTION / Thrillers / General

#WickedBook

Follow Rising Action on our socials!
Twitter: @RAPubCollective
Instagram: @risingactionpublishingco
Tiktok: @risingactionpublishingco

For Mom and Dad.

For the endless love, countless hugs and being the ones that lift me up whenever I fall.

WICKED

Chapter One

BLAINE ROCHE

The article on the local news page of the *Ottawa Citizen* beckoned him, trying to draw his attention away from surveillance. Blaine drummed his fingers against the glass table in the quaint corner café, eyes darting from the headline to the front door of the office building across the road.

He'd been keeping an eye on the door for nearly twenty minutes now, having finished his coffee after only ten. She was taking her time today. He had been about to leave, thinking perhaps he'd missed her, when the server sauntered by with a refill and the local news page.

Blaine had declined both, but the young woman didn't acknowledge him. He wasn't surprised, having spotted the two white earbuds nearly hidden beneath her messy, purple hair. The paper wouldn't have been of interest to him if not for that one little word sticking out.

Giving in to the temptation, he reached and grabbed the newspaper, flipping it flat and laying the article in front of him.

HERON MAN ARRESTED IN CONNECTION
WITH SANDY HILL MURDER
A suspect has been charged with first-degree murder after

a top ACE Pharmaceutical investor was found dead in a Sandy Hill condo.

Police said Julie Kanner, 28, was found dead the morning of September 5 by her roommate. Rickie Hastings, 34, was arrested yesterday morning (September 9) at 11:50 a.m. Police won't say at this time how, or if, these two people are related.

The investigation is ongoing.

Anyone with information is asked to contact Ottawa Police or Crime Stoppers.

Blaine placed the paper down and reached for his phone, googling Julie Kanner. Her LinkedIn page confirmed his suspicions. Julie wasn't just an investor; she was an employee of ACE pharmaceuticals. She had a connection to Solydexran.

He put his phone away and looked back at the article, wondering if the infamous drug would make an appearance in this case or if it was all just a terrible coincidence.

Before he could consider it further, the office door swung open and Doctor Miranda Konch emerged from within. Abandoning his coffee and leaving a crisp bill on the table, Blaine exited the café, darted across the road and fell into step behind her. He slipped his hood over his head.

Miranda had disappeared after Blaine's girls were arrested. In fear, perhaps, though Blaine couldn't be sure. She abandoned her downtown Toronto office and vanished into the depths of Ottawa, starting a new, quiet practice in the suburb of Orléans.

Blaine had expected the doctor to come out with the truth, to reveal that she'd been paid off to distribute a new and seemingly flawless medication. In fact, Blaine had counted on it. But the good doctor surprised him. She didn't try to save herself, as she had so many times before—instead, she slipped away silently. Blaine couldn't understand why.

He'd been watching her for two weeks now, noting where she went, who she met, and who was also keeping an eye on her. It was the only way he could stay under the radar.

Blaine had been desperate to confront her since the day he found out about her involvement with Solydexran, but after she went to the police, he had to be careful.

Now, several months later, Blaine was sure it was safe. It didn't appear she was under police surveillance or protection, and she lived alone.

When Miranda turned off the main street for the alleyway shortcut she often took, Blaine considered nabbing her then, pulling her aside and drilling her for all the answers he needed. But that wouldn't be discreet. He needed her to trust that he wasn't there to hurt her, despite what she'd told the police.

When they neared her apartment complex, Blaine stayed at a comfortable distance, slipping into the building behind her just as the door was closing. He followed her to the elevator. The once-paranoid doctor seemed unaware of his presence behind her as she waited for the lift, or maybe her guard had lowered after months of nothing.

When the elevator doors slid open, Blaine followed behind her and pressed a button on the floor above hers. He was careful to keep his face hidden beneath the oversized hood.

The doors opened on her floor and she stepped out without so much as a nod in his direction. Blaine waited only a few moments, slipping out before the doors closed. She was at her apartment door now, sliding the key into the lock. Then she disappeared behind the door.

Blaine strode towards it and knocked three times. She couldn't have gone far into the unit. When the door swung open, Miranda looked around with wide eyes. As they fell on Blaine's face and registered who was standing at her door, she quickly tried to close it.

"Miranda, wait," Blaine said, placing his palm on the door and holding it open. He was too strong for her to fight him off. "I just want to talk to you."

Miranda seemed to struggle for a moment longer before admitting defeat. The fear in her eyes said she didn't trust him, but also conceded she couldn't stop him from entering her apartment. As Blaine slipped through the door, he saw her eye the discarded cell phone on her counter.

"I'd rather you didn't," Blaine said, putting himself between her and the phone.

"What do you want, Dr. Wright?" Miranda backed herself away from him, though the wall behind her stopped her from going too far. The way her eyes darted around the apartment told him she was considering any escape possible. Still, she didn't scream, which meant that despite being frightened, she was curious. That would work to his advantage.

"I just have some questions for you." Blaine glanced at the couches beyond the open kitchen, ignoring the formality. "I promise, I'm not here to hurt you. I just need you to tell me some things."

"I don't believe you," Miranda said. "You called me and threatened me."

Blaine frowned. He'd done no such thing. The most he'd done was keep an eye on the doctor; he'd never made contact before today.

"Then you tried to break into my house," Miranda snapped. "Why do you think I left Toronto?"

Slowly, he raised his hands. "I didn't call you and I didn't try to break in, but I think I know who did. If you could talk to me for a minute, maybe I can help you out too." He waved to the couches.

Her raised shoulders didn't lower as she cautiously stepped around him and moved to the couches. Her eyes found the phone again as she passed him by. Blaine followed her steps, keeping the distance between them. She was an older woman, with grey hair and a frail frame. He could overpower her any day and Blaine knew his stature didn't instill much confidence in his assertion of meaning her no harm.

"What do you want to know?" Miranda moved to fold her hands in her lap, but instead she fidgeted and threaded her fingers together.

"Were you paid off to distribute Solydexran?" Blaine asked.

For a moment, the doctor seemed taken aback by the questioning. "You want to know about the drug?"

"Yes," Blaine said. "Were you offered something to start prescribing it?"

"Yes, of course," Miranda said. "It came with a selling bonus. I wasn't interested at first, as it's important my clients only receive the best care, but after I refused a few weeks later, the gentleman returned with substantial results and an increased incentive."

"So, you took it," Blaine said, trying to keep the judgment from his tone. It was difficult to see past the falsified testing and understand how professionals could have classified such a new medication as effective and safe.

"I saw no reason not to," Miranda said. "I started prescribing it to my clients who showed increased anxiety and began to see substantial results."

"You treated Brielle Jeffries for many years, correct?" Blaine asked, referring to one of the women he'd taken into his care.

Miranda nodded. "Since she was a child."

"And you knew about her second personality." Blaine paused, remembering the person that had lived inside Brielle. Though he'd known the truth about her from the beginning, Blaine had struggled not to find the alter, Jackie, endearing. Like Mel, he'd let her in when he should have kept them at arm's length.

Again, Miranda nodded. "Yes, she sought treatment at my facility for several years as an attempt to recover from drug use and to help quell the voice inside her."

"And did you help her?" Blaine asked, though he knew that whatever aid Miranda had given failed years later when Solydexran came into the mix.

"For a time. Until Jackie surfaced again, only a year after her departure."

"You realize now why that was?" Blaine asked. He'd seen the results; he knew the consequences. It was only a matter of time before everyone else did too. He hoped.

"Look, before Brielle began on Solydexran, things were looking up and the results with the drug had been as flawless as the original testing implied. I saw no reason to not start her on it. If anything, I hoped it would alleviate some of the pressures of her home life."

Blaine didn't answer, as they both knew how poorly that had turned out. Solydexran had only worked to amplify Brielle's childhood traumas and bring life to the other being that lived hidden within in her subconscious. The one Blaine had come to know.

"You said you knew who was threatening me," Miranda said.

Blaine nodded. "The same people who have been after me for years. A lot of shady shit went down when the drug came into creation, and someone is trying hard to keep it hidden."

Miranda shook her head. "What does that have to do with me?"

"You know the truth," he said. "You've seen the original reports, you've seen the damage it has done and it's already destroyed you. You have nothing left to do but come clean about Solydexran and the conspiracy around it. But you haven't. Which means you're scared and someone is keeping you scared."

"I'm scared of you," Miranda said, straightening her back as if to show her strength in the words.

"That's probably what they want," Blaine said. Fear had been their tactic in the past. If they knew he was still working against them, then it was only a matter of time before they got to the doctor—or perhaps the detective. Anyone and everyone to clean up their tracks. "Tell me about the guy who brought you the drug. Do you have his contact or a card?"

Miranda shook her head. "It was years ago. I had a sales rep come into my office; he was new to the area and new to the drug trade. He was looking to enter the market with a breakthrough drug."

Blaine couldn't stop his grimace at her response. He'd hoped she would give him more to go on.

"What about names?" he asked. "Do you have information on who you have provided the drug to? Others who could have suffered?"

"That's confidential," Miranda said stiffly. "I could lose my license."

Blaine raised an eyebrow at her. "Are you really worried about that now? The best thing that can happen for you is that the truth comes out and you're far away when it does."

Miranda seemed to consider his words but didn't respond.

"I am trying to fix all of this. Solydexran should have never been created for mass distribution." Blaine shifted, remembering when he'd first discovered the forged reports and the mayhem that followed: the payoffs, the denial, the deaths. "If you give me the names of those who have used it, then I can trace how far and deep the damage goes. I can get closer to revealing the truth, and you may survive."

Miranda still didn't answer him. Instead, she stood and retreated from the room. For a moment, Blaine was worried she'd call the police, but when she returned with a folder in hand, he forgot his concerns.

"This is what I gave the cops months ago," Miranda said. "I'm sure they looked into it, so I'm not sure what you'll be able to find."

Blaine nodded his thanks and took the folder.

"Should I be worried?" Miranda asked. "About my safety?"

Blaine hesitated. "You should be cautious. Continue to keep your profile low and I think you'll be fine. You aren't the biggest player in this and you don't have the evidence to be a major threat to them."

For a moment, he pondered the report he'd so willingly given Detective Ryan Boone back in Toronto. That man was the first officer of the law he'd felt confident in trusting. Now, he'd realized his mistake, as the reports remained buried and Boone's work on the case had all but vanished.

Blaine turned and headed for the door.

"You surprised me," Miranda called after him.

Blaine stopped but didn't turn back to her. "Why, you really thought I'd hurt you?"

"I suppose I always thought that was inevitable, considering what I'd done to someone you loved. But no, I am surprised you didn't ask about *her*—or where she is."

Blaine looked over his shoulder at the doctor. He'd tried not to think about Mel in the months that had passed since their separation, but it had been futile.

"She isn't who I thought she was," Blaine said.

Miranda nodded. "You're right about that. But you're not who she thought you were either, are you?"

Blaine stiffened at the question. "You don't know what you're talking about."

"I know more than you think," Miranda said.

"Then I'd be careful to keep your mouth shut." Blaine didn't give her a chance to respond before he dashed out the door. He gripped the folder tightly as he returned to where he'd parked his car and he didn't risk a look inside at the contents until he was parked at a motel outside of the city.

When he flipped it open, stuck to the list of names was a yellow Post-it note. Patsy's name. The hospital where he could find her and a phone number to reach her.

Mel had been Patsy's alternate personality brought on by abuse and the use of Solydexran. Blaine had met her when he'd been hoping to help her through her struggles, only to fall head over heels for the woman that was Mel. After her arrest, Blaine couldn't be sure that the woman he loved still existed.

As he stared over the nine digits, his heart fluttered with hope for the first time in months. He really could hear her voice again; the only question was if he really wanted to.

Chapter Two

CORA PORTER

The man seated at the table of the prison's visitation room was nothing special. His black hair was messy and stuck to his sweat-covered forehead. His dark, unfocused eyes darted around the empty space. He was small in stature, with narrow shoulders and a long face. Detective Aidan Hunter, seated across from the confused man, asked several questions, but Rickie Hastings didn't give straight responses. All of his answers were jumbled, disordered.

Cora watched through the window, the results of the drug test in her hands. Traces of Solydexran ran in his blood.

"Ms. Porter," someone said from behind her.

Cora turned towards the voice, brushing her cropped black hair from her forehead. "Yes?"

The man who'd addressed her was tall, with dark, slicked-back hair. Light stubble coated his chiseled chin and dark purple lines haunted his eyes, as if he hadn't slept well in months. Still, his lips were turned up and his gaze was bright, interested.

"Detective Ryan Boone." He offered his hand to her. "Your chief sent me in."

She'd heard of him, of course. He worked in the grittiness of Toronto and had been dispatched once his superior had heard about Hastings. Apparently, they'd seen a crime all too similar, with suspects just as messed up as Rickie. Cora had looked into the news for any report of his findings only to come up blank. A part of her wasn't even sure the case existed.

"A pleasure, Detective Boone," Cora said, taking his hand.

"'Detective Boone' is so formal. Someone like you can call me Ryan." He winked, and Cora raised an eyebrow, unsure how to interpret his comment.

"Where's your partner? I was under the impression the department wanted both of you," Cora said.

"Archer is taking some much-deserved stress leave. He has a new baby and this really demanding wife. And we just had a crazy case—" Ryan stopped speaking and smiled sheepishly. "Sorry, I'm not great at reading social cues and tend to overshare. I sometimes forget that not everyone is used to it." He nodded towards the window. "What's going on here?"

Cora cracked a smile at the strange detective. His quirky outbursts were definitely different than the straight-to-business attitude she was used to when working with cops in Ottawa.

"No problem." She passed the drug test to him. "The suspect is Rickie Hastings. He was picked up five days ago at his apartment for the murder of Julie Kanner. Very disoriented and unable to provide us with any information about the occurrence. But the evidence is undeniable."

Ryan flipped through the pages. "He's on Solydexran."

"Yeah, a substantial amount in his blood, too."

"Have you met his alter?"

Cora frowned. "I'm not sure I know what you mean."

"I have found reports that speak of the disastrous side effects of Solydexran," Ryan explained.

"Mood swings, loss of memory, nausea," Cora said. "It's all pretty standard."

"What about schizophrenia or other mental disorders?" Ryan asked. "I had three cases of pretty intensive dissociative identity disorder."

She glanced sideways at him. This was the first she'd heard of DID being involved. Strange that she couldn't find any details on his case. "I had no idea."

"Well, that's no surprise," Ryan said. "I must have really pissed someone off during my investigation."

"Why do you say that?"

"It seems someone was more interested in sweeping my case aside than addressing the real issues." Ryan shook his head as he passed the file back to her. "But we found original reports from the creator of the drug himself that claimed the drug trials were forged. There is a serious consequence to taking this. For some more than others."

"How so?" Cora asked.

"The reports claimed these symptoms only showed up in subjects who were predisposed to mental disorders and had past trauma that could resurface." Ryan glanced at the man sitting in the visitation room. Detective Aidan had started asking about an accomplice, but Rickie just continued to deny any involvement. "How much do you know about Rickie Hastings?"

"He sounds like a bit of a lost soul," Cora said. "Struggling with depression on and off for the last seven years." She looked at Ryan and noticed how his face shifted. His brow furrowed, but his eyes remained focused. "Do you think that would be enough to trigger a negative mental response to the drug?"

"Possibly. My case dealt with a woman who had been abused, a woman who was abducted and a woman who was attacked."

Cora frowned. Those sounded different than what had happened to Rickie.

The conversation inside the room caught her attention. "Thank you, Rickie," Aidan said, standing from the table. "We appreciate your cooperation in this case."

"I'm innocent," Rickie said as the waiting prison guard rounded the table and took him by the arm, ready to escort him back into general population.

Aidan didn't answer him, stepping out of the room and nodding to Ryan.

"Ah, Detective Boone," he said. "Good of you to come." Then he smiled at Cora. "Did that help at all?"

Cora shook her head. She'd known Detective Aidan Hunter from several years of working together with the police department. She'd started as a cop, then gone into forensics. Aidan often did as she asked.

"Ryan here thinks we're dealing with an alternate personality," Cora said.

Aidan looked to the other detective. "Really?"

"Maybe we should discuss this at the station," Ryan said.

"This way." Aidan motioned for them to follow him to a small office opposite that of the warden. They took the chairs around the nearly empty desk.

Cora couldn't help but compare the two detectives. Aidan was easily attractive, with short blond hair that he spiked up carelessly, so it looked like he spent no time on it—Cora knew he spent longer than she did—and grey eyes; he reminded her of a high school ex, a muscular surfer. Even if Aidan's suit didn't strain around his arms, Cora *knew* how strong he was.

Ryan was different, mysterious. He was certainly attractive and had a steady smile despite his concentrated eyes. His dark hair was nearly black and although he wasn't as tall and broad as Aidan, Cora found herself very curious about what was hidden away under his clean suit.

She shook her head to clear the thoughts as Aidan said her name again.

"What about an accomplice?" Ryan asked, seeming to realize that Cora wasn't tuned in. He cast her a knowing smile.

"We've been on the lookout. We have DNA and a partial print, but it doesn't match anything in the system," she replied.

"Who is the victim?"

"A woman in her early thirties. Julie Kanner." Aidan slid the case file across his desk towards Ryan. "Strangled."

"Any relation to the suspect?" Ryan asked, combing through the case file.

"None," Aidan said. "She had a boyfriend, according to her roommate. A man named Noah. She couldn't help us find him and we have no idea where to look. Whoever he is, he's gone."

"Our own Cherie Curry?" Ryan chuckled.

Cora raised an eyebrow.

"Who?" Aidan said.

"A runaway?" Ryan gave a stiff laugh, then waved them off. "Sorry, bad joke. Anyway, how does Hastings tie into this?"

Cora smiled, amused by Ryan's cheesy comment, though not surprised that Aidan had missed the Runaways reference. "Hastings was found near the scene and had the murder weapon on him."

Ryan flipped the page. "A necktie?"

"We thought it was strange too," Aidan said.

"With this evidence, I'm surprised Rickie would *hang* around to get caught in his own noose," Ryan quipped.

Cora cracked a smile. Okay, that one was *really* bad.

"What's this?" Ryan asked, flipping the page when neither answered him. It was another picture of the tie, of the small tag, which had three letters embroidered into it: *ISK*.

"We're not sure," Aidan said. "Seems like it may not belong to Mr. Hastings."

Cora gripped the arm of her chair. They were familiar initials. *His* face flashed in her mind. She hasn't spoken to him in days. No, she wouldn't believe it. A coincidence, that was all.

"Is there any evidence that suggests an accomplice?" Ryan asked.

Aidan turn his laptop around. "Security footage."

Cora leaned forward. This was the first she'd heard about surveillance. The footage showed a black car pulling up to the front of the building. Two people with their hoods drawn got out of the car and entered the apartment. Then Aidan hit fast-forward until they saw one of the people run back to the car and hop in before driving it, screeching, down the street. Several minutes later, another person emerged. He was stumbling, confused, and then he looked directly into the camera. Rickie Hastings.

"So, whoever brought him left him behind?" Ryan asked, looking back to the file when Aidan turned his computer back towards him. "Talk about a job gone wrong."

"That's what it looks like."

"Did you get a license plate?" Ryan asked.

Cora frowned. She hadn't heard about any of this yet. Aidan must have been holding out on her. That was out of character. Was he upset with her?

Aidan nodded at Ryan. "It's for a silver sedan we picked up near the crime scene. We've been scanning the car but haven't found anything yet."

"Who owns it?"

Aidan leaned back with a smug smile. "Can you guess?"

"Mr. Hastings," Ryan said.

"Mr. Hastings."

Cora leaned back in her chair her eyebrows drawn together. Rickie Hastings didn't look like a man who'd committed murder. He looked as confused as he'd been for the past few days that they've had him in custody. Something didn't fit. The boyfriend they couldn't find, Noah, had to be involved. Wasn't that the way these things usually went, especially since the guy seemed completely MIA?

Cora realized she'd missed something when Ryan stood to leave. He and Aidan shook hands and then Aidan pointed at the case file.

"Review that, and we'll get to work on it first thing. You can speak to Hastings in the morning if you think it will help."

"Great."

"Are you staying in town?" Cora asked.

Ryan nodded. "A hotel nearby."

"Give the information to the station when you leave," Aidan said. "The department will cover your tab." He looked to Cora. "Will you stay a minute please?"

He *was* upset with her.

Cora stood and grasped Ryan's hand. "Thanks for coming. If you have a minute, could you forward those reports on Solydexran you were talking about? I think it will help the investigation."

"Of course."

"And call if you need anything," Aidan said.

Ryan left, closing the door behind him.

"What did you need?" Cora asked, poised to leave as well.

When Aidan turned to face her, his expression had changed. Cora knew this look well. The torture in his eyes. His slightly parted lips. His hand quivered and he stepped towards her, looking from her eyes to her lips and back.

"You didn't call me back last night." His voice was low, husky.

Cora stepped back. "Is now really the time?"

"If not now, then when?" Aidan asked. "Because I know you won't call me."

"Isaac was over last night," Cora said. "I couldn't call you." But he wasn't. She hadn't heard from Isaac in several days. She'd tried calling, but he never called back. Cora was starting to worry. Worse, he was supposed to be picking up their daughter. What time was it now? She should check in.

Aidan's jaw tightened at the mention of Cora's ex-husband. "I thought you weren't seeing him anymore."

"I'm not," Cora said. "But I also won't deny Lyssa her father."

The man stepped closer to her. "Lyssa doesn't need a deadbeat like Isaac. She could have me." Another step. "You could have me." He leaned down and kissed her.

Cora allowed him, but only for a moment. Then she pulled away. "Now really isn't the time."

Aidan ran a hand through his hair. "There's never a good time, is there?" He moved away from her, falling into his chair and waking up his laptop.

"Aidan . . ." Cora said, but she stopped herself from going any further. They had a complicated relationship. Which was really no surprise since Cora's entire life was filled with complicated relationships.

"It's fine," Aidan said, his business voice on now. "We have a case to solve. I get it."

Cora hesitated by the door for a moment, unsure what to say. She and Aidan had never been official. Only friends, but more. He knew Lyssa well because Cora's seven-year-old daughter had spent hours at the station while Cora was working, on the days Isaac failed as a father.

"It's fine, Cora," Aidan said again, closing his laptop and slipping it into his briefcase. "You know that."

Cora nodded but didn't answer, turning for the door. He'd call her later; he always called.

She headed to her car, but before she got there, her phone started ringing. She half expected Aidan to be calling her already, but instead Isaac's name flashed across the phone.

"Isaac, where the hell have you been?" Cora asked.

"Cora, don't hate me," Isaac said through the receiver. He didn't bother to answer her question.

She bit down on her lip. He was about to bail. This was his usual line.

"You promised last month," Cora said. "Lyssa is expecting you today."

"I know, but I can't make it. I need you to go get her."

Cora glanced to the time on her watch. Lyssa's day was nearly done. Cora wouldn't make it in time. She would be waiting. Lyssa was always waiting.

"Isaac, you can't keep doing this," she said. "It's not fair to her."

There was a frustrated sigh on the other end of the phone. "Lay off, Cora. I said I can't be there. I'll make it up to her."

"You say that every time." Cora pulled open the door to her car and slipped into the driver's side before clicking a few buttons to get the phone on speaker. She glanced at the clock. "What's your excuse this time?"

"I said lay off." His voice hardened.

"Fine," Cora said. "I don't know what I expected anyway. You've been doing this for years." She clicked to end the call before he had a chance to answer. Gripping the steering wheel harder than necessary, she turned the car onto the main road, heading towards Lyssa's school.

She frowned and took a quick glance at her phone as she pulled up to a red light. Where had Isaac been this last week? Why was he being so evasive? Part of Cora didn't care. If Isaac wanted to do this with his life, he could. It wasn't her problem . . . but it was her daughter's. She looked over her list of calls. Ten times she'd called him over the last few days, without success. The name "Isaac Kirby" populated her recent call list. She tossed her phone aside, unable to shake the uncomfortable feeling. Isaac Simon Kirby.

Cora didn't know where he was. Cora didn't know what he did, but it probably wasn't good. She was starting to believe Isaac had cracked—and the initials "ISK" weren't as mysterious as the police department thought.

Chapter Three

NOAH BAKER

Every siren made Noah jump. It didn't matter whether it was an ambulance or a police cruiser, they all put him on edge. He was still sleepless, haunted by memories of that night. He hadn't planned plan on killing Julie. It just happened.

Grace had lost control. She was temperamental, jealous. She'd never liked Julie. Noah couldn't stop her. He didn't want to hurt her. He simply loved Grace more. Besides, things with Julie had gone downhill. This was her fault.

Julie shouldn't have said the things she had. She shouldn't have threatened them.

Noah slumped against the wall beneath a bridge, which rattled as a car thundered by overhead. He'd been here since it happened, surrounded by the unhoused and those with drug addictions. He was one of them now. He couldn't go back to his house. He had a prior relationship with Julie. The police would figure that out if they hadn't already.

"You're new," a woman's voice said, breaking through Noah's repeating thoughts.

He glanced towards the woman. She was slender, from starvation or drugs, maybe both. Her cheeks were sunken and black circles rested beneath her eyes.

"Actually, *you* are," Noah said. "I've been here for a week." Or at least he thought it had been a week. Maybe less. His mind had been a fuzzy mess since that night.

She settled down on the ground next to him, leaning her head on his shoulder.

Noah stiffened at the contact but didn't move away.

"They call me Marigold," she said. Then she pointed to a man who was curled up under a ripped sleeping bag. "That fella there tells me you dream of a girl named Grace." She slid closer to him, pushing her frail body against his. "I could be Grace if you wanted."

Noah pushed her off him, then stood and moved away. "I'm not interested."

No one could be Grace.

"What the hell?" Marigold snapped, pushing herself to her feet. She swung her hand back to slap him, but he caught her wrist and pushed her away. She stumbled backward and fell to the ground, scraping her elbow in the process. It quickly pooled with blood as she yelped in pain. Noah made a swift exit as another man sauntered over. He didn't want to stick around and find out what happened next.

Noah ducked under the overhang of the bridge and onto the street. He was immediately pelted with rain, soaking his jacket and black hair, the ends of the strands tickling his neck as they stuck to him. For a moment, it reminded him of Grace, the way her fingers would slide across his cheek and down his neck, caressing him gently with her short nails. How she would tug playfully on the ends of his hair, which had grown too long.

Noah sometimes wondered why he was so drawn to her. They'd known each other only a few months. They hadn't even had sex—Grace said she wasn't ready.

But something about her held Noah. Her tender smile. Her loving gaze. Her gentle southern drawl. She was like no one he'd ever met. He knew how cliché that sounded.

Tires screeched as a car raced around the corner past Noah. He shuddered as the perfect image of Grace faded from his memories and Julie's frightened eyes took over again. It was a haunting image, one he'd been unable to shake. The way she stared at him, realizing he was going to let her die.

Noah hadn't registered it then. The whole incident seemed like an awful dream. Like he was watching someone else's life. But it wasn't a dream. Julie was dead and he'd let it happen.

The clouded sky hid the stars from view, darkening the night. Very few streetlights lit this area and Noah found himself squinting in the blackness to make out his steps. He was on the run, but he remained in the city. Why hadn't he left yet? He told himself it was because of Grace, but it wasn't.

He already missed his life. He missed *her*. He couldn't even remember the last time he'd really seen her. Not that she ever knew when he watched her from afar.

The image of her face appeared in his mind and he willed it away. It wouldn't do to dwell on fantasies.

Instead, Noah thought about Grace. Her hearty laugh, her rose-petal lips, her warm, playful kisses. Noah missed Grace. He wished that was enough to stop the anger from twisting through him. He wished he could justify Julie's death, if only because of his love for Grace. But he couldn't.

Then there was the guilt. Guilt for Julie's death, guilt for leaving Grace behind, guilt for feeling relief at being alone.

When had his life gone all wrong? Julie was a sweet girl. Too many years younger than him. She'd gotten involved way too quickly. Noah had never intended for things to be serious with her. Life was too complicated for that.

When he met Grace, it was different. Grace understood him. She saw him for what he was and could see how he struggled to be better. She was the same, with her own demons to fight, and she helped fight his.

Julie was just an unfortunate accident. She shouldn't have gotten in the way. She should have just left them alone. If only she hadn't threatened Grace. If only Noah had stopped her.

Shivering in the night air, he ducked under an awning in an alleyway and leaned against the cool brick wall, hoping to wait out the rain.

Noah closed his eyes for a minute, trying to remember the events of the previous week.

Julie had wanted to tell him something that night. What was it? She'd left him a message claiming she had something important to say. She told him not to bring Grace.

When Grace overheard, she got angry. She wouldn't listen to Noah before storming off to confront Julie.

Noah shouldn't have gone with her—maybe it wouldn't have gone as far. He'd thought he could stop her. He should have known better.

Once Grace got something in her mind, that was how it was. Grace always got what she wanted, especially when it came to Noah. He couldn't seem to deny her, no matter what. Even if it meant someone died.

That was just Grace.

Noah shook his head but couldn't rid his mind of the awful memories.

Grace and Julie had argued. Julie had called Grace a freak and screamed several slurs towards them as a couple. Nasty, confusing words. Julie ran for Grace. Her eyes were wide, crazed, her hands outstretched, reaching for Grace's neck as she screamed that she was a monster. But Grace was faster.

Grace pushed Julie to the ground and grabbed the discarded necktie from the back of the chair, wrapping it around her neck and squeezing it. Julie clawed at the tie, desperately trying to break free.

Noah could only watch, paralyzed by the struggle before him, until a siren sounded in the distance. Then he ran. He hopped into the car, not waiting for Grace.

He left her there, still strangling Julie.

Why had he left her behind? Noah squeezed his eyes shut and tried to think of what had been running through his mind. They lived in a city. Sirens went off every day. Most likely, the one he'd heard hadn't been for them. It was just a coincidence.

Noah couldn't remember what he'd been thinking and why he'd abandoned the woman he loved. It all seemed like a horrible dream.

He reached up and scratched his neck, brushing his long hair aside. His collar was open, his dress shirt half-buttoned and dirty. He'd worn these clothes for too long. He'd need something better, and soon—he could smell his own stench.

Another siren in the distance made him freeze. He knew Grace had one friend in a nearby neighbourhood. Caroline. A woman near forty, living in a house uptown. They'd discussed her once, when Grace insisted that he know exactly where she was one night. Noah remembered her address.

Grace always said Caroline would be the first person she would go to if she was ever in trouble. She'd once advised Noah to do the same. Though he couldn't be sure what to expect from a woman he'd never met, he had no other options.

Noah glanced down the alleyway. It was dark, but it looked empty and the back portion was more covered. He would stay here for the night; he'd been in worse places. He'd head to find Grace's friend when the rain had cleared and the sun rose.

Chapter Four

CORA PORTER

Isaac's knock resounded like a herald of uncertainty as it echoed through the front hall. Lyssa ran to the front door, grabbed the handle and pulled it open.

"Daddy!" she cried out when she saw him. Her black, braided pigtails bounced as she jumped into his arms.

"Hey baby girl," Isaac said, smiling at his daughter and lifting her off the floor.

Cora watched them from the stairs, just inside the house. Isaac seemed to feel her gaze. He glanced at her, placing Lyssa back on the floor.

He was dressed in his usual black T-shirt and a pair of ripped jeans. His long hair was pulled back and the stubble on his face had grown longer than usual, camouflaging the scar that traced from his cheek to his chin. His narrow brown eyes were almost bloodshot and Cora worried for a second that he was high.

When he nodded in her direction and smiled, she released the breath she'd been holding. It was sober Isaac.

"Sorry I'm late," he said.

"You aren't," Cora said, shrugging. He *was* late by almost twenty minutes, but at least he was here.

"You'll pick her up in two days?" Isaac asked.

"I'll get her from school." Cora walked closer to them, taking Lyssa by the shoulders. "Run upstairs and grab your backpack, honey."

Lyssa scurried up the stairs, leaving Cora and Isaac alone.

"Where were you last night?" Cora asked. "You sounded stressed. Did something happen?" All she could think of was the embroidery on the tie.

Isaac rubbed the back of his neck. "It's a long story. But nothing to worry about."

"When it involves Lyssa, I will always worry." Cora stepped closer to him. "You have to be careful with her. She loves you and we don't want her to take after you."

His jaw tightened. "What's that supposed to mean?"

"You know what it means, Isaac."

"I'm clean," he said. "Not a drop or a hit in weeks."

Cora frowned. That wasn't as convincing as he meant it to be. "You've been clean already. It's failed already, too."

Before Isaac could answer, Lyssa's steps thundered down the staircase.

"Ready!" She grinned and threw an arm around Cora's waist, squeezing tight. "See you soon, Mommy."

Cora leaned down and kissed Lyssa's forehead. "See you soon, honey."

Lyssa pulled away and took Isaac's hand.

"Call me when you get back to your place, okay?" Cora said.

"I always do," he replied.

"And tomorrow," Cora rushed out before he could turn away, "let's grab lunch while Lyssa is at school. I think we need to catch up."

Isaac eyed her with suspicion, but after a second, he shrugged. "Sure thing."

Cora stood at the door and watched them climb into Isaac's car. Lyssa waved to her from the back seat. Cora didn't close the front door until they'd backed out of the driveway and started driving down the road. She'd be anxious until she heard her phone chime, confirming they were at Isaac's house.

Cora went to the kitchen, where she had already poured her second glass of wine. She had plans for tonight. A bath, maybe candles and wine. A lot of wine. It had been a while since Isaac had taken Lyssa for a night. Longer since Cora'd had a night alone.

The phone chimed when she was halfway done with her first glass. Isaac, confirming their arrival with a text and wishing her a good night. She took her wine to the couch and considered running that bubble bath. The thought was interrupted by another knock at her door.

Frowning, Cora placed her wine aside and went to answer it. She wasn't expecting any guests.

Standing on the front step was Detective Ryan Boone. He looked better than he had the previous evening, clean-shaven and in a fresh suit. The bags under his eyes were gone. She hadn't seen him at the police station that day, so he must have rested well.

"Hi," Cora said. "What are you doing here?" It was strange he'd shown up unannounced. How did he know where she lived?

"Sorry." Ryan shifted in place. "I sort of realized how weird this might be right after I knocked. I got your address from Detective Hunter." He held up a file. "You weren't at the station when I stopped by and I wanted to give you these."

She took the file to find the reports that he had been talking about the previous day. The ones on Solydexran and Dr. Calvin Wright, the creator.

"Thank you," Cora said.

When Ryan didn't make a move to leave, she glanced over her shoulder, considering the night she had planned, but she stepped aside anyway. "Did you want to come in?"

"If you don't mind," Ryan said. "I'd like to discuss that with you."

Cora allowed him to enter and directed him to the sitting room where she'd come from.

He glanced at the glass of wine as they passed. "Did I interrupt anything?"

"No," Cora said. "My daughter was just picked up by her father. I hardly ever get a night alone."

"I feel bad I'm intruding on it." He seemed to hesitate, but Cora shook her head.

"It's okay; I invited you in."

"If you're sure," Ryan said as he settled onto the couch.

Cora sat beside him and flipped open the folder he gave her. "Where did you find these?" She shuffled through the papers. They were old, stained, and tattered. Weathered by age.

"The research doctor owns property in Toronto. It was connected with my case," Ryan explained. "We searched the place and found them."

Cora scanned the files. They outlined the information that he'd spoken of the day before. Reports that showed irregularities in testing and links to extreme mental disorders.

Ryan reached for the file. "Hunter mentioned that no other personality has surfaced. But many of the facts in this case are remarkably similar to the one I worked on. I feel like there is an alter that hasn't come out yet."

"And you think the alter committed the murder?"

"It seems like the most likely option right now, from what I've been told." Ryan reached forward, grabbing one of the pages from the file. His arm brushed Cora's leg and she immediately flushed. He passed her the page. Their fingers touched for only a moment, but Cora felt the heat pass between them. She resisted the urge to fan herself. Was it discomfort or something else that put her on edge? Maybe she shouldn't have invited someone who was practically a stranger into her home.

The report spoke of a test subject with severe depression. After only a month on the trial, his depression was gone, but two personalities had surfaced.

"It's impossible that these results didn't get out," Cora said, placing the report down and picking up another. "The trial was clearly a failure."

Ryan shook his head. "There is no record of these findings, which is why the drug made it to the market."

"The trial results were falsified," Cora concluded. "But why?" And how?

"I'm not sure." Ryan flipped through the files until he found the picture of a man in a lab coat. "But this man, Calvin Wright, has something to do with it."

Cora had heard the name before. He was a former research doctor working with narcotics. Deceased. She remembered hearing when he died. It was a terrible accident, around five years ago.

"Dr. Wright is dead," Cora said. "He can't help you."

"I have reason to believe he's still alive. He goes by an alias, Blaine Roche."

Cora shook her head. "It's not possible. I remember Wright's death."

For years, Cora had had an affinity for the obituaries. After seeing so much death in her day job, from dangerous cases to abuse, the obits offered her a moment of reprieve. No one ever spoke poorly of their dead loved ones. It helped center her in a weird way and counteract the trauma of the job.

Ryan raised an eyebrow. "Did you ever see a body?"

"No." But what did that matter? Someone had to have confirmed that he died. Wasn't that enough?

"Then who's to say if he's really dead or not."

Cora frowned. "Are you saying that this whole case is only a smaller part of a much larger conspiracy around this medication?"

"That's my theory."

"Have you told Aidan this?" Cora asked.

"Hunter wasn't too interested in hearing my theories." Ryan shrugged. "He seems to only want hard facts."

Cora cracked a smile. "Is there a problem with that?"

"Not at all," Ryan replied. "I'm sure it makes him an exceptionally good detective. And a bit of a pompous ass. He should take more risks, though I gather he doesn't."

No, Aidan wasn't known for his risk-taking. He followed procedure and he followed the facts.

"This theory seems pretty based on fact," Cora said, looking back to the reports in her hands. Unless *these* reports had been falsified. Something about this drug was a lie, one way or another.

"I've been trying to track down Blaine Roche ever since we brought in the women from my case," Ryan said. "He knows something more than any of us and I think we need to find him to figure this all out, at least until there is another lead."

Cora nodded. "How do we find him?"

"We'll need to find all we can on Calvin Wright and his death," Ryan suggested. "Maybe that will tell us what Blaine Roche is planning."

They sat in silence then, but Cora found herself curious about the man beside her. "Could you tell me more about Toronto and the case you just had?"

Ryan grinned. "What do you want to know?"

She hesitated, knowing she should ask about the job but instead finding herself inclined to ask about Ryan. "You mentioned your partner was off with his family—yours didn't mind letting you go?" Cora tried to imagine what it would be like to be called out of Ottawa to assist on a case. She couldn't imagine leaving Lyssa behind.

"You're looking at a lone wolf." Ryan chuckled. "No one is missing me."

"I'm sure your partner would disagree."

"Archer has been a friend for a long time," Ryan said. "It's good for us to get a break every now and then."

"I guess it makes it easier to be a workaholic?" Cora asked, raising an eyebrow.

"Guilty as charged." Ryan lifted his hands in mock defense. "I'm married to the job, as they say."

"You never thought about finding someone to spend your life with?" Cora asked, unsure why she was getting so personal with him. His lone-wolf status intrigued her. Other than Lyssa, she felt the same.

A pained look flashed across Ryan's face as he looked away from her and Cora's ease suddenly vanished.

"I'm sorry," she said quickly. "I shouldn't pry."

Ryan looked back at her and waved off her concern. "You aren't. I was married, but I lost my wife a few years back. It's funny how wounds heal. I know I'm okay, but the scar sometimes feels fresh."

Cora could relate. Though Isaac wasn't dead, sometimes it felt like he was further gone than she could ever reach.

"I'm sorry," Cora said, unsure how else to comfort him.

"Don't be." Ryan's smile returned. "I don't often get to think about her and tonight you've given me a reason."

Cora forced a smile. "Glad I could help." Though she felt stupid bringing it up. His single status definitely interested her, but he was a colleague after all. What was she really expecting? Another fling like Aidan?

Ryan reached out and patted her knee, the movement stilted but oddly affectionate. "And you?"

"Other than Lyssa, I'm pretty untethered." She looked down at her hands. "A bit of a workaholic myself."

"I guess we're just two peas," Ryan said with a wink. Then he stood. "I should probably get going, but thank you for letting me in. I wanted to get you that info. I'll leave you to the rest of your evening."

Cora followed him back to the front entrance. At the door, Ryan turned back and smiled. "Thanks for inviting me in. I'm glad you're open to my ideas and that we can discuss this."

"Of course," Cora said. "I'm happy to help however I can."

"It doesn't hurt that you're nice to look at," Ryan added. "Certainly better than my last partner."

She let out a stiff laugh. "We'll look into this tomorrow."

"Good night, Cora," he said. Then he headed out the door and turned towards his car.

"Good night, Ryan."

Cora watched him from the door for a moment, thrown by their strange interaction. It was professional; after all, they'd mostly discussed work. But his sudden arrival, the heat she'd felt and his comment about her looks all seemed like something else and he seemed as untethered to the concept of relationships as she did.

She shrugged off the strange feeling swirling around inside her as she closed the door. Maybe that was how things were done in Toronto.

Chapter Five

BLAINE ROCHE

Blaine waited until the nurse stepped out of the on-call room of the mental health hospital in Newmarket before glancing around and entering. Inside was empty. The lockers were at the back. He was quick to find scrubs that fit and changed into them, shoving his other clothes into his backpack. He pinned a false pass on his breast pocket and exited the on-call room. None of the passing doctors gave him a second glance.

He checked the area before slipping into the hallway that led to Mel's room. He counted the doors as he walked down the hall until he reached seven. With one last glance, he slipped into the room to find it vacant. His stiff shoulders relaxed. He'd expected her to be here.

The care center advertised security and privacy. Blaine found it amusing how easily he'd been able to gain access to the inside unnoticed.

The room was uninteresting, with plain grey walls, one tiny, barred window, and very little furniture—only a desk, a small dresser, and a single bed. All white.

Blaine closed the door behind him and moved toward the bed. He checked under the mattress but found nothing. Then he moved to the dresser, pulling the drawers open one by one. They were filled with plain clothes. Nothing like what she used to wear. Where had she hidden it?

A pit formed in his stomach. He almost wanted to see her. It had been one thing to hear her voice for those brief five minutes, but it would be another to see her standing before him. It'd been over five months since he laid eyes on her. He'd tried to follow the trial and keep an eye on the girls, but there hadn't been any coverage. In fact, he'd found no record of their arrest anywhere. Like the case had been covered up.

He moved to the desk on the opposite side of the room and dropped to his knees. He felt underneath, his fingers finding the slick surface of tape. A slip of folded paper, something she had promised would help. Blaine pulled it out and shoved it into his pocket. He was standing to leave when the door opened and she entered the room.

"Oh." Her voice jumped an octave higher than he was used to. "What are you doing in my room?"

Blaine turned and regarded the woman he loved. A long white robe wrapped her body. Her once long and luscious hair was pulled back and frizzy; her wide, blue eyes were glassy. She looked as unsettled as the others living here.

She cocked her head to the side. "Blaine. You came?"

"Melanie?" he asked.

She smiled and shook her head. "I haven't seen Melanie in days."

"But you know me."

He'd made himself known to Patsy more than once in their time together, but she never seemed to recognize him. Not like this.

Patsy pushed the door shut behind her. "Of course. You were very important to Melanie, or to me, I suppose."

Blaine frowned. "How much do you know about Melanie?"

Patsy moved farther into the room, stripping off the white robe before going to the desk. She slid her hand beneath it.

"You found it." She smiled in a way that made him pause.

Mel hadn't been one to wear a steady grin, but Blaine knew every curve of her body. Including the one on her lips that she reserved mostly for him. It sent a pang of regret trembling through him, making his legs weak. All those months ago, he thought he'd done the right thing, letting that detective find her. But seeing her again, he wished he'd never let her go.

A part of him wanted to reach out for her, to draw her against him and take her in his arms. Blaine forced himself to stay still. No matter how much he missed her, this woman wasn't Melanie Parker.

"I wondered if you'd come," Patsy said when he didn't respond. She glided across the room, moving towards him.

He stepped back, careful to avoid her. "Melanie told me to."

"I know." Patsy still wore that playful smile.

Blaine wasn't sure what else to say. Patsy had always been quiet, frightened, but it seemed like the months she'd spent here had done wonders. She seemed almost at ease. Almost like Mel.

"The doctors helped," Patsy said. She continued to watch him with amusement.

"Helped what?" Blaine asked. He shifted under her gaze, unsure what to feel. Part of him longed to hold this woman who looked so much like Mel. But he knew Patsy wasn't the one he'd fallen for and her clear change in personality put him on edge.

"With knowing Melanie. I'm on different medication. It's seemed to change things. I've been able to access that side of me, away from all the terror I endured." Patsy took another step closer to Blaine. "She really loved you, you know. You protected her. You kept us safe."

He stiffened at her words, but she spoke the truth. "I loved her too."

"She wants to help," Patsy said. "That's why she called you back."

"Melanie always wanted to tie up loose ends." Blaine thought to the paper he'd taken only minutes before. Last week, he'd left a message for Patsy, against his better judgment. He'd had one too many drinks and the loneliness had taken hold. When Mel called him back only two days later, he worried that he'd messed up her treatment. Worse, she had given no clues to what she wanted him to have, only that it would help him. Now Blaine wondered if it had been Patsy all along. Was she playing him?

"That's not it. When you told her your secret before the arrest, about what happened, she knew she needed to help. She understands. She wants to do this for you." Patsy reached up and twirled her messy hair. "She knows more than she let on. It's time you do too."

"How can you help me?" Blaine asked. "You're locked up in here." He wished he'd looked more closely at the paper before he took it, wished he could better understand her.

A knowing smile crept across Patsy's lips. "I'm not the one helping you, Blaine. It's Melanie. She's the one who knows."

"And what does she know?"

"She knows that you'll find him and the truth will come out," Patsy said in a lower voice. "Even I'm sure of it."

"How?"

Patsy reached out and slipped her hand into his pocket before he could stop her. She pulled out the folded piece of paper. "It's all right here. Melanie wrote it for you. You really should have come sooner. She's been waiting for days."

"I didn't think I should come," Blaine said, taking the paper from her hand and putting it back in his pocket. He didn't want her to touch him again. It was too weird. "I thought it might screw something up."

"But I'm just fine." Patsy stepped closer to him. Her eyes darted to his lips for a second before taking him in fully again. "They take care of me in here. And you take care of me out there."

"I was taking care of Melanie." Blaine leaned away from her.

"Yes, you were and she never appreciated that." Patsy shook her head. "You were very good to us."

Blaine didn't like how Patsy used the word "us" to refer to her relationship with Mel. He turned for the door.

Patsy reached out and grabbed his arm. "Are you leaving so soon? I thought you'd stay awhile." A familiar smirk spread across her face and Blaine hesitated a moment. The touch was familiar too. The grin and the games.

Blaine cocked his head to the side. "Mel?"

Patsy shook her head, but the smirk didn't fade. "I told you, I haven't seen Melanie in days."

Blaine stared at her, unsure what to say.

"So, are you staying or not?" Patsy put on a playful pout.

He stepped away from her, the confused feeling twisting around inside him. "I have to go. But don't worry. I will make this right."

Blaine turned and left her room without waiting for a response. He wasn't sure who that woman was. It seemed like Melanie, but Patsy denied it. He shuddered as he slipped out of the psychiatric ward. There was an eerie feeling of familiarity, yet he felt like they were strangers.

When Mel and Patsy were separate, they'd had clearly defined personalities, but now . . . it seemed like Patsy had engulfed the person that Mel was. Were they really one and the same? He shook his head. Of course they were the same person. But whatever this place was doing to her was just too strange.

It didn't matter. He'd given up Melanie months ago when he'd let them all go. He had what he came for. He had to leave before anything, or anyone, stopped him.

At his car, he changed his clothes and slipped into the driver's side. He glanced up at the imposing care center and considered that Mel hadn't ended up in such a bad place, not for committing murder—they'd been lenient on her. There would be a trial. She was cooped up in a mental health hospital until then, but Blaine suspected it would end up being self-defence or manslaughter if the case went to trial. He doubted Patsy would be released from the hospital anytime soon.

He'd tried to follow their charges and convictions, but as soon as the girls entered the system, they all but vanished. If there had been hearings, they had been kept quiet. If what Boone had found out about Solydexran had been passed on, then someone had swept the results under the rug.

Blaine had hoped the news would surface, that the drug would be pulled from the market and the company investigated, but so far, nothing. He regretted giving up the one shred of evidence he'd been holding on to. He'd trusted the wrong cop.

But this wasn't the end. As more came out about the effects of Solydexran, the case would change from the women being criminals and instead they—like too many others—would be the victims.

Blaine pulled onto the street, taking a moment to consider Jackie and Candy. He didn't know what had happened to the latter. She had no one to vouch for her, no family behind her and no name to consider. He'd tried looking into Lexi Chase more than once but could never find out much.

Jackie had been different. Brielle Jeffries had money, connections, prestige. It was easy for her family to push for a private facility with personal care. They could afford it, after all. She was the least accessible, but Blaine doubted that Jackie or Candy's real personas would know who he was. Or care to help.

Blaine turned down a side street and pulled over. He fished the paper out of his pocket, desperate to read the clues Mel had left behind. He broke the tape that held it together and found an address scrawled in blue ink. Beneath it were three sets of numbers. Possibly coordinates, though they seemed too short.

Frowning, Blaine typed the address into his GPS. It was a private care facility in Kingston. Why would Mel send him there?

He then tried the numbers. All came up with nothing he could tie them to.

The care facility was just under two hours' drive away. The sun was already going down. Blaine would be sleeping in his car either way—if he got any rest at all. He turned back onto the road and headed to the care facility. All the while, he tried to figure out why Melanie would send him to an old facility in a town he was certain she'd never visited.

Chapter Six

CORA PORTER

Cora glanced at her phone for the third time since she'd sat down. Isaac was late for their lunch meeting. Typical. She only hoped he'd dropped Lyssa off at school on time.

She had just swiped up, posed to write him a message, when the bell over the door rang and Isaac sauntered through. He found her quickly and in a few short strides was through the restaurant and taking the seat across from her.

"Sorry," he mumbled, reaching for the glass of water that had been waiting for him. "Got held up on a work call."

Cora nodded, knowing better than to question him about work or the real reason he was late. Isaac was a carpenter with his own business. He made his own schedule and worked a lot of custom jobs. Cora didn't ask him about money, as he paid child support regularly and kept his own apartment. Those had been the stipulations when custody was determined.

"Everything okay?"

Isaac eyed her but then nodded. "Yeah, fine. Nothing I can't handle."

Before Cora could question what he meant by that, the server came by and asked for their order. Cora and Isaac had been meeting at this bistro every month for nearly three years. Their orders rarely changed and today was no different.

After Isaac requested the Reuben on rye and Cora ordered her usual club wrap, the server vanished, leaving the two alone.

"Do you want to tell me what's going on, or am I going to have to guess?" Cora asked, jumping right into the problem at hand.

"What are you talking about?" Isaac asked.

Cora pursed her lips. She hated when he played dumb.

"Where were you?" Cora thought back to the phone call when he'd bailed on picking up Lyssa. "You were supposed to pick her up. She was devastated and I had to cover for you . . . again."

Isaac rolled his eyes. "Then stop covering for me."

Cora's chest tightened as the anger swelled up inside her. "I don't do it for your sake."

She bit down on her lip to keep the string of frustrations bubbling inside her from coming out. She was tired of lying, tired of seeing the disappointment on Lyssa's face and tired of being the bad guy. Why couldn't Isaac just show up and be a decent dad?

"Look, I'm sorry," Isaac said, putting his hands up in defence. "I get it. I screwed up. All I can do is tell you I won't again."

Cora stared at him for a few moments, taking in the man she used to love. He'd lost weight since their youth, from lack of sleep or drugs or stress, Cora never really knew and the dark blue bags under his eyes told her that something or someone was keeping him up at night. She didn't care if it was the latter. All that mattered to Cora was Lyssa.

"You promise you're clean?" She kept her voice quiet.

Isaac's eyes flashed with annoyance, but the look quickly vanished as his gaze softened and he reached across the table to grip her hand. For a moment, Cora appreciated the warmth he offered.

"Yes," Isaac said. "I know I haven't always been the best father, but I assure you, Lyssa is the most important thing to me. I would never do anything to harm her. If I didn't trust myself with her, I wouldn't take her. I promise you that."

Cora closed her eyes and allowed his words to sink in. All she wanted was for Isaac to be the dad Lyssa needed. But Cora also had to let him try and prove himself. She had to let her past judgment go.

When she opened her eyes again, she gave Isaac a small smile. "Okay. I trust you."

He nodded and pulled away from her. An easy smile fell into place. "Now, with all the scrutiny out of the way, tell me what you're working on."

Cora smiled. She shared about the strange case they'd encountered and the Toronto-based detective who'd come up to join their team. She didn't mention his abrupt visit to her house the night before, or the fact that he hadn't been far from her mind since. Instead, she tried to focus on Isaac and their conversation, all the while realizing that Isaac had never really answered her first question.

Isaac leaned in and kissed Cora on the cheek before leaving the restaurant. She handled the bill and was making her way out to her waiting car when her phone started ringing. Hadley's name and number popped up on the screen.

"Hey Hads," Cora said, bringing the phone to her ear, as she waded through the parking lot towards her sedan.

"Girl, where have you been?" her best friend said. "I've messaged you like ten times."

Cora rolled her eyes. Hadley had texted her twice.

"I was having lunch with Isaac."

"Ew, why?"

Cora laughed. Hadley had never been a fan of her ex. Well, that wasn't true. When they were younger, Cora, Isaac, Hadley and her husband, Sawyer, were a close-knit group. They'd all met in university and fallen into an easy quartet. However, Hadley was fiercely loyal and never thought Isaac was good enough. Looking back on it now, Cora wondered how she'd been so blinded by him. Then again, he was funny and handsome, and he always had a good time.

"We just had to talk about Lyssa," Cora said. "Nothing serious."

"Ah, so nothing romantic?" There was a tease in Hadley's voice that Cora ignored.

"I don't think that's in the cards for us anymore."

"Hmm," the other woman hummed. "Because you have the hots for Aidan?"

Again, Cora laughed. "Aidan is complicated."

"Girl, your whole life is complicated."

Cora couldn't disagree. She opened the driver's side door and slid into her car. "Yeah, I know."

"Maybe if you decided to settle down with Aidan, it would get less so?" Hadley had met Aidan only a handful of times and while Cora had to agree he was devilishly handsome, Hadley just didn't see the angry, controlling side that could surface.

"You know it's not like that." Cora couldn't have that type of relationship around Lyssa. She'd shielded her daughter from all her flings. Aidan was only different because they had so much history.

"I know," Hadley said, defeat in her tone. "I just want you to find someone to take care of you."

Cora thought back to the handsome detective who'd come from out of town. There had been a moment between them, hadn't there? Though if it were to be like any of Cora's other relationships, it wouldn't go further than flirtation, a few dates and a couple nights spent together. Besides, he had to go back to Toronto eventually. Maybe that was the appeal. Cora had long since tired of the games she and Aidan played. Maybe it was time for someone new. With Ryan's time limited, it meant they could form a simple relationship, something to satisfy Cora and keep her life with her daughter safe and separate.

"You still there?" Hadley asked when she hadn't responded after a few seconds.

"Yeah, sorry," Cora said. "Just thinking . . ."

"About?"

"Just what you said." Cora laughed, brushing it off. "I don't need anyone to take care of me."

"Don't I know it. Anyway, the real reason I called . . ."

Cora smiled. She'd been waiting for Hadley to bring up the texts. "Yeah, yeah. I'll go pick up your order and come by."

"Aww, really?" Hadley said. "You're the best. I have wine on ice."

"You better."

"See you in a few."

Cora ended the call and started off to the craft store. Hadley had messaged asking her to pick up a last-minute order to distract Danny, who was home with a pesky cold. Together, Hadley and Cora took care of one another, so she was happy to help her. Plus, girl time was always needed, especially when all the men in her life seemed so confusing.

Chapter Seven

BLAINE ROCHE

B laine sat in his car outside the Kingston facility, his driver-side window rolled down. Smoke trickled from the sides of his mouth and into the night air. He'd taken to smoking since the girls had been arrested. It was a habit he'd kicked years ago, but one that sprang up when his anxiety was particularly uncontrollable.

Blaine had been sitting here for almost two full days, monitoring the comings and goings from the facility. But there was little movement. The center was small and only a few people came and went.

The gates rattled as they slid closed on rusty hinges. Blaine glanced at the clock—9 p.m. Right on schedule. It had opened at six that morning.

Blaine butted out his cigarette and waited another seven minutes before stepping out of the car. The cameras were on a seven-minute timer. He approached the gate, where he'd found a way in the previous night and slipped through.

The sun was falling behind the centre and casting a large shadow across the yard. Blaine went around the side of the white brick building, where a door was propped open with a rock. The nurse he'd bribed had done as he asked.

He slipped into the hallway and headed for the front desk, which was vacated, as the nurse had promised.

He glanced around before stepping behind the desk. The computer login was scribbled on a Post-it that was stuck to the keyboard. Blaine had access to patient history within moments.

The problem was, he wasn't sure what he was looking for. Mel had only given him an address.

First, he searched for her name, but nothing came up. He read the files for Jane Does who were listed but never properly named; none of them matched Mel's description. After only a moment of hesitation, he typed in Patsy's name, and her information scrolled down the screen. He scanned it quickly. She'd been a patient here a few times, starting seven years earlier. She'd come in with a fractured wrist and many broken fingers. Her face was swollen, with two black eyes. The pictures on file were almost unrecognizable.

She'd returned seven more times over the course of four years. There was an address on file. It wasn't Patsy's dead husband's house.

Blaine jotted it down with the intention of checking it out later. Perhaps that was what Mel had wanted him to find.

He was about to close the window when he noticed that Patsy had a familiar name listed as her emergency contact—Alison Wright.

Blaine paused, his mouse hovering over his sister's name. No. That couldn't be right.

He minimized the screen and searched Alison's name. His stomach lurched. Alison had been in for a minor fracture in her wrist four years ago. It had mended quickly and she was out of the centre before they discharged Patsy. It listed that the two had roomed together for a few days. Blaine wondered why Alison would stay overnight in the facility for such a minor injury, but with no other details, he couldn't know for sure.

Blaine took down Alison's contact information, noting the familiar address. He was certain this was the information Mel had hoped to pass on. It was too convenient otherwise. But why hadn't Mel told him about Alison when he'd divulged all his secrets months before?

He shrugged off the thought and stared at Alison's address. He smiled at the prospect of seeing her again. It had been years.

When he was finished with the files, he shut the computer down and disposed of the login information. He headed back down the hallway the way he'd come.

His breath caught when he heard approaching footsteps and he ducked into the closest room.

There was no one inside. The bed closest to him was empty and the curtain on the other was drawn.

Blaine turned toward the door as a voice called to him from behind the curtain.

"Go away." The curtain was drawn back with a hard yank. A gaunt boy glared at Blaine. His legs were beneath a blanket, but from the outline, Blaine could guess he was tall.

"You don't work for the hospital," the boy said. He didn't reach for his call button but instead eyed Blaine curiously. "How did you get in after hours?"

Blaine looked to the door, planning to leave when the footsteps passed.

The boy followed his gaze. "You'll have to tell me, or I'll hit the call button and two nurses will be in here."

Blaine frowned. "Is it smart to threaten someone you don't know?" The boy had guts; he'd give him that.

The boy shrugged. "I'm only a few years from death. I've been in this hospital since I was eight. There's not much you could do to me."

Blaine stepped closer to him. The boy looked like he could be a teenager. It was hard to tell.

"How long have you been here?" Blaine asked.

The boy glanced to his nightstand at a clock radio with the date displayed. "Eight years in two weeks."

"Wow." Blaine moved further into the room, reaching for his chart at the end of the bed. The boy shifted his hand closer to the call button as Blaine grew nearer, but didn't touch it or stop him from taking the chart. His eyes glittered with curiosity.

"Ace?" Blaine asked.

"That would be my name. Dad liked to play poker." He crossed his arms. "So, you can read. What else?"

He put the chart down. Ace was in the care centre for a rare disease. His bones were slowly deteriorating. His body was brittle and weak. "You're very sick."

Ace rolled his eyes. "Tell me something I don't know. Like who you are."

Blaine shook his head. "It's not important." He moved back towards the door.

"You look familiar." The boy's eyebrows scrunched together like he was trying hard to remember something. "You used to visit with Ali whenever that quiet woman was here."

Frowning, Blaine turned back to him. It wasn't the first time someone had brought up an event he couldn't remember. "How often did I visit?"

"Not often," Ace said. "Ali came more. She used to bring me things and give me a taste of the outside. She stopped coming like three years ago. That woman returned only once after that, and Ali didn't come. I don't think you did, either."

"Are you sure?" Blaine asked, making a mental note of the timeline.

"I think so."

"You sound a bit confused."

The boy's frown drooped lower, his forehead creased and concentrating. When he looked back up at Blaine, his gaze had softened. "I don't know what I remember anymore. I spend so many days in this bed, everything just melts together."

"Can you leave?" Blaine asked. "Go outside?"

"When I could still walk. With help, I can still take a chair outside. But I can't go alone as I once could."

"And you're alone?" Blaine asked.

"I've been alone for years." Ace looked away. "My parents left me here. Mom used to visit often, then one day she didn't return. I guess it was too much."

"I'm sorry," Blaine said, unsure how to comfort the boy.

"She was a good person," Ace said, looking back at him now. "Ali, I mean. If you did know her."

Blaine grimaced and glanced to the door. After having lost them years ago, he didn't like to think about his family. "Look, I have to go. But I hope she comes back to you, one day. Wherever she is."

Ace shrugged and lay back. "I've given up that hope." He drew the curtain shut, and Blaine left his room.

He hurried down the hallway and slipped out the side door, luckily not running into anyone on the way there. Outside, the sun had gone down. He darted across the dimly lit property towards the opening in the gate.

Back in his car, Blaine typed in the address provided in Patsy's file. It was close, around the corner. It was too late to go there now, but he would investigate when the sun rose.

The address that belonged to Alison was farther off.

Blaine reached for a cigarette as he looked at the suggested route. Alison wouldn't expect him and probably wouldn't welcome him home, even if she'd always been understanding and far too nice for her own good. They'd fought endlessly before their separation. Alison had an affinity for those who could care for her and as a young woman it had been no different. She'd dated her fair share of poor choices, the last that Blaine remembered being the worst.

Shifting his car into gear, he headed down the road towards Alison's address.

The thought of seeing her again excited and frightened him. What would she be like? What would she think when she saw him? He'd done a good job running and hiding, but he was still wanted by the police and Alison had always been wary of the police. He didn't know her connection with Patsy, but because of it, she had likely heard the news about her arrest and mental state. Blaine only hoped she'd hear him out before slamming the door in his face like the last time.

Chapter Eight

CORA PORTER

Cora glanced at her phone as it started to rattle on the glass table. Aidan's name appeared across the screen and she swiped to answer.

"Cora, I need you to come to OCDC right away," Aidan said, his voice rushed.

"What's going on?" Cora stood with the phone, moving to grab her bag. If he needed her at the Ottawa Carlton Detention Centre, then it had to be about Rickie.

"You need to see it to believe it," Aidan said. "But I think Rickie's alter just showed up."

Cora stopped. Ryan had practically said this would happen. "What?"

"Just get here fast. Boone is already on his way." Aidan ended the call before she could ask any more questions.

Cora glanced at the time. Lyssa would be in school for another three hours. Cora and Isaac had agreed to let him keep her for another couple of days. Still, she would hold her breath a bit until Lyssa confirmed that she was home safe.

She was in her car and at the OCDC in only a few minutes. A guard directed her to the visitation room, where she found Aidan and Ryan seated at the table in the small plain room with Rickie.

Although he was handcuffed, there was a silken pashmina wrapped around Rickie's shoulders. He stared at the tabletop and looked to be crying. Every so often, he'd pinch his cheeks and poof his hair. Every time he did, he'd groan with disappointment.

Cora knocked on the door and Aidan excused himself. Ryan did the same.

"You made it." Aidan smiled when he saw her. He stepped towards her, but Cora kept her distance.

"What's going on?"

"I think you'll want to see this one for yourself," Ryan said. He moved away from the door and allowed Cora and Aidan to enter the room alone.

"I'm Cora Porter," she said, sitting across from Rickie, unsure what to expect.

Rickie looked at her. His dark eyes shone with fresh tears, and he bit down on his lip. When he spoke, his voice was significantly softer than the last time they'd met. It was higher and carried a strange Southern accent, as if he were purposely changing it to sound more feminine.

"Hello," he said. "I am Grace Rainer."

Cora frowned.

"I know," Rickie said. "It must seem funny. I must look awful." He pinched his cheeks again. "Rickie never took good care of himself. I've been trying to care for him for years, ever since he lost his mother. Rickie never really appreciated it."

Cora cast a glance to the window, where Ryan stood watching. "Do you know Rickie well?"

Grace smiled. "Why yes. I've been a part of Rickie's life for many years. He used to talk to me, though that hasn't happened since he was a little boy."

"We've spoken with Rickie—he doesn't know you." Cora tried to keep her voice steady, thrown by the strange interaction. Rickie's alter was female.

Her expression faded and she pulled the pashmina tighter around her shoulders. "I tried to remind him. I left him presents and letters through the years, but he's never replied. He only ignored me. Maybe as a grown man, he thinks he doesn't need me anymore."

"Can you tell us about the victim?" Cora asked. "Julie Kanner."

Grace's expression darkened. Her eyes narrowed, and she pursed her lips. "I have nothing to say about that wicked woman."

"But you know her?"

"Of course I know her," Grace snapped. "She was trying to take my Noah from me."

Cora raised an eyebrow, remembering what Julie's roommate had said about a boyfriend. "Where is Noah now?"

Grace shook his head. "I don't know. He ran away after that woman who attacked me." She swallowed hard, and Cora saw more tears form in her eyes. "She said some awful things. She called me a monster. An abomination. A mistake."

"Why did she say that?" Cora asked, trying to keep her eyes on Grace. She wanted desperately to watch Ryan's reactions to all this. He'd dealt with three alters; what did he think of this one?

Glancing over her shoulder, Aidan still stood with his arms crossed over his broad chest. His posture was stern, but his eyes were surprised. She'd seen his look of disbelief before. He was struggling with this revelation as much as she was.

"She said she knew the truth," Grace said. "She said she knew what was wrong with me. But I think she was lying. No one ever knows what's wrong."

"We're going to help you find out," Aidan said, placing a hand on the table. "We have a very qualified psychiatric specialist on their way. We will get down to the truth."

Grace flashed the detective a smile. "Thank you, handsome. But I already know what's wrong."

"You do?"

Grace's smile faded, and she turned back to Cora. "Of course. Rickie and I are intertwined. Our lives connected." She shook her head. "But there can only be one. There *is* only one."

"What does that mean?" Aidan asked.

"It means that I was already seeking help to change my situation," Grace said. "Caroline told me that she would make things better. That she would fix us."

"Who is Caroline?"

Grace shook her head. "I can't say anymore. I promised her complete privacy."

"Can you tell us about Noah, then?" Cora asked as Aidan moved away from the table with a frustrated groan. Grace was both revealing information and twisting the truth. Cora was beginning to struggle with the ups and downs of this confusing case.

Grace's expression lit up. Her eyes shone in the bright light, and a faint smile creased her lips. "Noah was very special to me."

"So it seems," Aidan said, his tone sarcastic.

Cora raised a hand to silence him. "What made him so special?"

"He had this smile," Grace said. "It only came out when I made him laugh. No one could make Noah laugh like I could." She looked at her hands. Her lips sank downward, and she pulled her pashmina tighter around herself. "Then he left me. He looked horrified and for a second I think he saw the monster that Julie referred to."

Grace met Cora's gaze and wiped away her tears with the back of her hand. "I didn't understand. I was his Grace. He told me he'd never leave and then he did. I tried to find him, but I lost him and Rickie surfaced."

"You couldn't stop him?" Cora asked.

Grace shook his head. "He was very afraid. He didn't seem like himself."

A tap on the window halted their conversation. Aidan excused himself and Cora did the same. She was desperate to ask Rickie's alter more questions but wanted to get Ryan's take on the whole thing.

Outside the room, Ryan waited with a middle-aged man in a pinstriped suit. He offered his hand to Aidan and then Cora, introducing himself as the psychiatrist they'd requested.

Aidan nodded and led the man into the visitation room. Cora stayed on the opposite side with Ryan.

"Does this seem familiar?" Cora asked.

Ryan shook his head. "I've never dealt with cross-gendered personalities. All my girls still identified as women."

"She seems very aware of her alternate," Cora said. "And she mentioned the death of Rickie's mother. Maybe she came about as a protector for him, a mother-figure in place of the one he lost?" From her research on DID, Cora knew that trauma could bring about the dissociation and grief was known to be traumatic. She made a mental note to look into Rickie's past and the loss of his mother.

"Maybe." Ryan shrugged. "Sometimes they're very aware of their alternates. Sometimes it's deeper than that. One of my girls knew her alter but didn't realize they were the same person. It's complicated."

Cora nodded, watching as the psychiatrist sat down across from Grace and started asking similar questions to those which she had posed.

A loud ring came from within Ryan's jacket pocket and he was quick to retrieve it. He glanced at the number, smiled an apology, and stepped away from her as he answered the call.

"Boone here."

Her phone beeped and she reached for it. A single unread text sat in her inbox from Isaac, confirming that he was still planning to pick up Lyssa. Cora breathed a sigh of relief.

"Are you sure?" she heard Ryan ask. Cora glanced over her shoulder at him. His dark eyebrows were furrowed and his free hand had clenched into a fist, which he immediately relaxed upon seeing Cora's attention on him.

"Okay, thanks for calling," Ryan said. "I'll head over right away." He ended the call and moved back to Cora's side.

"Everything okay?" She cast him a sideways glance.

He nodded. "Yeah, I just got confirmation that they saw Blaine Roche at a care centre in Kingston. I'm going to head there now." He motioned to the window. "You and Hunter have this handled?"

"We'll be fine," Cora said. "Let me know what you find." With a small smile, she added, "Good luck."

He turned to leave, and Cora watched him go. She hoped he'd find what he was looking for, but a quiet part of her brain wished the opposite, in case finding Blaine put a stop to their case and sent Ryan back to Toronto prematurely.

Chapter Nine

BLAINE ROCHE

Blaine leaned against his car and took the final drag of his cigarette before tossing it aside. He'd waited for first light so he could properly understand what he was seeing. The large, familiar, two-storey house loomed before him. The windows were boarded, the front door as well.

Pushing off his car, he headed around the yard. He knew there was a cellar door at the back. As expected, the overgrown vegetation covered it. He pulled the reeds aside to expose the aging wood. The door was held shut with a rusted, brown padlock.

Blaine frowned. He took three short steps to the right, then bent down and moved the long grass away from the bottom of the house. A single rock rested against the concrete base. For a moment, Blaine reveled in his luck. But as he grabbed it and shook, a feeling of dread overcame him.

The rock was light, and something rattled around inside. In both hands, he turned the rock hard, feeling it slowly release and fall apart.

Inside the hollow stone lay a single brass key. The very one Alison had used all those years ago. For her to leave it, Blaine imagined, she had to have been in an unexpected rush. She wasn't typically so careless. Unless, when she'd abandoned the house, she had left nothing of value.

All those years ago, Blaine had known she was running too.

Blaine scanned the area, wondering if someone could be watching. When he felt he was alone, he slipped the key into the padlock, careful not to snap it. Both seemed brittle after so long. The lock fell away and the latch crept open. All that held the doors closed was the thin board hammered across the top.

Blaine took the knife from his pocket, flipped open the blade and carefully slid it beneath the old nails, pulling them out one by one until the rotting board came free.

He took a deep breath and opened the cellar door.

The stale air hit his face, swept up by the cool wind. He shivered as he recalled the last time he'd been in this house. The last time he saw Alison. The look of anger painted on her face. The way she'd screamed at him to leave and never come back. Blaine shook his head free of the memory. That wasn't why he was here.

Flipping the blade of his knife closed, he tucked it into his pocket and withdrew his phone. He clicked the button that turned on the flashlight. Taking a deep breath, he reminded himself that he was no longer the young boy who'd approached this cellar with fear. He was a man now. He took his first step into the cellar.

The stair creaked under his weight, echoing down the empty, darkened room. Blaine hesitated, filled with memories of hide and seek gone wrong, of getting locked in the cellar when his mother had been home sick, of Alison jumping out at him from the dark, laughing in glee at her attempts to frighten her younger brother. All memories that had happened long before their parents died and the agency took him and Alison away.

He moved lightly through the cellar, recalling the path well. Soon he was at the steep ladder steps that led into the main floor.

It was lighter up here, as sun managed to creep through the cracks in the boarded windows. The rooms were nearly bare, with nothing but old, ragged furniture and broken bottles. A scorch mark in the center of their former living room made him wonder who'd found their way in here and how long they may have squatted.

Blaine moved towards the front of the house, to the stairs. If Alison had left anything behind, it would be in their secret place, somewhere no one would think to look. He hoped he could still find it.

He reached for the railing before quickly retracting his hand. A thick layer of grey dust coated the once-polished mahogany. Cobwebs coated the walls and flecks of dust floated into the air with each of his steps. It had been years since anyone else had entered this home. He still didn't understand why Alison had taken up living here after their family had been torn apart.

Upstairs, Blaine entered the furthest room, the one that Alison had never used. His old bedroom. There was nothing inside the boxlike space, save for the empty shelving built into the far wall and the broken wooden bed frame on the opposite side. One of the closet doors was missing and the other hung on its hinges.

There was nothing inside the closet save for piles of dust and a lonely black spider. The shelves stood empty. Blaine frowned. He couldn't remember the right place, though he nearly laughed at the thought. When they'd been children, Blaine was certain he'd never forget their little secret room. They'd thought themselves so clever. But of course, their parents knew their children's secrets all along.

He stepped closer to the shelves, running his hand across the length of the middle one and feeling for any imperfections. His finger hit a small hitch and he stopped. It was here, the door. But how did he open it?

Blaine slid his hand further. In the corner of the shelf was a notch only big enough to slip a pencil tip into. He retrieved a pen from his pocket and gently prodded the hole. There was a low groan and the sound of hissing air. Blaine stepped back as the left side of the bookshelf swung open, revealing the small room behind it.

Everything was exactly as they'd left it. A promise kept between them. Long forgotten, until this moment.

Whoever'd been through the house clearly hadn't known about this room. It was barely big enough for Blaine to stand inside. A square desk had been pushed up against the back wall. On top was the jewelry box that Alison's adoptive mother had given her when she turned fifteen. But Alison never wore jewelry. As she grew up, the box became home to random collections of things she loved. Even later in life, it had changed every time Blaine had opened it and this time was no different.

It was filled with paper. Some newspaper clippings, reports, and printed emails. Blaine reached for the first news story.

Innovative New Drug Hits the Market, the headline read. Blaine frowned. It spoke of the launch of Solydexran after countless successful trials. It discussed test subjects who had taken the medication and now lived fulfilling, anxiety-free lives. They were excelling, married, and happy.

Blaine placed the article aside and reached for one of the emails. It was addressed to Calvin. The paper was rough and wrinkled, dated seven years earlier.

That bastard got away with it like you said he would. I've heard talk that they plan to release the narcotic to the public as soon as they can process the trial results. How many test

subjects can you confirm suffered from serious side effects? Ten? Twenty? He won't listen to reason!
I think you're right. We need to speak to him together. He has to understand the weight of what he's doing. I await your instruction.
- A

Blaine ran his fingers over the typed words. He remembered the email vividly, as well as the fear Alison had expressed. They had such trouble trying to release the truth. He pushed it away, anger and sadness welling up inside him as it had all those years ago.

He reached for another email, dated the same year. It spoke of the conversation with the CEO of the company and his refusal to call off the launch. Dylan Parsons was not known to be a kind man and Alison claimed he'd pushed the drug through without a thought to Calvin's findings.

She'd written a total of ten emails over two years. The last one was dated a week before Calvin's death.

The time is now. Leave. Meet where the river runs parallel to your heart. Look to the south on the third moon. You will find all you need to disappear.
Take care.
- A

He could hear the sweet and strong timbre of her voice in the words. She had tried to warn him; Alison always tried to help.

Blaine was about to place the emails back inside the box when he saw the corner of a photograph sticking out from under another news article. He reached for it, revealing an aged picture of two young children. One girl and one boy with matching happy grins. He and Alison.

Blaine smiled at the memory. It was from when their parents were still alive, before the tragedy and all the changes. Before their lives took on a direction that they'd never known possible. Their chubby child faces made Blaine think of the photo he'd kept in his wallet over the years. It was from later, after he and Alison had really reconnected, when they'd allowed themselves to put the past behind them and rekindle the sibling love they'd once had.

He'd cherished that photo, with its ripped edges and permanent crinkle from where he'd kept it folded down the middle. They'd been young adults then, Blaine having only just turned twenty-three. But it was the most recent photo he had of his older sister.

This one was different. A memory, a time capsule of something Blaine could barely remember.

He flipped the picture over and on the back was written: *For Blaine.* Alison had left this for him. Had she known he would come? He looked back at the picture, examining it closely. There was writing on the photo as well, though it was so small, Blaine could have missed it. *Come find me,* it read, just above Alison's head.

He placed it back in the box, then took the whole thing before turning to leave the house. He moved carefully through the cellar until he reached the door.

It was mid-afternoon and the sun had settled low in the sky. With new information in hand, Blaine returned to his car to ponder his next step. Pulling out the phone, he pushed the box and the rest of the contents beneath the passenger side seat, next to the gun that used to belong to Jonathan Roche. Another thing Blaine had inherited along with the farm.

Alison wanted him to find her. For all these years, they'd been separate, broken by the drug that had ruined too many lives, including their own. They'd stayed apart because Alison had threatened him. She'd forced him out. Told him to run. Eventually, as the truth began to chase him down, Blaine believed it was safer to be apart than together.

Alison had once promised she would come find him. When she had the answers they needed, she would find him. But she had never came and one day Blaine had given up on her.

Now, it seemed she'd tried. He'd done a good enough job of hiding. Maybe too good. Had she been looking for him all this time? Did she regret how they'd parted?

He reached for the photo again, running his fingers over the tiny words that invited him to search for her. Alison had always been one for games. Hide and seek had been a sibling favourite when they'd been carefree. Maybe now it was safe enough for them to be together. Maybe now they could figure out what to do next. Maybe now she really wanted him close to her.

Blaine lit a cigarette and started down the street. He thought of those who had suffered the consequences of Solydexran over the years. People like his girls—Melanie, Jackie, Candy—even if they weren't who he knew them to be.

Enough people had suffered for something that should never have been allowed. He would find Alison, as she wanted, and then they would put a stop to all of it.

Blaine glanced at the GPS directing him to turn right on the next street. He was at a loss for where to search for Alison next, but he still had Patsy's mysterious address, whoever it belonged to. Perhaps that could lead him to his sister.

Chapter Ten

NOAH BAKER

Noah took the back roads, avoiding the congestion that the over-population and constant traffic caused. He'd lived in this city his whole life. He'd never imagined leaving it, as too much held him to the city. Now, if he wished to avoid prison, he couldn't get out soon enough.

Though he tried not to think about *her*, he often found himself wondering if she was drinking a vanilla latte at her favourite coffee shop or reading on the bench in the park. He immediately pushed the image of her dining with other men out of his mind but lingered on the picture of her painted lips sipping the edge of a crystal wine glass.

Her fine, sharp features vanished when Noah looked up at the brown brick home in front of him. The last known residence of Grace's companion. Noah hesitated. This part of the neighbourhood was low income and lined with crumbling houses and overcrowded yards. At first glance, Noah knew the kind of people who made this place home and couldn't imagine how this woman could be of any help to him. Under normal circumstances, he wouldn't be here. But as a wanted—or soon-to-be wanted—criminal he didn't have a choice.

He climbed the cracking concrete steps and knocked on the rotting door. There were footsteps in the house, then hesitation before the door creaked open.

Standing there was a short woman. Her hair was dyed a bright, fake red—it had become popular many years before—and pulled back into a tight bun. Her eyes were so light, the brown was near orange. There was a small, crooked scar on the back of her right cheek. It disappeared beneath her hairline. She blinked at him a few times before cocking her head to the side.

"Caroline?" Noah asked, his voice hesitant.

She continued to stare at him for a moment. "And you must be . . ."

"Noah," he said.

Her eyebrows rose as if she were surprised. "Noah?"

"Yes, ma'am. I'm—"

"Grace's boyfriend," Caroline said quickly. "Yes, of course." She stepped aside. Her eyebrows had knit together, causing her skin to wrinkle in several places around her eyes, her forehead, and her pursed lips. "Would you like to come in?"

"Thanks." Noah stepped through the door into the dingy entrance, unsure where to go from there. The lighting was dull, casting obscure shadows around the room.

Caroline motioned with her hand, directing him into another room and to a seat beneath the window. She sat across from him, crossing her ankles and folding her hands over her long black skirt.

"I'm sorry for this sudden drop-in." Noah took in the room, unease whirling around inside him. The walls were a dull beige, like they'd faded over the years. Aged wallpaper curled and peeled away at the top, giving sight to the drywall beneath it. The furniture was dated and ripped and stained from years of who knew what. Noah shifted in his seat. What was Grace doing with someone like this woman?

"Grace was often abrupt." Caroline smiled. There was kindness in her gaze, an endearment that Noah recognized from Grace.

"Did you know Grace well?" Noah studied the older woman's face as he asked the question.

She nodded, and her expression never faltered. "Well enough. She used to come by every week or so. Sometimes for a night. Sometimes for six."

A fireplace took prominence at the opposite end of the room and several picture frames lined the mantle. This woman was in each one, with different people. There was one of Grace near the front. Her dark eyes were bright and smiling. Her long blond hair was as sleek and straight as it always was, and her eyebrows were still dark. Noah had asked about them once, but Grace said it was just her DNA. He never questioned it again.

"I came to ask about Grace," Noah said. "I hoped that you would know where she is."

"Why are you searching for her?"

"She's done something," Noah said. "Something terrible and I need to find her before anyone else does."

Caroline's lips twisted down as she shifted her eyes towards him. Her eyelids had drooped low and her gaze was laced with sadness.

"You are too late. She was taken into police custody over a week ago."

Noah's heartbeat slowed. This was what he'd been afraid of. "For killing Julie?"

Caroline nodded. "What happened?"

He leaned forward, his face in his hands. He regaled her with the story of the murder and how he'd left Grace behind.

"It's all so blurry," Noah said. "I must have been in terrible shock."

Caroline reached out and touched his wrist. "It's not your fault. Grace was struggling with her own problems."

"I was trying to help." Noah knew of the demons Caroline spoke of. Grace often discussed her discomfort and how she used to be suicidal. How she'd felt trapped inside herself. Noah understood. He had his own darkness. In some ways, he'd never really felt right. Like himself.

"I know." Caroline stood, heading from the room into the attached kitchen. She continued to speak to him as she moved around the kitchen. "Grace talked about you often. She was very fond of you."

"I was fond of her." Really, he loved Grace. It was a different love than the obsession he had whenever he watched *her*, the random woman he'd come across one day and had never been able to forget. Noah had never been able to understand the differences between her and Grace. He only knew he held a love for both.

Feeling awkward still sitting, Noah stood and leaned on the counter, watching Caroline move around the kitchen, preparing a tray of tea and biscuits.

"How long have you known Grace?"

Caroline smiled. "I met Grace four years ago. I've seen her almost every week since. Until now."

"How did you meet her?"

Caroline smiled as she poured the steaming water into a small porcelain teapot.

"It's a very long story." She set the pot on the tray and moved back into the attached room. Noah followed as they returned to their seats. She prepared two cups, milk and sugar. "Why don't you tell me how you met her. It would be good to think only good thoughts right now."

Noah frowned. He'd never told this story before. No one had ever asked.

"I'm sure Grace told you."

Caroline shook her head, a small smile still playing on her lips. "I'd like to hear it from you."

"It's nothing special," Noah said. "She came out of nowhere when I was standing on a platform waiting for the train. She stumbled over her own feet and crashed right into me. She was lucky I have good balance."

"She said you caught her." The light from the window reflected in Caroline's eyes. She looked happy, enjoying the memory as she drank from her cup.

Noah reached for the one offered. It was peppermint—too sweet for his taste. He drank it anyway.

"She was so flustered." Noah laughed. "And so embarrassed. All I could think was that she had that most beautiful blond hair." The perfect straight hair that framed her face. There was something about her, like he was supposed to meet her.

"Sounds like love at first sight," Caroline said.

"Is there such a thing?" Noah looked away from her steady gaze.

"For some."

"I don't think that's how it was with Grace." Noah loved her—he knew that much. But it was a different love, one he'd never felt before.

"You understood each other."

Noah nodded. "Yeah, it was crazy. I'd be thinking one thing and Grace would say it. We were so in sync."

"Then why did everything happen with Julie?" Caroline asked, setting her tea down and reaching for a plain biscuit.

Noah dropped his gaze again. "It was my fault. I never really broke up with Julie. I just stopped seeing her. She seemed fine with it, until one night she called. She told me to come alone. She told me Grace shouldn't hear about it."

"Do you think it was about Grace?"

"Yeah, I do." Noah's fingers threaded together. "Julie never got a chance to tell me, but she called Grace a monster, a freak."

A hint of sadness flickered across Caroline's face. "She isn't a monster. Some people just can't understand."

"Understand what?"

"I'm sure you noticed differences with Grace," Caroline said. "She was confused and it often brought out the worst in her."

"Did you ever find out what it was?"

Caroline shook her head. "I only supported her. That was the best I could do."

"Have you been to see her?"

"No, I haven't."

"Will you?"

"Maybe when it's clearer what happened." Caroline reached for her tea again. "And why."

"I'd like a bit of clarity," Noah mumbled. Everything in the past couple of weeks had been very confusing.

"I bet." Caroline's smile returned. It was sympathetic, friendly. "Why don't you stay here tonight? If you have nowhere else to go."

If he didn't take her up on her offer, he'd be sleeping on the streets and then leaving town. He couldn't help Grace if she was already behind bars. And he knew there was no reason to stay behind for *her*.

"That would be nice," Noah said. "If you don't mind it."

"Not at all." Caroline moved to stand. "I'll set up the spare room."

Chapter Eleven

CORA PORTER

The ringing came from the floor below and Cora had to run to get to her phone in time.

"Hello?"

"Cora, it's Ryan." The voice was distant, like she was on speakerphone.

"Hi." Cora hadn't spoken to him since he'd left for the hospital the day before. "Everything okay?"

"Yeah, of course," Ryan said. "Do you have a minute?"

"Sure." Cora perched on the barstool at her kitchen counter. "Are you back in town now?"

"Just about," Ryan said. "I'm actually near your place. Mind if I stop in? I have a file I'd like you to see. No problem if not; it can wait until the morning." He chuckled. "I just love to get a jump on things, often at the least appropriate times."

Cora glanced at the time. It was a bit late, half past nine, and she wasn't prepared for guests, but she could make do. Her mind drifted to the heat she'd felt the last time he showed up at her house. She immediately shook her head, scolding herself.

"Yeah, for sure," Cora said. "We can talk here."

"See you soon."

Cora placed her phone down and started moving around the house, collecting the clutter she'd let accumulate over the last two days without Lyssa. Finally, she moved back into the kitchen and gathered the scraps of newspaper, discarding the clippings in the recycling and placing the untouched pages aside. She stacked the obituaries she'd meticulously cut out to add to her collection and climbed the stairs to put on leggings in place of her torn sweatpants.

By the time Ryan knocked on her door, she had somehow managed to make not only her place but herself look presentable.

"Come on in." Cora stepped aside for him.

"Thanks." Ryan entered and shed his long coat before passing it to her. "Sorry, it's wet out there."

Cora looked around him. She'd known it was raining by the way the drops pinged off the roof, but the sound didn't do the storm justice. It was coming down in buckets outside.

"That's okay." She hung it on the coat rack before directing Ryan into the main room. He settled onto the couch and ran a hand through his damp hair. For being wet, it didn't look any different than it normally did, slicked back to perfection. "How did your trip go?"

"As well as can be expected," Ryan said.

"I take it you didn't find him."

Ryan shook his head. "We did confirm Roche had been at the hospital. It looks like Patsy Morrison had been there a few times, but we're not sure what he was looking for or if he found it. There was an address on file that we've sent an officer over to look into."

Cora frowned. Patsy was one of the women from Ryan's previous case.

"Perhaps he was just looking to get closer to her," Cora said. "Didn't you say you suspected this man of having a relationship with her alter?"

Ryan nodded. "He certainly did."

"What did you find?" Cora sat next to him on the couch and took the file he held in his lap.

"Not much," Ryan said. "One boy staying in the hospital claimed he saw Mr. Roche. He also said that Mr. Roche used to visit on a regular basis with a woman named Ali."

Cora frowned. Could Ali be short for Alison? Calvin had an older sister according to the obituary Cora had collected all those years ago.

"Do you think he meant Alison Wright?"

"Yes, Calvin Wright's sister." Ryan leaned back on the couch. "She was listed as an emergency contact on Patsy Morrison's old hospital records."

"Hmm," Cora hummed, flipping open the file folder and reading through his findings. She stopped when she came across his strange suggestion. "You don't think Blaine is just an alias. You think it's Calvin and he's suffering from the drug as well?"

Cora looked up at Ryan. The report suggested that Blaine Roche was an alter of Calvin Wright, that he too may have been subjected to the devastating effects of Solydexran.

Ryan frowned, rubbing at the stubble that had formed on his chin. "I'm not sure. Maybe he's just a liar."

"And faked his death." The whole thing seemed farfetched, but Cora couldn't fault the detective. What else did Ryan have to go on other than the things he'd already seen?

"It's not unheard of." That much was certainly true. With the right connections, circumstances, and timing, anyone could disappear. If anything seemed clear, it was that Calvin Wright was smart. He had connections and money.

Cora flipped the page. "What about the sister?"

"We can't find her," Ryan said. "We sent people to her last known residence and it's completely boarded up."

"Weird," Cora said. The next page claimed that the last time there was a record of Alison was shortly after Calvin's believed death.

"It is. Maybe she's working with him and hiding under an alias."

"Maybe." Cora wasn't sure. She frowned, thinking back to the obituary that had shared Calvin's death and picture. There had been family. She'd pulled it out after the first time Ryan mentioned his name. Maybe now her strange hobby was going to prove useful. Without a word, Cora stood and left the room to grab the article.

"Cora?"

She didn't answer Ryan, only ran up the stairs and opened her top drawer. Inside were countless obituary clippings. She'd placed the newest ones carefully on top.

Deaths of significant people were the main collectible, but Cora kept the kindest ones as well.

She grabbed the obituary for Calvin's death, which she'd set aside and returned downstairs.

Ryan stood in the archway leading to the sitting room. "I wondered where you'd disappeared to."

Cora handed the yellowing paper to him. "Is that Alison?"

The obituary stated that the picture featured a photo of Calvin and his family. Two women stood at his side, one a brunette with a petite, pointed nose and jutting chin, the other tall and fair, with curls reaching to her waist.

At the edge of the group stood a younger woman. Her dark eyes matched Calvin's, as did her rounded face.

Ryan frowned. "They were adopted?"

"His files didn't say?" Cora had learned as much from the obituary. It mentioned his two mothers and sister.

Ryan shook his head. "Calvin Wright is a very difficult man to find."

"And this Blaine fellow?" Cora brushed by Ryan. Their arms touched, but she continued into the room. His footsteps told her that he had followed.

"A mystery as well. But if there are adoption records for Calvin and Alison ... and if Blaine is truly a different person ... then there will be a record of him as well." Ryan shook his head. "I hadn't thought to look into adoption."

Cora sat on the couch, and Ryan did the same. He was close, so close their thighs touched. This time, Cora didn't move away.

"Where do you think Alison is now?" Cora asked, taking the picture and looking at the young woman. She was smiling, but the expression was stiff. The picture looked to be of Calvin's graduation day. He wore a cap and gown, and both mothers smiled with clear admiration. Alison was simply off to the side. "Could she be dead too?"

"If *he's* even dead," Ryan said.

Cora cast him a sideways glance. "How will you find her?"

Ryan's gaze jumped quickly to her lips before meeting her eyes. She thought she'd imagined their closeness, but now she was certain he meant something by it.

"I have one idea." Ryan's voice had lowered and when he paused, his lips stayed slightly parted.

Cora's knitted sweater suddenly became unbearably hot. Drawing a sharp breath, she moved away, putting space between them. That seemed to be enough to break the spell.

"What would that be?" Cora asked. She hoped she wasn't turning red.

He leaned back. "If I am correct in my theory about Blaine, then perhaps Alison has been seeking to help those affected by the drug too."

Cora drew a steady breath. Ryan had theorized that Blaine Roche was acting out of mercy, possibly guilt. Seeking out those damaged by Solydexran and hoping to aid them, support them. Perhaps a strange form of creator's guilt, but from what Cora understood, Blaine hadn't helped people. He'd only made it worse.

"That could be why she was visiting Mrs. Morrison," Cora concluded. The heat started to melt away as she allowed herself to focus back on the mystery. "Have you found any recent photos or information about her?"

Ryan nodded. "My team is doing a thorough search. She may be the piece that ties our two cases together."

He took the picture from her hand and their fingers touched for longer than necessary.

"It's possible Alison would do what Blaine has done," Ryan said. "Protect and try to help those affected by this drug. Brother and sister, angels of mercy?"

"Why do they feel so much guilt in connection to it?" Cora wondered out loud. "Calvin's reports clearly outline the dangers of the medication. The fact that his findings were ignored is not their cross to bear."

"We have to be missing something."

Ryan was right. The whole story behind Solydexran and its release felt like an incomplete jigsaw puzzle. They had the pieces but seemed to be missing enough that they couldn't get a look at the bigger picture.

Cora straightened as she thought back to the previous day. How could she have forgotten? "Grace said there was a woman. Someone who was helping her make things right. She called her Caroline."

Ryan's confused expression broke and a wide smile spread on his lips. "Of course." He reached out and grasped Cora's hands, shaking them with excitement. "That could be her alias. You're brilliant."

"Well, I do try," Cora said, trying to keep her tone playful and not focus on the warmth coming from his hands.

"You don't have to."

The blare of her phone made her jump. She pulled her hands from his grasp and her eyes from his penetrating gaze.

"Sorry, it's my daughter." Cora reached for her phone and pushed herself off the couch, putting distance between them.

"Hey baby, everything okay?" Cora asked when she answered the call.

"Mommy." Lyssa's quiet voice shook as she sniffed back her tears. "I'm scared."

Cora's heart started to race. "Baby girl, where are you?"

"In Daddy's room," Lyssa said. "But Daddy hasn't come home."

Cora glanced at the time. Quarter past ten. Where was Isaac? How long had he been gone? The questions didn't matter. All that mattered now was that her seven-year-old daughter was alone in an apartment in the middle of the city. What was Isaac thinking? Cora knew he was irresponsible, but this was next level. He *had* to be using.

"Okay, Lyssa," Cora said slowly. "I'm going to come and get you."

"Will you be long?" Another sniffle.

"I'll keep you on the phone until I get there, okay?"

"Okay."

"Just hold on a minute, baby girl." Cora pulled the phone away from her ear and looked at Ryan, who had stood and started moving towards the door.

"Sorry," Cora said, keeping her voice soft.

"It's okay. It's your kid. Kids come first." Ryan reached out and gave her bicep a gentle squeeze. "I'll see you tomorrow. Thanks for your help tonight."

She passed him his coat, and he turned for the door.

"See you tomorrow," she said, then pressed her phone back to her ear. "Okay I'm back, baby. I'll be there soon."

Chapter Twelve

BLAINE ROCHE

B laine drew a deep breath before knocking on the door. The home belonged to J Reese, according to a quick internet search. Patsy's family name. Whoever lived here might be a relative.

The woman who answered was older than Patsy, with prominent wrinkles forming around her eyes and lips. Despite the age difference, she looked quite similar, the same rounded chin and dark brown hair. Her eyes were identical in shape and size, but the colour was different. Instead of blue they were brown.

"Can I help you?" She even cocked her head to the side in the way Mel used to.

Blaine knew of Patsy's sister, having used her as an excuse multiple times when he'd been protecting Mel's secrets from Fraser. He drew the easy conclusion.

"You must be Jenny," Blaine said. "I knew your sister, Patsy."

Her manicured eyebrows pressed together and she looked him up and down a few more times.

"Do you know Alison?" Jenny asked.

"A long time ago I did." He glanced over his shoulder. "I'm Blaine."

Jenny's frown lifted and she stepped aside. "Please come in."

"I take it you've heard of me," Blaine said, entering her townhome. He couldn't be sure how much she knew. Patsy's case may have been swept under the rug, but Blaine had not been so lucky. He knew Boone was hunting him, by whatever means necessary.

Jenny nodded. "You're wanted by the police."

Blaine hesitated. Of course Boone would have spoken to Patsy's sister during his investigation. Still, he would have expected more resistance to letting him in. After all, he *was* a wanted man.

"You don't seem concerned."

Jenny shrugged. "My sister trusted you. As I understand it, you tried to help her."

Blaine nodded. "I didn't commit any crime."

The woman snorted with laughter but quickly covered her mouth, seemingly embarrassed by her outburst. "You seem to misunderstand the rule of law. You aided and abed my sister's crime. And ran. That's enough to get you time."

"Yeah, well, I don't plan on doing time."

"Does anyone ever really plan on that?" Jenny moved into the kitchen and Blaine followed. The large, open space featured granite countertops and a small table in a solarium. Blaine imagined it was the perfect place for an afternoon coffee. He'd dreamed of a house with Mel, once, when he thought he could still save her. The memory made his heart ache and he pushed it away.

"Why are you here?" Jenny asked.

Blaine looked back at her. She'd moved to stand behind the counter, a cutting board and several different vegetables lying in front of her. There was a pot on the stove. He'd interrupted her cooking.

"I'm sorry," he said. "I didn't mean to intrude."

Jenny shook her head. "It's just prep." She motioned to the barstools and Blaine perched awkwardly on one. "So, why?"

"Honestly, I was going to talk to you about Alison and her relationship with Patsy."

Jenny frowned. "That was a long time ago."

"I understand, but Patsy insisted I find her and I want to know why," Blaine said. His investigation of the house hadn't given him any insight into why Alison had taken such a liking to Patsy or been so intent on helping her.

"Alison met Patsy when she was visiting the centre after a particularly bad night with Fraser," Jenny said. "He'd broken a few of her bones, but she still wouldn't report it. We got her treatment at the centre here. They mended her wounds and kept her for a few days. I'd taken her there for years, then one day, Alison was admitted. She snapped her wrist slipping outside her office. Bones are easy to break, aren't they?"

"Yeah," Blaine mumbled. Especially when someone was breaking them for you.

"When I first met Melanie, Alison seemed to understand what was going on," Jenny said. "She did her best to help whenever Patsy was with me, but after about a year she just disappeared."

Blaine leaned against the counter. "There were no signs?"

"Oh, sure there were signs," Jenny said. "She once told me she was being followed and swore that someone had searched her house. Then one day she was gone. I figured the paranoia took over and she ran for it."

"They didn't find a body?" Perhaps Alison really had run for it and not died like he once suspected. But why hadn't she contacted him? Why had she left him alone all these years?

Jenny shook her head. "They never found anything to suggest that."

Blaine frowned. He didn't need Jenny to explain it to him. Alison kept a low profile and likely would have gone unreported. She didn't keep friends and could disappear quietly. If she'd left a body, who knew what the police would find? Who knew what the pharma thugs would do?

It was different now. If the police made a connection between Alison and the drug, her disappearance wouldn't go so unnoticed. There would be questions and they'd open a case looking into her.

"Any clue where she could have gone?" Blaine reached up and rubbed at his temples. He wasn't sure how he would find her. If he could.

"She always said there was this guy, Simon, who needed her help in Ottawa. She told me she wanted to seek out and help people like Patsy, however she could." Jenny frowned. "I was so thankful for all her help and how she managed Patsy's switches that I never questioned anything about her or her past. She was too kind to suspect otherwise. Desperation kind of runs in our family."

Blaine ignored her comment. "Any idea where in Ottawa?"

"I'm sorry, no." Jenny shook her head. "She once brought Patsy back a souvenir magnet from parliament." Jenny turned to the fridge behind her and plucked one from the mass cluttering the surface. There were magnets from France, Spain, and England, as if her collection was a way to keep a record of her travels. Jenny passed the magnet to Blaine.

It was a laminated rectangle that featured Parliament Hill and the surrounding buildings. Nothing more than a generic tourism gift. Blaine placed it on the counter and slid it back toward Jenny.

"Why would she do that?"

Jenny shook her head. "No idea. Patsy said it was an inside joke between them. I never asked any further."

"But she left it with you," Blaine said, nodding towards the fridge.

"Patsy was scared of taking anything back to Fraser that would make him think she'd been untruthful. She believed the magnet belonged with my collection. She touched it every time she visited."

Sadness hit Blaine again, as he thought about Patsy's fear. It was quickly replaced by anger at the man who'd caused that fear, but that didn't matter now. Fraser had paid for his abuse with his life.

Blaine glanced back at the magnet that still rested on the counter between them. For Alison to bring something from parliament, part of her travels would have taken her into the busy capital city. It would be like finding a needle in a haystack, but Blaine had no other leads.

He stood. "Thank you."

"You're leaving already?"

"Unless you know more." Blaine shrugged. He had to find Alison and at least this was *something* to go on.

"I'm seeing Patsy tomorrow," Jenny said. "If you wanted to, you could come. She could probably help."

Blaine's heart twisted at the thought of seeing Patsy again. When he'd seen her before, it had been too strange. She was a mix of the girl he'd loved and the frightened woman he tried to save. Seeing her complicated things. Blaine had to do what he set out to do all those years ago. When he'd explained it to Mel, she had agreed. That was why they parted ways in the first place. She had to get help. He had to keep helping.

Blaine shook his head. "I don't think I should see her. I think I make things worse." He turned and headed the way they'd come without waiting for instruction.

Jenny followed behind him.

Before reaching for the door, he thought of one last thing. He took the paper from his pocket and passed it to Jenny.

"Are these coordinates familiar to you?"

Jenny frowned as she scanned the page. Then she shook her head. "They aren't coordinates. Wait here a minute."

She went back to the kitchen and returned with a slip of paper. She passed it to Blaine, pointing at the numbers and address.

"The first four numbers are for the storage unit that Patsy rented two years ago. Up on the corner of Fifth and Wellington. That's the address."

Could Patsy have rented this facility shortly after Blaine and Mel had met? Had she known of a connection between Blaine and Alison even then? Though Blaine wondered, if she had, why Mel hadn't said anything when he first told her about Alison.

"And the others?" Blaine looked up from the paper Jenny had given him.

Jenny shrugged and handed the paper back to him. "Maybe the lock code? She never took me there. I only know about it because I've been paying for it on my credit card for years."

"And you never thought to ask her?" That seemed strange to Blaine, to be paying for a unit when you had no idea what was inside.

Jenny shrugged. "Patsy has been through a lot. If I can help afford her one little sense of privacy, then I'm happy to. The unit isn't costly; most times I don't even notice the charge. Besides, if there is anything inside there that's dangerous or questionable, my ignorance is bliss. I've never been to the property or seen what Patsy hid away."

Blaine raised an eyebrow at Jenny, realizing she'd likely grappled with what was in the unit over the years. But she was firm in her response.

She'd made her decision long ago and stuck to it. All for the love of her troubled sister.

"Fifth and Wellington, you say?" Blaine asked. "About half an hour west?"

Jenny nodded. "I could come with you if you wanted."

"Don't worry about it," Blaine said. He'd put her family through enough. Jenny didn't need to get wrapped up in this mystery. "I think what you said about your ignorance being bliss was right." He turned and reached for the door. "Thanks for your help. I'll manage the rest on my own."

Jenny called after him as he stepped into the crisp air. "What are you hoping to find, Blaine?"

He stopped and looked back at her. "All I've ever wanted. The truth."

They gazed at one another for a moment. Then he turned and left for his car without another word. If there was anything that Blaine deserved, it was the whole truth.

Chapter Thirteen

CORA PORTER

Hearing the door to her office open, Cora swiveled in her chair. Ryan stood hovering in the doorway. With her phone pressed to her ear, she held up a finger, asking him to wait.

"As I said before, Ms. Porter, I will call you as soon as I hear anything," the man on the phone said.

"I just—" Cora didn't get the sentence out before the call was disconnected. For hired help, they were curt.

Cora had filed a missing person report for Isaac with the police earlier that day. Lyssa said he'd only been gone since yesterday morning, but the fact he'd left a seven-year-old alone was enough to get the police interested in finding him. Aidan had nearly flipped his desk when Cora had come to him with what happened. Aidan didn't mess around when it came to Lyssa's safety. That was one of the only reasons Cora still tolerated the hot-headed detective.

She was anxious, however. She was sure something was off and had hired outside help to find him.

"Everything okay?" Ryan asked when she put down her phone.

She looked up at him and nodded to the chair across from her. "Yeah, fine." Ryan didn't need to know about the turmoil in her personal life, no matter how comfortable she'd gotten with him.

He continued to hover. "Hunter was asking for you."

"Are you his errand boy now?" Cora cracked a playful smile.

Ryan grinned and shook his head. "Only when the errand requires me to fetch a beautiful woman."

Heat rose to Cora's cheeks as she pushed her chair back and stood. She definitely wasn't imagining the flirtation from Ryan.

"Do you have the picture?" Cora asked, trying to focus on her job. She had suggested they ask Grace about Alison directly, to see if she'd ever contacted her or Rickie. Ryan's team had found a more recent photo in their search, as well as more background on the elusive Alison Wright and her family. Calvin and Alison had been adopted after the death of both their parents, trauma that would be more than enough to cause any past dissociation, or so Ryan had suggested.

Cora only hoped it would be enough to give them another lead. Anything before the case dried up.

Ryan nodded and handed her a file. Flipping it open, she found a picture of a middle-aged Alison resting on top.

"Great." Cora brushed by him. She grabbed her jacket and purse, then nodded to Ryan. "Are you coming?"

"After you." He stepped aside and waved her by him.

She led the way through the station and out the front entrance. "I can drive us."

Ryan didn't respond, just took the passenger side. They were at the prison in a few minutes, their ride a comfortable silence, listening to the soft rock song playing on the radio. It was one Cora didn't recognize.

Once they got through security at the prison, Aidan stood outside the visitation room with a sour expression on his face. Rickie sat at the usual table, awaiting the next round of questioning. Cora breathed a moment of thanks for the willingness Rickie had shown in helping their investigation.

"What took you so long?" Aidan asked. "He's been sitting in there for nearly ten minutes. Who knows if Grace is still around."

Cora thrust the file into Aidan's hands. "There's all you need. If Grace can confirm that she knew Alison, then we might have a decent lead for Ryan."

Aidan's jaw tightened when she said the other detective's name.

"Hopefully for us, too." Aidan took the file and turned to enter the room.

Cora watched from the window. Rickie sat alone at the table. This was the third time she'd been present for a round of questioning. Each time, Aidan had asked if Rickie wanted his lawyer present and each time the man had refused, claiming since he didn't remember the crime, he couldn't imagine saying anything that would incriminate him further.

Ryan stepped to Cora's side. He stood so close that their arms touched, but only slightly.

"Hey," he said softly, leaning his head towards her. "Everything okay?"

The warmth from his body made her flush. When she didn't immediately answer, Ryan stepped away, leaving her feeling cold. Cora straightened her shoulders. For a moment, she wished he'd step back so she could inhale his warm scent. The deep, musky citrus of his cologne had plagued her dreams since the first night he appeared at her door. A part of her wanted to feel his strong arms wrapped around her, to be pressed up against what she imagined to be a firm abdomen, burying her face in his neck, touching his soft skin.

She puffed out a long breath, trying to shake the thoughts from her head.

Cora kept her gaze ahead, unwilling to give a hint as to her desires. "Yeah, just worried about Lyssa."

Ryan nodded but didn't ask for more information. Cora appreciated that about him.

"Do you recognize this woman?" Aidan asked the man seated in front of him. Cora leaned closer to the glass, hoping to read Rickie's reaction.

It was slow at first. Rickie took the picture, a confused, concentrated gaze etched on his face. As his eyes cleared with recognition, his lips turned down and he choked back a sob. The photo dropped to the table as he looked away, covering his face from view. Grace had surfaced.

Grace shook her head vigorously, wailing. "I can't say. I won't!"

Aidan slammed a hand down on the table, his voice rising. "Is this woman helping you? How do you know her?"

Cora flinched at Aidan's forcefulness. He'd been an intimidating cop for as long as she'd known him.

Grace's shoulders shook. Her hands trembled as they dropped away from her face, and she looked up at Aidan. Her tear-streaked cheeks were red and blotchy. Her lip quivered as the words came out.

"Yes, she was helping me." She spoke so softly, Cora instinctively leaned forward, nearly touching the glass. Alison was alive and possibly close.

Grace dropped his gaze to the table.

"How was Alison Wright helping you?" Aidan asked.

Grace's head tilted as she frowned and met Aidan's hard look once again. She no longer fidgeted and instead look confused, surprised.

"I don't know anyone named Alison," she said.

Aidan's eyebrows folded together, making his already menacing gaze more intimidating. He tapped the photo. "That is Alison Wright."

Grace shook her head. "No, *that* is Caroline."

"An alias," Ryan muttered as he reached up and scratched at his chin. "Just like her brother."

Cora cocked her head towards him. "You sound sure."

Ryan stepped back from the mirrored window. "Why shouldn't I? This can only help my case."

"Do you think she could suffer too?"

Before Ryan could answer, Aidan spoke again. "How was she helping you? How did you find her?"

"She found me," Grace said. "She knew about me and what I was going through. She was trying to help."

"Help with what?"

Grace shook her head. "Help me get better. Me and Rickie. I think she was trying to help one of us take over the other."

Cora shifted, looking back at Ryan. That sounded exactly like what Blaine Roche had been trying to do with the sex workers.

"Maybe it's not about an alter but an attempt to hide," Ryan said. "They seem too aware of what's going on, to be suffering like these others we've found."

Cora looked back at the visitation room as Aidan moved towards the door and exited.

"Get what you needed?" Aidan asked.

His tense shoulders told Cora that he was riled up from the questioning. Aidan worked better with a more passive partner like her. Good cop, bad cop. He got too worked up when he had to go it alone.

Ryan spoke first, stepping forward and putting himself between Cora and Aidan.

"It definitely helped." He held up his phone. "I'm going to call the department and let them know. Can you get an address? Maybe a search warrant."

"Sure," Aidan said. He stepped around Ryan, closer to Cora. "What about you?"

"You're doing great," she said.

Aidan nodded and turned, but as he did, he reached out and brushed Cora's hand.

She looked down, but it was so quick that he was gone before she could react. She didn't get a chance to speak before the door to the visitation room closed behind him. Cora looked away from the window to where Ryan stood and met his gaze.

The touch clearly hadn't gone unnoticed.

He raised an eyebrow. "Am I sensing something here?"

Though she found little humour in the situation, she couldn't stop the smile that tugged at her lips. "You are a detective."

Ryan's eyebrow lowered, and he stepped closer to Cora. She drew a sharp breath and willed herself to keep breathing. Though breathing only made it harder. All she could smell was his cologne and she found herself wondering what his lips would feel like pressed against hers.

"You're off the market?" Ryan asked, his voice low. Did she hear a hint of disappointment behind those words?

Cora shook her head. "Hardly." Then she paused. "I told you I was untethered. Honestly, I don't know that I was ever on the market. Having a daughter and a difficult romantic past makes dating tough."

"Don't I know it," Ryan said, running a hand over his slicked hair. "The past part, not the kid."

Cora nodded and thought back to the late wife he'd mentioned.

"Cool." Ryan kicked at the floor. "I wouldn't want to get in the way, or cause problems."

"You aren't," Cora said, then corrected herself. "You wouldn't be."

Ryan's gaze found hers. He raised his eyebrows. Cora wasn't sure if in interest or curiosity, but both suggested what she'd already been thinking—Ryan was taken by her.

He reached out and took her hand, giving it a gentle squeeze. "Good." Then he took a step back and turned for the door.

Cora watched him retreat, wondering if he'd only continue to flirt or actually ask her out.

She turned back towards the room and placed a hand on the ledge in front of her, willing her rapid heartbeat to slow. Ryan's scent still lingered in her nostrils and the flushed feeling that seemed to arise whenever he was around hadn't subsided.

When the door swung open again, she jumped and her racing pulse resumed its rapid pace. She sucked in a sharp breath when she realized it was just two uniformed guards, prepared to escort Rickie back to his cell.

One eyed her with concern and she quickly excused herself. Cora needed air.

"Cora," a voice called after her, causing her to stop and turn to face Aidan.

His steps were brisk. "Are you leaving?" He glanced around her to the door.

"Yeah," Cora said. "I have to get Lyssa from school."

"Oh right," he said, running a hand through his hair. "I forgot you had her tonight. I guess you didn't know when you told me you'd meet me for dinner."

Cora looked away. She'd only half forgotten about the dinner she'd agreed to the previous week. It had been so hectic with Ryan's arrival and Isaac's disappearance; it was a fair excuse. But when it came to Aidan, she rarely forgot anything. Her guilt wouldn't allow her.

"Aidan, I'm not sure."

"Hey, I get it," he said. His strained tone and folded brow line said otherwise. "It's not your fault that Isaac is a terrible father."

Cora stiffened at the comment. Isaac was unreliable, but he loved Lyssa. Cora was sure of that. He was sick. Addiction was a disease. He needed help, sure, but that didn't mean he was a terrible person.

Aidan didn't seem to notice her reaction. "Well, let's reschedule for next week. Unless you think you can still make tonight work? A drink at least." He forced an awkward laugh that Cora was sure he meant to be charming. "You kind of owe me one."

Cora frowned, finding the idea of owing him a bit ridiculous. But as she considered it, she did sort of owe him one. She constantly put him off, over and over. And he did give her unprecedented access to cases when she requested it.

A voice drew her attention and she looked up to see Ryan standing at the opposite end of the station, his phone pressed to his ear. As if sensing her gaze, he glanced over at her.

Aidan cleared his throat, then looked over his shoulder. When he saw Ryan standing there, his expression shifted from hopeful to irritated.

Cora shook her head, clearing the not-safe-for-work image that had just appeared in her mind. She wanted to put Aidan off and continue her daydream about running her fingers over Ryan's abs, but Aidan had been patient and Cora didn't want to damage her access to case details. He could be difficult, but he was a good ally at the police station.

Cora reached out and touched Aidan's arm gently. "I can't tonight. How about tomorrow? I'll make it up to you and take Lyssa to my parents for a couple of hours. Let's say six at Pardeezo?"

"We're on," Aidan said. He forced a tight smile, but from the way the muscles in his neck bulged beneath the loose collar, she could tell he was still annoyed by her wandering gaze.

Cora nodded and he walked away. She looked to Ryan one last time, wishing the previous thoughts had gone interrupted, then turned and left to pick up her daughter.

Chapter Fourteen

BLAINE ROCHE

I t was nearly noon the next day when Blaine arrived at the storage unit lot. He'd tried to enter the previous evening, but it wasn't a twenty-four-hour facility. He found a motel nearby and spent the night, preparing to discover Mel's secrets in the morning.

He'd been hesitant, however. As desperate as he was to know the truth, he worried what the truth might bring. Eventually, his curiosity got the best of him.

The gate that had been closed and locked the previous night was now wide open, inviting visitors. Soon he walked among rows of orange storage units. He found the number Melanie had given him near the back and just as Jenny had suspected, the remaining numbers opened the combination lock.

Blaine removed the lock and slid the door open. It creaked on rusted hinges and required strength to move. The stale air inside rushed towards him, stinking of mold and musk.

Blaine clicked on his flashlight and shone it around the unit. It was empty, save for a small square table in the center with a slim laptop on top. He entered the unit. It creaked underfoot.

Shining his flashlight all around, he confirmed there was nothing else inside. He checked below the table and gathered the laptop. There was no charging cord, but a quick glance told him the make and model were similar to his computer; Blaine's own cord would work.

He left the storage unit and locked it tight, then headed to his parked car. His body buzzed with curiosity. What could the computer hide? Would it work? Melanie had always been elusive, but this level of secrecy was beyond what Blaine knew of her. Or was Patsy truly the one to hide this away? Blaine couldn't be sure.

Back in his car, Blaine set the laptop on the passenger seat and headed towards a plaza he'd passed on the highway. In it was a small restaurant. They advertised free Wi-Fi.

Gathering his cord and the strange computer, Blaine entered the restaurant, hopeful for answers. When he asked for an outlet, the young hostess directed him to a table near the back. Soon he had the computer plugged in.

"Can I get you anything?" a woman asked.

Blaine didn't even look at the server. "Just a coffee, please."

When she was gone, he powered up the computer and waited for the screen to load. He assumed there would be a password, another obstacle in this convoluted mystery, but there wasn't and he was soon present-ed with a blank blue screen. No desktop background, no disorganized icons. Nothing. Only a menu bar and endless blue.

"Would you like a menu?" the woman asked when she placed the coffee on the table.

Blaine cocked his head briefly to the side. "I'm fine for now."

He caught only a glimpse of the slender woman before looking back at the screen in front of him. The only thing on his mind was the contents of this mysterious computer.

He double-clicked on the folder icon in the menu to bring up the documents. Inside was only one file simply labelled "New Folder," like Mel didn't have the care to rename it.

That was where he found what she'd left for him. In true Melanie fashion, everything was misnamed or jumbled. A bunch of letters and numbers that made no sense. Likely most were internet files she'd downloaded and never renamed. She'd never been one for organization. How she'd managed to run their intricate party business was still beyond him.

The computer contents were her organized chaos at its greatest. This would take Blaine some time.

He waved down the server and ordered whatever was on special. He'd never been a picky eater and for a place like this, it couldn't be anything more extravagant than fish and chips or a "fancy" burger.

The woman lingered longer this time, as if studying him. When he didn't acknowledge her again, she turned and left.

Blaine meticulously separated the files. Photos in one place, PDFs in another. Text documents were few. There were a few miscellaneous files he left alone, to review later should something not come from his other searches. It took another twenty minutes before he had a clearer sense of what he was looking at.

The server appeared again and placed a plate down.

Blaine glanced at the greasy-looking burger and pile of fries. "Thanks."

"Anything else?" she asked.

From the corner of his eye, he could see the way she shifted as if waiting for him to meet her gaze.

"Just the bill." He brushed her off. Blaine didn't want to take the time to chat with anyone. He had more pressing things to consider than a server who wanted to talk to him.

He sifted through Melanie's research. It was thorough but confusing, as if she had gathered information for something but didn't know precisely what she was looking for. Her search was broad, missing key details.

Why wouldn't she have asked for his help? Unless Blaine was correct in thinking that this belonged to Patsy's confused mind.

The pictures told a story of their own. Most followed Alison. Melanie must have spent several days keeping an eye on her.

The others were of a middle-aged man in a dark suit that strained around his bulging stomach. Anger boiled inside of Blaine. It was Dylan Parsons, former CEO of ACE Pharmaceuticals, the company that tested and released Solydexran. The very man who'd pushed forward distribution despite the trial findings.

The server came by with the bill and asked how everything was. Blaine waved her off with a "fine" as he flipped open Google and searched the CEO's name. He scrolled through several articles featuring him. Some discussed Parsons's failing health and a sudden hospitalization. More recent results mentioned his return home while he healed. Or died. The articles didn't imply the latter, but Blaine suspected it might be a possibility.

What he knew of Parsons didn't give Blaine much hope for his survival. While he'd been a brilliant man in his forties, launching ACE pharmaceuticals to a point that it competed with the others in Big Pharma, he'd let himself go as he aged. His failing health was no surprise.

Blaine flipped to another article that caught his eye. Vivian, Parsons's daughter, would be speaking at the Carlton University that weekend. Blaine paused, staring at the picture of the young woman. She had long, straight blond hair that fell around her face like a heavy curtain. Her thin lips were pressed into a tight smile that looked neither joyful nor encouraging. Blaine had seen her before.

She was the poster child of Solydexran. Her miracle case had been shared when the drug was first released. She was one the drug helped and didn't hinder. She was Parsons's only child and, Blaine suspected, the reason the drug had been pushed to market despite the strange test trials.

Blaine jotted down the address of the university and the lecture hall she'd be speaking at. He didn't know what he'd say to her, but at the very least he figured he could follow her and maybe she would give him clues as to where Parsons was hiding. Blaine would hate for him to pass away peacefully after everything that had happened.

Blaine exited the browser and glanced into the folder with the PDFs. At the very top of the list was a single file called "Alison." Inside was a list of her last known whereabouts. Including their childhood home that he'd recently visited. Blaine almost smiled at the information.

Below were known aliases and photos. Melanie had spent a long time following her. How had Blaine not known? It didn't matter now; if Mel could find Alison, he could too.

He shut the file and did a quick search of Alison's last known where-abouts to confirm the location. A couple of hours away in downtown Ottawa. Possibly the place Jenny had believed she was visiting. Still, he'd check all the addresses to be sure.

Blaine stretched his aching neck, ready to head back to the motel for the rest of the day. He closed the laptop and pulled out enough cash to cover the bill as the server sauntered over.

"I'm sorry," she said. "I didn't recognize you when you first walked in. Though it's been a while."

Blaine looked up at the woman, seeing her fully for the first time. Her blond hair was pulled back in a tight bun and despite her light hair, her eyes and eyebrows were dark. Fine lines were prominent around her eyes and lips. She was maybe in her early forties. Her smile was steady, but it faltered when he didn't respond.

She pointed to her chest. "Natalie . . . not sure if you'd remember?"

Blaine didn't. He'd never seen her before in his life, but he forced a smile, as he did with most who claimed to know him. "Of course, sorry. It's been a while."

"Uh, yeah," she said. "Like five years. You used to be my favourite regular, here three times a week without fail, until one day we never saw you again. I hope it wasn't because of that girl."

"Which girl?" Blaine asked. The conversation, while strange, wasn't off-putting.

Natalie put a manicured finger to her chin, tapping it as she thought out loud. "Hmm, that brunette who was always with you. The one who looked like she'd had a rough go. Then there was another time with that woman you introduced me to. I can't remember her name, but you kept calling her soror."

Blaine cracked a smile. Latin had always been a favourite of Alison's. "Do you remember the last time I was here?"

Natalie's eyebrows folded together, and she bit down on her lip. "You were quiet," she said. "Fidgeting. You greeted me with a smile, but it wasn't as genuine as usual. Something was wrong. I asked, but you insisted you were fine. I wouldn't have remembered it normally, but it was the last time I saw you. It was strange." Natalie shook her head. "Don't you remember?"

"Been suffering some memory loss over the years," Blaine lied. "Did I say anything important you can think of?"

Again, Natalie shook her head. "No, though you were clearly stressed. You kept looking around and checking outside." Then she shrugged. "Eventually, a car pulled up and you left without a word. I never saw you again. Until now."

"What car?" Blaine asked, but Natalie shook her head.

"I don't remember."

"Of course," he said. "It's been a while."

"Natalie!" The woman behind the counter called to her. Natalie's head snapped in her direction.

"I'm coming." She turned back to Blaine. "Sorry, I have to get back to work." She took the money he'd set out and the empty plate he'd set aside.

"That's okay," Blaine said. "I was heading out anyway."

She offered him a smile. "Well, it was good to see you again. Don't be a stranger, Calvin."

Blaine frowned as she walked away. He hadn't heard anyone use the name Calvin in years and it sounded foreign to his ears. Gathering his things, he returned to his car. There he reached under the passenger side seat and let his fingers first graze the old jewelry box, then over the cool shaft of the gun. He hoped to never use the latter, but he found comfort in the firearm. He had a means of defense if he needed it.

Withdrawing his hand, he turned the car and headed for the motel. One night's rest, and then off to find Alison. Blaine was so close, he could almost taste victory; it wasn't bitter enough to be failure.

Chapter Fifteen

NOAH BAKER

Noah still couldn't believe it. He'd stared at the picture for an hour, maybe two. He'd read the article six times. It was all there, but it wasn't right.

Staring back at him from the fifth page of the newspaper was the mugshot of Julie's believed murderer. His face was long and narrow, with dark eyebrows and short, dark hair. A light stubble coated his chin. Rickie was his name, Rickie Hastings.

Except, it was Grace.

Not as Noah knew her, but it was her. He could see it in the eyes. Dark brown and familiar. But how was it possible? This man was Grace.

He folded the paper as the bus pulled up to the curb and climbed aboard. Noah had been in the process of leaving the city, but since finding the picture, he'd decided to go back. The only person who could explain this to him was Caroline.

The bus ride would be another hour. Once seated, he opened the paper and looked again. He could see it, where her long hair fell to her shoulders. The bright red lipstick she wore. How dark and long her eyelashes were. Surely this was a different person—a brother, an unknown twin. Whoever he was, he was being accused of Grace's crime.

The bus dropped him off three blocks from Caroline's. He was there in minutes and knocking on her door. The sun had gone down. It was past ten.

The door crept open, and Caroline peered out at him.

"I'm sorry," he said. "It's late, but it's important." He needed an explanation, clarity. Anything.

Caroline stepped aside. "Come in."

Noah entered, this time moving right to the sitting room they'd occupied before. She followed and flicked on lights as they passed. When he turned back to regard her, he saw that she was dressed in a long blue nightgown and fuzzy slippers.

His cheeks burned. "I'm sorry. I didn't mean to disturb you."

He glanced away from her, looking in any direction he could. The pictures on the mantel were gone. The house looked plain. Too plain.

"It's fine." Caroline directed him to the chairs. "What is it?"

Noah took out the folded newspaper and handed it to her. "You told me Grace had been arrested for killing Julie, but the paper is claiming this man, Rickie, did it."

Caroline took the paper and flipped it to the page he indicated. She smiled as she ran a hand over the photo, but it was sad.

"You didn't know?" She looked at Noah, tears shining in her eyes.

"Know what?"

"Who she really was." Caroline pointed to the image. "This man, Rickie, this is her."

"No," Noah said. "It's not possible."

"It is, and I'm afraid there's more."

Noah was unsure what to say. How could there be more?

"I'm sure you knew Grace was unwell," Caroline said.

"Unwell?" Noah asked. "What does that mean?" Grace had seemed perfectly healthy when they'd been together. Noah knew she had her demons, as he did his own, but beyond the scars of their pasts, Grace seemed well adjusted, normal.

"She suffered from a devastating illness." Caroline leaned away, her expression grave.

"What kind of illness?" How did this strange explanation make sense of what Caroline had said about Rickie?

"One which was caused by the consumption of a drug called Solydexran, advertised and sold as an anxiety medication."

Noah frowned. "A drug that was intended to make her better, only made her sick?"

"That's exactly right," Caroline said. "Except it didn't really make Grace sick, it was Rickie. Rickie was a regular user, and Grace was the result."

Noah stiffened at the implication that Grace was simply a disease. "I don't believe that." How could Rickie and Grace be one and the same? "You're saying she wasn't real? She was just an illness that lived inside this man?"

Caroline reached out and placed her hand on Noah's, sympathy in her gaze. "I didn't mean to imply that Grace isn't real."

"Then what?" Noah snapped, the confusing conversation starting to irritate him. Why couldn't Caroline just give him straight answers?

"I only meant to say that due to this drug and this illness, Rickie and Grace are one and the same."

Noah shook his head. Nothing she said made sense. "Everything with Grace was a lie? It was a fabrication of this medication?"

"Yes and no," Caroline said. "Grace was very much a real person, a part of Rickie. Perhaps a part of him he doesn't know. The drug amplified this personality and gave her a life of her own."

Had Grace lied to him? Told him only what he wanted to hear, when she was really Rickie, a man, the whole time?

The pity in Caroline's eyes never shifted as the realization dawned on Noah. He'd had such a strong connection with Grace. He'd loved her from the moment she stumbled into his arms. He'd told Caroline it wasn't love at first sight, but maybe it was. Something about her. They had an instant connection. How could it have all been a lie?

"You must understand," Caroline said. "Rickie and Grace are two very different people. I understand why you feel cheated, wronged, or lied to, but you weren't. The woman who was Grace is everything that she told you. Everything that you fell in love with. The only thing you didn't know was that there was a different side of her."

"And that she was a man," Noah retorted. Still, even as he thought of what Caroline had told him, he did not picture Grace as a man in disguise because that was not what she was. Grace was a woman in her own right. The way she spoke, carried herself. Sure, they'd never been truly intimate beyond a few chaste kisses, but their relationship had never really been about sex. It had been love, understanding, acceptance. That was all Noah had ever asked for from her.

"Grace is not a man," Caroline said firmly. "If you truly believe that, then you didn't really know her."

Noah didn't believe it. He *did* know Grace. He'd held Grace. Loved Grace. Cared for Grace. No matter her biology, or what hid away inside her. Grace was a woman. A beautiful, strong, wonderful woman.

Noah wouldn't let a strange drug and realization ruin the woman he'd fallen for. The woman who'd understood him and helped him.

"A drug caused all of this?" Noah asked, unsure how such a thing could be possible. Weren't there trials for that exact reason?

"Not exactly, but it helped. There is a lot going on with this drug. The test results were falsified to force the drug to market and there have been others who suffer side effects like Grace's," Caroline explained. "She is not the first."

"That seems impossible."

Caroline nodded. "It does. But that's where Julie comes in. You see, Julie worked for ACE Pharmaceuticals, the company that pushed Solydexran to market. She has a personal stake in the company."

"Did she know the truth about Grace?" Noah asked.

"I think so yes." Caroline said. "There's a young woman named Vivian who is the reason this drug went to market. She suffered horrible anxiety and nothing seemed to help. When Solydexran was formulated, she was put in the test trials, and things improved. Suddenly, the crippling weight that haunted her was gone. She was able to function normally and have a successful life. It was a miracle to those who knew her."

"And why is she so special?" Noah asked. It seemed risky to put out a dangerous drug just because it helped one person live a more successful life.

"Vivian Parsons is the daughter of the CEO of ACE Pharmaceuticals," Caroline said. "When he found out how beneficial the drug could be, he was desperate to overlook the devastating results. He falsified the findings of the drug trials and pushed for approval."

Noah frowned. "This doesn't sound like a condition that's easily hidden from the public."

"You're right," Caroline agreed. "And as such, they sought to remove the doctors involved in the trials. And worked to find any Solydexran user that they classified as afflicted."

Caroline paused and closed her eyes for a moment. Noah didn't rush her, as it was clear to him that this was a difficult conversation.

"You said Julie called and wanted to discuss Grace."

Noah nodded.

"You said Julie called her a monster."

Again, Noah nodded.

Caroline drew a breath. "I believe Julie knew of Grace's condition and that she intended to report her. I believe Julie cared for you enough to try and keep you away from her. I don't know that Julie knew the whole truth."

"Which was?"

Caroline looked away, seeming unwilling to clarify. Finally, she said, "Julie likely worried that when she put Grace's name forward, you would get caught up in the extraction. That you would try and stop the enforcers from taking her and that you would be harmed in the process."

"What happens when someone who's suffered side effects gets taken?"

A darkness passed over Caroline's face. "I don't know."

"And they take anyone who shows signs of this?" Noah found the whole idea so farfetched. Unbelievable. How could a company be so influential that it could falsify drug trials and abduct anyone who could reveal the truth?

"That is what I believe," Caroline said. "I've seen people disappear and never return."

"This sounds like a giant conspiracy." Noah frowned. "People can't just vanish. They have families, friends, associates. Someone would notice."

Caroline nodded. "They go in under the guise that the person's anxiety has worsened to the point that the medication is not enough. Their stories are sold as a need to attend a psychiatric facility where they can get more serious care."

"How do you know all this?"

Caroline closed her eyes and drew an unsteady breath before answering. "I know because I was part of the trials. I knew the doctors who created and distributed the drugs. I've seen how this drug can affect someone."

"Then why haven't you spoken up?" Noah demanded. If Caroline was so privy to this information, why did she hide out in this dump? Why didn't she make the truth known?

"I've tried," Caroline said. "Each time, my reports would go missing and I would be followed, sometimes attacked." She shook her head. "I knew if I didn't run, if I didn't hide, then I would suffer the same fate as those before me. The doctors that no one can find. The patients who suffered needlessly. I am powerless against a multimillion-dollar corporation."

Noah gazed at the older woman for a moment, unsure if he should trust her. The story she told was so detailed but also sounded like a work of fiction. He didn't know her well enough to know if what she spoke of was really fact.

As if reading his mind, Caroline stood and left the room.

Noah watched her go and continued to ponder the words she'd spoken. People were vanishing and there was a massive conspiracy that was slipping under the radar. He wasn't sure how any of it was possible.

When Caroline returned, she carried with her a slip of paper, which she promptly passed to Noah. He frowned as he took the paper from her hand and read over the contents. It was a printed correspondence between two email addresses tied to ACE Pharmaceuticals. The message begged the company to reconsider the decision to push forward with the drug. It quoted devastating test trials and expressed concern about the results getting out, how it would make the company and team look.

The response was brief, claiming the original results had been falsified due to the conditions in which the trial was performed. A second trial had provided much stronger results that ensured the drug going to market was soon to be the best anxiety medication available.

Noah looked up from the page. "This contradicts what you were saying."

"No, it doesn't," Caroline said. "This was the response I got when I pushed back with the true trial results. Soon, I was terminated and all my files were wiped clean. That little bit of email trail is all I have that proves I tried to fix this."

Noah shook his head, reading over the short emails again. He wasn't sure what to believe. When he looked back up at Caroline, he got his answer. Her gaze was genuine, her words sincere and Grace trusted her above anyone else. Grace had always said Caroline had helped her. For Noah, that was enough to allow himself to believe. After all, Caroline knew about Grace and Rickie, so who was Noah to say that she was lying about this?

"People must know, if what you say is really true," Noah said.

Caroline shook her head. "Sadly, there seems to be no one who believes my stories. I fear I put myself and others in danger with my accusations."

"What if we do this together?" Noah asked. "Maybe together we can make sure everyone knows the truth about what this drug does."

"No, I'm afraid we can't. You must leave immediately. Hide and stay out of sight. It's possible that more than just the police hunt you if they knew of your connection with Grace."

Noah looked around again. Despite the furniture, the house was packed up. The realization dawned on him.

"You're leaving." Suspicion crept into Noah's mind. What if she was telling him only what would allow her to escape?

Caroline nodded. "I must. Once the police meet Grace, she will lead them right to me."

"Why are you worried about the police?"

The woman paused, her eyes revealing her fear. "I cannot trust anyone. I've made that mistake before."

Noah frowned, unsure what to say. The story seemed fictional. But before him stood a very real woman with very real terror in her eyes.

"You must go too," Caroline insisted. "I fear Grace will tell them about you too."

"Why would she do that?" He couldn't believe that all of Grace's feelings had been faked. She must have cared enough for him to confront Julie. She wouldn't just give him up to the police.

"She doesn't know the *real* truth," Caroline explained. "Not fully. She will share more than she should and she will think she's helping. She doesn't understand the seriousness of this."

Neither did Noah, but the message was clear. Caroline's fear was clear. He stood. "Then we have to go. We have to go now."

A weary smile appeared on her tired face. "At first light, Noah. We must be smart about our movements and not rash in our decisions."

Noah shook his head in disbelief. How could she be so calm after sharing the news she had? How could she brush off their danger now? Unless there really was none. His head was starting to spin. He didn't know anymore.

Caroline didn't offer any further information as she stood. She waved to the archway leading from the room. "Stay here tonight. Tomorrow is supposed to be lovely. A perfect time to start something new."

Still shaken by their conversation, Noah followed her down the stairs to the basement. He had thought it odd when he first met her, that Caroline's bedrooms were downstairs rather than up, but now he found the silence of the surrounding earth peaceful. He went to the guest room, where he noticed that she seemed to be leaving all her furniture behind. Only the small, sentimental pieces had been packed away from sight.

He sat on the bed and Caroline entered the room. On the bedside table sat a small lamp and a dog figurine, a basset hound or bloodhound. The wooden carving didn't give away the breed. He picked it up. The item was light, as if it were hollow.

"My old dog, Scout," Caroline explained. "My brother carved it for me when we were very young."

Noah placed the figurine back on the bedside table. "Why do you keep it in here?" A quick glance around the bare spare room showed nothing else sentimental.

Caroline smiled. "He used to protect me as a child. So, I felt he was the perfect one to protect my guests."

Noah only nodded, needing no further explanation from the woman offering him kindness. He wondered why she hadn't packed it away with the rest of her belongings, though—it was as if she had expected a final guest before her departure.

Caroline hesitated at the door for a moment. looking at him. Then, without saying another word, she turned for her bedroom and left him alone.

Noah lay on the bed and stared up at the ceiling, pondering what he'd been told. Grace was not who he thought she was and somehow, a drug tied into it all.

Whatever the case, anger boiled up inside him. Some sick corporation had forced an unsafe drug to market and now people like Grace suffered. He rolled onto his side and stared at the blank wall. Whoever it was would pay for what they'd done. Noah had ruined lives before. There would be no remorse when it came to ruining someone who'd wittingly ruined him.

Noah had lost so much in the short week since Julie's murder. He missed Grace, and though he knew he shouldn't, he missed *her*. He'd tried not to think about her, but running away from his life made his obsession with her come to the forefront. If only he could see her one last time.

Chapter Sixteen

CORA PORTER

Cora swirled her wine as she contemplated Hadley's pointed question. Why *was* Cora going out with Aidan tomorrow? She wasn't interested in dating him. She wasn't interested in pursuing their relationship anymore. Why couldn't she let him go?

Hadley's son Danny and Lyssa were in the sitting room, surrounded by Danny's latest LEGO set. Together they were painstakingly pressing ridged blocks into each other, in hopes to build Black Panther's Dragon Flyer. Cora had already been in the room twice to remind Lyssa not to be so bossy.

"I guess I feel like I owe him," Cora said.

Hadley scoffed. "Don't get me wrong, the guy is hot. But you don't owe him squat."

She cracked a smile. "You don't really know everything that's happened between us."

"It doesn't matter what has happened," Hadley said. "You don't owe any man anything."

Cora couldn't disagree, though sometimes they made her feel otherwise. Aidan, in particular, was good at manipulating a situation.

"He's a good ally to have," she said. The excuse sounded flat even to her.

"Ally?" Hadley laughed. "You're not going to war."

"No, but it helps when I'm not constantly faced with his opposition."

"You'll sleep with a guy just to get a leg up at work?" Her friend raised an eyebrow. "I didn't think that was your style."

"I'm not sleeping with him." Cora put her now-empty glass down. Not anymore, at least.

"Then why bother going for a drink with him?" Hadley asked, reaching for the bottle of wine in the process. "Besides, it sounds like you've got the hots for this Ryan fellow."

Cora had told Hadley about Ryan and his visits. She'd mentioned the intense heat she felt whenever he was around and the fact that his delicious scent and likely firm abs had not left her mind for long.

"I do," Cora admitted. She'd been coming to terms with the immediate attraction that seemed to blossom between her and Ryan since his arrival in Ottawa. But their interactions had been so populated with the strangeness of the case and the watchful eye of Aidan, it was hard to really read it.

"Then what's the problem?" Hadley had never sugar-coated any of Cora's worries.

"I think I owe Aidan an explanation."

Again, Hadley scoffed.

"No," Cora said, understanding her friend's reaction. "I have to let him down easy. It's complicated enough that we work together. Harder that we have a history. He already suspects something is going on with Ryan."

"Well, he's right." Hadley grinned, then made a smooching noise.

Cora shrugged and sipped her wine. "I mean. not really."

"Hey, Sawyer agrees with me," she said. "Girl, you have to cut out the losers and maybe get porked."

Cora nearly choked on her drink. "Oh my god, you didn't just say that."

Hadley just gave her a wicked grin. "You know I'm right."

She rolled her eyes. "Please refrain from discussing my love life with your husband."

"Sure thing." Hadley winked. "So what's holding you back?" she asked after Cora was silent for a moment. "You do like him, don't you?"

She considered her friend's question. "I think so, but I don't really know him and we're also dealing with this incredibly strange case right now. And with Isaac missing . . ."

Hadley put her hand on Cora's. "I'm sorry about all that. But I'm sure he's fine."

"Yeah." Though Cora wasn't so sure. Isaac could be unreliable at times, but to be gone this long without a single word was unusual. "It's sometimes hard to tell if I'm really feeling something or if my emotions are getting influenced by the work I do."

Hadley nodded. She'd been the only person Cora had been able to confide in for years, telling her one too many details about a case she was working on, things that could have been detrimental to her career if they'd gotten out. But Hadley was a vault. She never told a soul anything Cora mentioned about work. Cora's love life, however, was a different ball game.

"Have any leads on what to do next?" Hadley asked, though the case wasn't really Cora's. No case really belonged to Cora anymore, beyond being pulled in for forensic work. She kept reminding herself the change had been her choice.

Cora shrugged. "Until the search warrant gets approved, we've hit a wall. Hopefully that turns up something."

"Do you really think Isaac could be involved?"

Cora had mentioned her suspicions to Hadley. The strange initials on the tie that was so characteristic of Isaac's upbringing. The disappearance when the case got tough. Rickie's mysterious boyfriend, who seemed nowhere to be found. Something in Cora's gut told her that Isaac was somehow connected to this case, but how, she was still unsure.

"I really don't know," Cora said. "I can't shake the feeling that he could be involved. That somehow, he knows this person. I keep hoping I'm wrong."

Hadley grimaced in a way Cora recognized. She didn't think Cora was wrong. She believed that Isaac was capable of more than Cora allowed herself to believe. Hadley loved Cora and Lyssa and once she'd loved Isaac too, but she'd never trusted him. Especially when the drinks began to flow.

Isaac could get angry, Cora remembered that well, but she'd never taken his drunken outbursts seriously. He'd never hit her or made any indication that he wished to. He would yell, throw a tantrum, and the next morning clean the mess and apologize for the upset.

But murder? No, Cora couldn't believe that.

Hadley reached out and took her hand once more. "He'll turn up. And then you'll get your answers." Without giving her a chance to respond, Hadley changed the subject, darting across the kitchen to the pile of folded newspapers. "Oh my God, C, are you still chopping obits like a lunatic?"

Hadley grabbed the top paper and flipped open to a cut-up page. She looked at Cora and gave her an amused smile along with a gentle shake of her head. "You do understand that this is absolutely loopy, right?"

Cora reached out and swiped the paper from her hands. "Won't you ever just leave me alone?" She couldn't stop the smile that spread on her lips.

"Oh never, you know that."

Cora allowed Hadley to pour her some more wine and pretended to let their previous conversation fade away. Yet though she smiled, Cora couldn't stop the feeling inside her. Hadley hadn't denied any of Cora's worries. Her gut was telling her it was the worst-case scenario.

Chapter Seventeen

NOAH BAKER

Noah needed to leave town. When he'd woken up that morning, he'd found the house empty, save for a note from Caroline and a burner phone she'd left behind. The instructions were clear—they'd go their separate ways, but together they would make sure the people responsible for Solydexran went down. He couldn't get caught, but fear of the police wouldn't stop him. With his impending departure, he needed to see *her* one last time. It had been a while since he last followed her. Since he'd fallen for Grace.

Even now, he wasn't sure what drew him to her. It was like a magnetic force. Every time he thought he'd forgotten her, he'd find himself outside her house or her favourite coffee shop, waiting for her. It had been months ago when he'd seen her first—in the park where she'd been playing with her young daughter. At one point, Noah thought she'd glanced in his direction and he was quick to step behind a tree, worried he'd be caught staring, but she'd never acknowledged him. She didn't see him—or didn't care to. Noah wouldn't be surprised if it was the latter. She was way out of his league.

He'd come to learn her name—Cora—from the barista she frequented. It was dangerous to be close to her now, as she worked with the cops, after all. Noah had never seen her in uniform, so he couldn't be sure what her association with them was.

Noah had seen her around town with that blond detective who was often in the news. Maybe she was his girlfriend, or a wife, though she didn't wear a ring.

Once, he'd considered approaching her. He'd wanted to talk to her, just to see what she was really like, but something always stopped him from doing it. Like he knew that as soon as he did, it would shatter the illusion he'd built, the story he'd told himself.

Instead, he continued to admire her from afar, to help her in ways that she would never realize. A purchased coffee, a strategically placed newspaper, and one time he'd scared off a loitering creep. To say it was weird was an understatement, but something about her just held him.

Cora exited her house, swinging her purse over her shoulder. "C'mon baby girl!" she called, and soon the young daughter came trotting out with a sullen expression painted on her face.

She carried a pink unicorn backpack and dragged her feet. "Mama, I don't wanna."

Cora sighed with her shoulders in an overexaggerated way. Noah could read her exhaustion as she stepped back to her daughter's side and knelt in front of her. What she said then was too quiet for him to hear from where he stood watching.

The young girl seemed to concede to Cora's wishes and dragged her feet to the backseat of the waiting car. Cora climbed in as well.

Without his own car, Noah had no way to track where she was going, so he stayed where he was, watching the quiet house. He couldn't put his finger on what was so fascinating about her. She was certainly beautiful, though not in a traditional way. She was unique. Like a perfectly crafted painting. A masterpiece that immediately drew the eye. Impossible to replicate. She carried herself with confidence and seemed to have an empathy toward even the most destitute.

That was the image of the person he'd created when looking at her. Noah couldn't say for sure who Cora was, but he couldn't stop himself from watching.

He was about to leave when her car returned to the driveway.

Strange. He watched her climb out, though this time she was alone. The sullen little girl had been left somewhere. But why? Cora was never without her daughter, at least most of time Noah had seen her. The only time she was, Noah realized, was during the weekdays, when she was probably at school.

Noah wondered about a father figure and if the little girl had anyone in her life. he had never thought about being a father, never thought he'd be good at it. He could barely care for himself, let alone others. His worst fear was to leave a child the way he had felt. Fatherless and unloved. At least this girl had Cora, even if she had no father.

When Cora disappeared behind her front door, Noah abandoned his spying and proceeded back to the motel room he'd rented earlier in the day. There was still work to be done.

Noah hadn't forgotten the things Caroline had told him, or the people who had tried to ruin his life. She would be in touch when she found out more about the drug and those who sought to harm Grace. When she knew what to do next.

He had plans to visit the local library and do some research of his own. His journey there had been interrupted by this detour. A chance he couldn't deny himself.

Noah took one last glance at the large house across the street. He was sad that his life was taking him out of Ottawa, that he would be leaving her behind, whoever she really was.

Chapter Eighteen

CORA PORTER

"Why do I have to stay with Nana?" Lyssa whined from the backseat.

Cora kept her eyes on the road as she made the turn into her parents' subdivision. "It's just for a few hours, baby."

"Why?" Lyssa whined. "Aunt Hadley and Danny would have watched me."

"Auntie Hadley went to visit her parents today," Cora explained. "She was very sad she couldn't take you."

Hadley had been helping care for Lyssa since the day she was born. Danny and Lyssa had latched on to each other quickly, something Cora and Hadley shared joy over. She'd been a second mom to Lyssa when Cora needed it, but Hadley had her own family and Cora took up too much of her time as it was. After last night, Cora thought her friend deserved a break away from all her drama.

Lyssa was supposed to be with Isaac. Cora was supposed to have this weekend to herself. But Isaac's disappearance put a hitch in that plan and now drinks with Aidan loomed on the horizon, yet all Cora could think about was Ryan.

Of course, she couldn't tell Lyssa any of this. The girl had been so distraught when Cora picked her up from Isaac's apartment that Cora had taken the blame. She said she'd forgotten that Isaac had said he had to work, that it was her fault Lyssa had been left all alone. Cora wasn't sure her daughter believed her.

She'd nearly cancelled on Aidan, worried about letting her young daughter out of her sight after the ordeal of being alone at Isaac's apartment, but she knew cancelling would only prolong the inevitable conversation they had to have. Better to just rip off the Band-Aid, as Hadley liked to say.

Cora knew it was for the best. Besides, if there was anyone qualified to care for Lyssa, it was Cora's own mother.

"Nana is so excited to see you." Cora turned to face her daughter in the back seat as she pulled into her parents' driveway.

Lyssa pouted. It wasn't that the girl didn't want to be with her Nana and Papa, it was that she wanted to be with Isaac. Cora knew this better than anything. Lyssa loved her dad. He'd never given her reason not to, except when he didn't show. Cora covered for him time and time again. She wanted Lyssa to love Isaac. Cora had once and she knew how he could be—before the drugs and alcohol had made him too anxious and unhinged. He'd always been so careful with Lyssa. Until now.

"You'll have fun, baby. I promise."

Lyssa didn't speak, only unbuckled her seatbelt, grabbed her bag and dog stuffy off the seat beside her, and slid out the door. Her shoulders slumped the entire way up the walk until Cora's mom threw open the door.

"Princess Lyssa," Molly said. "How honoured we are to be blessed with your arrival." She opened her arms for Lyssa.

Lyssa's posture quickly changed. She dropped her bag and jumped into her nana's arms. A smile replaced the sullen pout and soon she was through the door, looking for her papa without so much as a goodbye to Cora.

"Thanks, Mom," Cora said, embracing her spry mother. "You're a lifesaver."

Molly nodded. "What happened with Isaac?"

Cora leaned against the doorframe. "You know Isaac."

Her mother didn't answer, but her expression said it all.

"I want him and Lyssa to have a relationship," Cora said.

Molly put her hands up. "I didn't say anything."

"Sometimes you don't have to."

Molly gave a sad smile. "I just want you to find happiness, honey. What happened with Aidan? I always thought you'd make something work when you stopped being partners."

She nearly rolled her eyes. "It's not like that."

"Too bad," her mother said. "He's certainly nice to look at." A playful smile formed on her lips.

Nice to look at, sure, but the rest of it was exhausting. He was more emotional than Cora had realized and he had expectations she just couldn't fulfill. When she didn't, even though no promises were ever made, Aidan made sure she knew just how disappointed he was in her. Besides, he'd been her senior at work. It was always hard to date someone when they were so used to having some form of power over you. Sometimes, Cora noticed it play into their personal relationship in ways she didn't like.

But tonight would end all of that. Cora was sure of it.

"I'll be okay, Mom." Cora leaned in and kissed her mom's cheek. "Tell Lyssa I love her, and I'll be back in a few hours."

"Take your time, honey." Molly waved her off. "We have so much planned for our little princess."

Cora just smiled, then turned back for her car. Her mom always had some sort of extravagant adventure planned for Lyssa and ice cream. Lyssa would completely forget about the fact that Isaac was supposed to be taking care of her this weekend.

Back at home, Cora slowly got ready for the drink with Aidan, dreading sitting across from him and how he would act. He could be a roll of the dice. Some days she would get carefree, happy Aidan, who didn't have a miserable thought in the world. Then there were others where he would grow sullen and sometimes even angry.

Cora had come close to dating Aidan once, when they first stopped being partners, but she couldn't find it in herself to commit. At the time, she'd still been hopeful that Isaac would pull himself out of the darkness he'd stumbled into. Aidan got frustrated, tired of waiting around. He started talking down to her, like he had when they first became partners. Cora grew tired of him quickly after that.

Still, their affair never completely ended, despite Hadley nudging otherwise. With a full-time job and full-time daughter, dating prospects were low. The city didn't have a ton of eligible bachelors, at least none who were landing in her lap. Aidan made it easy to go back to. Easy company, easy sex, and easy to leave. None of that seemed to interest her anymore. Now she couldn't stop thinking about Ryan.

Cora took one last look in the mirror before conceding. She couldn't do any more to get ready and delay the meeting.

Her phone read 5:50. She'd be late already.

Her phone buzzed as she pulled into the restaurant parking lot. It was nearly ten after. Aidan was always punctual and would probably have words for her. Cora found she didn't care.

The text was from Ryan and she scrambled to open it.

Hey. Not sure if you heard but the warrant for Alison's house was processed. We're heading over there now. Hunter isn't coming.

Cora frowned. Why wouldn't Aidan be participating in the search? This was his case. She quickly typed back.

Hadn't heard. I'll see if I can join. Send the address.

She climbed out of her car, unsure what to think. If Aidan knew about the search, then surely he would have called off their non-date and insisted they go. Work always came first.

Cora brushed by the hostess, seeing Aidan seated at a booth in the corner. He stood as she approached and leaned in, kissing her cheek. She stiffened at his touch and didn't return the affection.

"You look great." He smiled.

Cora had to admit that he did too, but that didn't stop her irritation.

"Did you know they got a warrant approved?" she blurted out, unable to contain it.

Aidan's playful smile vanished in an instant. "How do you know that?"

She didn't answer. "Did you know one had been approved?"

"Of course, I know," Aidan said. "It's my case. *My* warrant."

"Then what are we doing here?" Cora scanned the restaurant, unable to stop her voice from rising. "We should be helping with the search."

His hand clenched into a fist. "*You* shouldn't be worried about anything. You are not a detective anymore."

"Well, I guess I'm just surprised that you would be so foolish as to let someone else do your work for you." Cora spat the words out, crossing her arms.

A server came by before Aidan could respond. "Can I get you anything to start?"

"Johnnie Walker Blue. Neat." Aidan looked expectantly at Cora.

"A pinot grigio, thank you."

The server turned away with their orders and Cora waited for Aidan to answer.

"Can we just have a nice drink?" he asked, keeping his voice low. The tremor behind his words told Cora he was doing his best to stay calm despite her accusations.

"Fine." She uncrossed her arms. She could definitely use a drink. Maybe wine had been the wrong choice.

The server was quick to return with their glasses and soon Cora felt the warmth in her stomach as the wine helped her settle in.

"How did you know about the warrant?" Aidan asked, swirling his scotch before taking a sip.

"Ryan texted me," Cora said without thinking. As soon as the words left her lips, she thought better of it.

Aidan immediately hardened. "So what, Boone tells you everything that's going on?"

"He just seemed surprised we weren't going." Cora couldn't blame him. "And to be honest, I'm surprised too. I don't want to fight with you, but you used to be so hands-on. I'm not sure why you're keeping me from this investigation."

Aidan sighed and ran a hand through his hair. "Because this is not your investigation, Cora. You are a forensics lab tech. Not a cop. You chose to change that."

Cora glanced away from him, watching the young bartender lean in close and talk to one of her patrons. "For good reason."

"I'm not staying it wasn't," Aidan said. "But it also changes your place in an investigation. I let you in on a lot more than I should."

Cora glanced back at him. "Because you've never liked your new partner."

Aidan cracked a smile and Cora did too.

"Well, he's certainly not as demanding as you." Aidan reached out and took her hand. "Not as nice to look at either."

"You like me helping out," she said after a bit of silence. "Don't you?"

"Of course." Aidan pulled his hand away and took his drink again. "I'm just worried that you don't feel the same."

"I love working with you, Aidan."

"And you've been enjoying working with Boone, as well."

Cora frowned. She should have known this was coming. Aidan had been standoffish whenever Ryan was mentioned. Cora wasn't surprised. She practically burned up every time Ryan was in the room.

"He's a brilliant detective," she said, nonchalantly.

"He's a bit unorthodox," Aidan retorted. "And what's with those terrible jokes?"

Cora chuckled. She actually liked the jokes, as bad as they were. "I'm sure if you'd dealt with the cases he had, you'd be the same. Besides, it works for him. He gets things done."

Aidan downed his drink and waved down the server for another.

"There are rumours," Aidan said quietly.

Cora frowned. "About what?"

"That he's been coming by your house. Late." Aidan's eyebrow rose with accusation.

"Who's been saying that?" It was no one's business if Ryan had come by her house. Besides, how could anyone have known?

"Is it true?" Aidan kept his eyes trained on her.

She didn't look away. "Yeah, it's true. He came by for work. There were questions and reports to show me. He's thorough. I'm surprised you can't appreciate him for that." Cora shook her head. "Your jealousy is blinding you."

His expression pinched as the server set another drink down in front of him.

"Anything else for you, miss?"

"I'm fine. Thank you." Cora had barely touched the first glass.

"So, what's going on between you and Boone?" Aidan took a big swig, downing nearly half the glass in one go. "Don't tell me it's just work."

Cora drew a long breath. "Even if it wasn't, it's none of your business."

He looked away, and his jaw tightened. "Like hell it isn't."

"We're both adults here, Aidan," Cora said. "You and I have never dated." Even as she said the words, she realized his frustrations. He wanted her more than she wanted him. She had him on a hook, not that she'd put him there intentionally. He made it easy.

"So now you're into him?" Aidan snapped. He downed the rest of his drink and waved for the server again to bring another.

"I don't know yet." Cora held out her hand. "Give me your keys."

His eyes narrowed. "Why should I?"

"Because when you finish your next drink, I'm driving you home," Cora said. They'd been at the restaurant only half an hour and already

Aidan had had two scotches. For an officer, he could be impulsive. "I don't think this drink is going as either of us wants it to. And there is no way I'm letting you get behind the wheel full of scotch and hopped up on some fantasy."

"I'm not an idiot," he snapped, but he withdrew his keys and handed them to her anyway.

The server placed the glass down in front of Aidan and then motioned to Cora's wine glass. "Another, miss?"

Cora shook her head. "Just water, please." The server left, and Cora looked back at Aidan, her voice lowered. "I don't think you're an idiot. But I also know that you don't make your best decisions when drinking scotch."

Aidan only glared. He tipped back his glass and finished it in two quick gulps, then waved again and handed the server his credit card.

"Let's just go," he said after he finished payment.

Cora followed him from the restaurant and directed him to the passenger side of her car. Aidan was silent the entire ride and didn't speak until she pulled up to his house.

"You coming in?"

She shook her head. "Not tonight. Not anymore."

"Why not?"

"Because I have to pick Lyssa up," Cora said. "And it's become pretty clear that neither of us is getting what we want out of this relationship."

Aidan's expression hardened. "You think Boone can give you what you want?"

She withdrew Aidan's keys and held them out to him. "That doesn't concern you."

"I deserve an answer." He ripped the keys from her hand, his narrow eyes locked on her.

"Get out of my car, Aidan," Cora said. "Before you embarrass yourself."

He clenched his jaw, then shoved the door open. He didn't say anything else before slamming it closed and storming up his front walkway. Cora waited until he entered the house, then drove off.

She glanced at the time. She was due to pick up Lyssa within the hour, so she turned her car towards her parent's house. Just as she did, her phone started to ring.

"Cora here," she answered as the Bluetooth came through the speakers.

"Hey honey," her mom said.

"Everything alright?" Cora asked, unease settling in her stomach.

"Oh just fine," Molly said lightly. "Lyssa asked if she could stay the night. We were just going to do bath time and settle down for a movie and a little Nana sleepover."

Cora smiled, glad her daughter's attitude had changed since she was dropped off, but a part of her would miss Lyssa for the night.

"Is that okay?" Molly asked.

"Of course, Mom," Cora said, taking a quick turn to reroute herself home. "I'll come grab her in the morning."

"Sounds good, honey," Molly said. "I hope you get some rest too."

"I will," Cora said, and then Molly passed the phone to Lyssa, and Cora bid her daughter goodnight before hanging up the phone.

Alone in the silence of her car, Cora pulled over and did a quick Google search to find the address Ryan had sent her. It was uptown, on the west end. If they were still investigating, she could get a chance to be involved. She clicked on the call button beneath Ryan's name.

"Hey," his smooth voice came through the receiver.

"Hey," Cora said. "Are you still at the scene?"

"No," Ryan said. "I left. The place was cleared out. A few officers are still looking around."

"Oh." Cora couldn't keep the disappointment from her tone.

"What happened tonight?" Ryan asked. "I expected you and Hunter to be a part of this."

"Tell me about it," Cora said, trying not to sound exasperated. "I feel like I missed out."

"Well, you're welcome to come by and I'll debrief you." There was a hint of humour in his tone.

"Yeah?" Cora asked. This was better than she had hoped. Could this be her chance to move things along with him? At the very least, if she couldn't be a part of every aspect of that case, Ryan would fill her in. "I'm not interrupting anything?"

He chuckled. "Just takeout—and maybe a couple drinks."

"I don't have to come," Cora said hesitantly. She really didn't want to intrude.

"I'm ordering Rudy's," Ryan offered. "Recommended by Graves."

Cora smiled. Rudy's was a small diner near the police precinct. It was a cop hot spot.

"You're welcome to join me?" Ryan inflected, inviting her presence.

"Sure, I'll have a combo four with garden salad." Her usual. Cora clicked on her GPS, bringing up the hotel information that Ryan had left with the station. "I'll see you soon."

"Great."

Chapter Nineteen

NOAH BAKER

Noah waited outside the large hotel, unable to decide his next move. He hadn't heard from Caroline all day. He'd been by her house again, only to discover that the police had found the place. Just as she'd said they would.

When they'd parted ways, Caroline had given him information on Grace and the name of the company Julie had been working for. He had sought out a library earlier in the day where he would find as much information as he could on the man named Rickie, Julie, and the drug called Solydexran.

Across town in a small motel he'd booked, he'd left several pieces of printed paper scattered across one of the double beds, details he'd pulled from the internet in hopes of reviewing again.

He'd learned that Rickie was a nobody. He had inactive social media pages, as if he'd never used them or only used them to keep tabs on others and there were few details beyond that. He was part of an alum group for a local high school, which told Noah that he'd likely been born and raised in this busy city. But there was no information about what Rickie had done for work or why Grace had become a part of his life.

Julie proved to be elusive too, beyond her limited social media interactions. Accounts that were now silent acted as a virtual memorial. Her Facebook wall was cluttered with "I miss you" and "RIP" posts. It made Noah's stomach twist with remorse when he read it. Julie may have been part of the evil corporation like Caroline said, but she'd been a kind and intelligent woman. Noah struggled to see her as an enemy.

The results on Solydexran were more forthcoming. Vivian Parsons—the woman Caroline had mentioned—was indeed a poster child for the success of the drug. There were countless reports of how she'd gone from a struggling, anxious teen to a thriving young woman. She worked in charities and spoke at university. She shared her success stories with students, showing that suffering from any type of mental malady was no reason to not try and pursue your dreams. That having to rely on medication to stabilize was okay.

Noah had to admit she was quite beautiful. Vivian had a captivating smile, which was well documented in Google Images, with some posed photos and some candid, and others where she was speaking at a podium. He found a video recording of one of her speeches. Even her voice was beautiful. Soft and angelic.

Noah reached into his pocket for one of the printed papers and scanned the report. It was an article from the *Toronto Star*. The news mentioned the discovery of the drug, Solydexran, as a way to tie three murder suspects together, but beyond that, not many other details were shared. Apparently each convicted woman suffered from a mental illness, but the article didn't explicitly state whether they were like Grace, or if the drug was simply a coincidence.

It named the detective on the case—Ryan Boone—and Noah had looked into him, wondering if the man could offer more insight on the drug and its effects.

Beyond that first article, there was nothing else about the women, Boone, or the case. Perhaps the trial hadn't happened yet, or the details had been swept under the rug. If what Grace had told him was true, he wouldn't be surprised if it was the latter.

When Noah finally went by the police station, he had hoped he could see Grace. But instead, he'd seen Boone. What was the big-city detective doing so far away from his jurisdiction?

Curious, Noah had followed him and ended up at the hotel. Now, he was unsure how to proceed. He didn't know how best to confront him, or what the detective could offer him in terms of insights.

When he was about to approach the hotel, he saw a woman enter from the street. The light gave way to her short-cropped hair, and immediately Noah recognized her. The object of his strange obsession. Cora.

Why would she be visiting Boone's hotel? Could she be visiting him?

Noah's shoulders stiffened with an unexplained annoyance. He'd thought she belonged to that blond detective. The pompous one with the jaw you just wanted to punch. He could feel the perfect image of Cora shattering inside him. Was she nothing more than a police whore? Moving from one badge to another, spreading her legs for the next powerful man?

Noah spat on the concrete, resisting the urge to spew his disgust across the sidewalk.

What about Grace, and Julie's death? What about the case Boone was supposed to be working on? Noah's hands clenched at the thought of the careless detective pushing away his responsibilities for a chance to get his dick wet.

Noah turned on his heel and stormed away from the hotel. The curiosity about the drug, the strangeness surrounding Grace and her condition, seemed to disappear from his mind as he stalked away. There was a burning deep within him that made his insides twist and turn.

The feeling confused and frustrated him. He didn't understand why he felt such an attachment to a woman he'd never met when he should have been thinking about Grace, locked away and lonely.

Chapter Twenty

CORA PORTER

The concierge nodded at Cora as she passed the desk and went to the elevators. It climbed quickly, hitting the twentieth floor in seconds. Ryan's room was at the end of the hallway.

She hesitated before knocking, suddenly feeling self-conscious about her choice to come here. Was she being too forward now? She pushed away the feeling, telling herself she was here for the case. Cora knocked twice.

"Hi." A playful grin greeted her and Ryan stepped aside to allow her to enter.

"Sorry it's late," Cora said, stepping around him. He motioned to the couch in front of the large flat-screen TV and she took a seat. On the coffee table were the take-out containers from Rudy's. Cora smiled when she saw that her order was perfect.

"A drink?" Ryan asked, hovering by the minifridge. "I have beer, or a bottle of red?"

Cora paused. This was the line she realized they'd been toeing cautiously for days, but she'd come for dinner, and in that case, a glass of wine wouldn't hurt.

"Sure, a glass of red would be great."

Ryan gave her a small smile and turned, producing a fresh bottle and two glasses. Cora watched carefully as he poured the drinks, wondering if he'd planned to drink the bottle alone, or if he'd hoped for this very circumstance to present itself.

Wine in hand, Ryan settled in next to her. "Everything okay?" He turned his body towards her and Cora inhaled his citrus cologne. Her mind immediately swirled with the dangerous thoughts she'd been having all evening.

"Yeah, fine," Cora said. "I was just so annoyed today."

Ryan chuckled. "By Hunter?"

"Am I wrong?" Cora sipped her wine.

Ryan shrugged and pulled the coffee table closer to them. "I don't pretend to know what's going on with you and Hunter."

Cora shook her head. "Neither do I."

"Tell me about it."

"Really?"

"There's a closeness there," Ryan said, passing plastic-wrapped cutlery to Cora. "There's definitely a history."

"I was his partner," Cora said.

"Like together?"

Cora laughed. "Oh no, like he was lead detective and I was his junior."

"Oh, that makes more sense." Ryan seemed to visibly relax as he leaned back against the couch. "Also explains why you're so attuned to police work."

"I used to love it," Cora said.

"Then why leave it?"

It was a long story, but Cora drew a breath, prepared to tell the shortened version. "Honestly, it was my daughter. When Lyssa turned two, I had a bad confrontation and was shot at three times. My ex—Isaac—and I were already apart and he was totally unreliable. Always drinking. So, I knew I couldn't keep up my job. She needed at least one parent she could count on. She needed me."

Ryan nodded.

"But I love cases," Cora said. "So, I took some time off and went back to school. I got my master's in forensics and specialised in DNA profiling. I knew I didn't want to get too far away from police work. Getting out of the field and into the lab seemed like a good alternative."

"I can't imagine it would change your hours much," Ryan said.

"It doesn't."

He gave her a knowing smirk. "I've seen you on a case—you act like a detective, not a lab tech. You miss it."

"Of course I do," Cora said. "But Lyssa would miss me more if I died."

Ryan nodded his understanding. "You and Hunter are close because you worked together."

"How do you feel about your partner? Brad Archer, was it?"

He cracked a smile. "Archer is the best around."

"Think of how you feel about your partner and then apply that to my situation," Cora said. "But change it to a relationship where complicated feelings and attraction developed."

"You loved him?"

Cora couldn't stop the laugh that came out. She quickly covered her mouth with her hand. "Sorry, that was rude."

"I'll take that as a no."

"I haven't loved anyone since Lyssa's father," Cora said. "And we can see how well that worked out."

"Then Hunter loved you," Ryan concluded.

"I guess," Cora said. "But I don't think he knows what he feels. I think that he thinks he loves me. That I fit into this vision he has for his life. I don't feel that for him." She gently nudged Ryan. "He doesn't like you though."

Ryan's hand went to his heart and he feigned being wounded. "What? No. Don't say that. I've been trying so hard."

Cora laughed and sipped her wine.

Ryan dropped the charade and reached for his glass, tipping it towards hers. "I guess it's lucky then, that I don't care if he likes me."

"I guess so." Cora reached for her turkey club and placed the wine aside. "Tell me about today, what did you find?"

Ryan shrugged, following her lead and reaching for his meal. Cora noticed that he'd picked the steak sandwich, likely the very item Officer Graves had suggested.

"Nothing really," Ryan said. "Just a staircase leading to an underground tunnel. It came out about a kilometer west."

"Why?" Cora asked. "What's the point?"

"Easy escape?"

"From the police?"

"Or someone else." Ryan frowned. "Maybe it was a part of the original build and Alison didn't know about it. Or maybe it was something that she sought out when looking for a house, so she would always have a backup plan."

"That's suspicious," Cora said before taking another bite of her sandwich.

"Maybe," Ryan said, but Cora could tell he wasn't surprised by the findings.

She gave his leg a gentle nudge. "What are you thinking?"

"When we found the women in my case, Blaine reached out to me. He sent us a video recording giving insights into the drug and the case."

"Seriously?" Cora said. "He taunted you?"

"Yes and no," Ryan explained. "He made it clear he had no intentions of being caught, but he also explained about the Solydexran trials and the effects. He implied there was something more going on behind why Calvin had to fake his death and why the results were falsified."

"Like someone involved is worried about the results getting released?" Cora asked. "It's pretty much a given that the drug is going to be pulled, isn't it? This is the second case it's been involved in."

Ryan frowned. "The most they can do is pull it for further testing. We need these reports to surface. We need to be able to prove the drug is dangerous and was brought to the market under false pretenses."

"Then why haven't the reports been released?" Cora asked.

Ryan shrugged. "Like I said before, someone was more concerned with sweeping my case under the rug than addressing what we found."

"Then why don't you release it? I'm sure a news outlet would run with the story."

"Because I need to find Blaine first," Ryan said. "There's more going on than I know. More than these reports tell me. He knows more than I do and if we release the results, he might be gone for good. At least right now, we know he's looking for something."

"So, until he finds it, you can find him."

"I can hope."

"Did the house offer any clue as to where Alison may have gone next?"

Ryan shook her head. "I imagine Hunter will have people scouring the tunnel and the forest where it lets out, but beyond that, Alison left no hints behind."

"I feel like we keep hitting dead ends in this case." Cora frowned.

"We're making progress too." Ryan reached out and place a hand on her thigh. He rested it for a moment, then gave her a gentle squeeze before pulling away. Standing, he fetched the bottle of wine to replenish their glasses.

"I have to drive, you know." She thought of her daughter, who would likely be on the couch with a movie and an unhealthy snack. The clock on the desk told her she had about half an hour before she needed to leave.

Ryan tipped the wine into her glass. "A bit more won't hurt." When he sat back on the couch, it was closer to her.

Cora reached for her glass and leaned back, allowing her shoulders to relax. She'd been angry that Aidan had denied her access to the new break in the case, but Ryan had come through, and it was relieving to know she hadn't missed anything major.

"Thanks for filling me in. I was pretty upset that Aidan didn't want to go."

"I could tell." Ryan shifted his position on the couch and placed an arm over her shoulders. Cora stiffened at first but was quick to make herself relax. She was nervous, not upset by the touch. Ryan didn't seem to notice and if he did, he didn't say anything about it.

"He never listens to me," she said.

"He should."

Cora only smiled in response. Aidan would never listen to her ideas. He barely did when they were partners. He was the senior detective; he always had the final say. She took another sip of her wine, only to find Ryan reaching for it. He placed it on the table in front of them.

Frowning, she thought to him to ask why, but before she could, he leaned close and caught her lips in a steady kiss.

Heat rushed up her neck. Conflicting thoughts swirled around her head. They were colleagues. He smelled delicious. This was wrong. This was what she wanted. Her desire overpowered her professionalism. She leaned into him. The softness of his lips made her head spin and her body weak.

Her lips parted and their tongues touched. Ryan slipped one hand around the back of her neck, drawing her closer, kissing her deeper. All the thoughts she'd had over the previous days assaulted her with an intense desire to reach for him and run her hands all over his body.

Her hands slid up his arms, feeling his tense biceps, then further over his shoulders, his neck. Her fingers threaded through his hair. Her head began to swim, half from the wine, half from the kiss.

When they broke apart, Cora's breathing was erratic, her cheeks flushed. Ryan still held her close and his dark eyes gazed into her own.

"Stay the night," he said. His voice was low, husky.

Cora swallowed hard. She wanted to. Was that moving too fast?

Ryan's hold on her loosened when she didn't immediately answer. "Or maybe I'm reading this wrong." He smiled, though there was clear disappointment in his eyes.

"You aren't," she said. "But I'll have to leave early to pick up my daughter."

Ryan's eyes dropped to her lips quickly before looking back up. "I've always been an early riser." He retrieved the bottle of wine. "We can finish this off, if you'll agree to stay."

Cora glanced at the half-empty bottle and the bed behind them. Then she nodded, realizing it was a proposition she didn't want to refuse.

Chapter Twenty-One

NOAH BAKER

It had been three days since Caroline and Noah parted ways and his burner phone remained silent. Noah paced the street opposite the police station. Was Grace inside? He quickly shook his head. That wasn't why he'd come.

He cracked his knuckles to relieve the tension. He knew who was working on the case; he'd seen the news; he'd seen *them* together. It made his blood boil. They didn't know what they were getting involved in.

But Noah did. He'd learned about the people who'd caused Grace to be this way, the ones he was going to destroy for destroying her. Despite himself, he still loved Grace, whoever she was.

Not having heard from Caroline, Noah believed he was on his own, but this wasn't new. He'd find the people responsible and fix what they had done. For Grace, for Caroline, and for every other person who had been affected.

His pacing stopped when he saw three people emerge from the police station. One left the others and went to a nearby car. The other two seemed to hesitate. From where Noah stood, he could make out a woman with cropped hair and a slightly taller man. Cora and Boone.

Together they walked away from the front of the police station. They seemed to be talking closely and soon Boone caught Cora's hand, turning her to face him.

Noah stepped back into shadows when he saw them look around as if checking to make sure no one was watching. When they believed it was safe, the two stepped closer and shared a quick kiss before going their separate ways.

Noah swallowed back the bile in his throat. He wasn't sure why their relationship sickened him so much. He thought of his girlfriend locked away behind bars, but as he tried to picture Grace's kind smile and caring eyes, Cora's sharp features took over. The object of his obsession. The thing that would never be his.

Cora's car passed by him on the street, but he doubted she even glanced in his direction, likely too caught up in her affair to notice Noah's presence. Boone, however, didn't drive. He plunged his hands into his pockets and started walking. He didn't look towards Noah and it was easy enough to follow the detective wherever he was headed.

Noah wasn't sure what he planned to accomplish, only that his feet took him in the same direction the other man walked. A part of him wanted to make it clear to Boone that what he had, in the jail cell and in his bed, were Noah's and no one else's.

At the hotel, the detective turned and entered. Noah stopped and waited. He leaned against the cold brick building across the road, watching the hotel doors.

Noah shivered in the cool night air. Crossing his arms over his chest, he considered leaving. Then her car pulled up outside the hotel. They couldn't have been parted more than twenty minutes. Cora didn't look around before entering the hotel.

His hands tightened into fists, which he quickly released. Whatever this anger was, it put Noah on edge and kept him rooted in place, watching, waiting.

He didn't know what he would gain from confronting the detective, but he couldn't let him continue what he was doing. If he got in the way, then Noah would never get what he wanted. Where was his revenge?

Boone posed a problem, nothing more. He would stop those responsible and bring them to "justice" before Noah even had a chance.

Noah wouldn't let it happen. Arrest and jail time wasn't for these monsters who'd caused such devastation in those using. They deserved worse; they deserved death; they deserved misery. To have everything they loved taken from them. They deserved to have their lives ruined as they had ruined Noah's and the others Caroline spoke of.

His anger was interrupted when he saw Cora emerge from the hotel. A quick glance at the time told him that an hour had passed.

Once she was gone, Noah only had to wait another half hour before the detective followed. His dark hair was slicked back with a wet gel that shone under the nearest streetlight. Noah immediately strode towards him. Boone didn't see him coming and Noah shoved him against the wall of the hotel.

"Get off," Boone said, grabbing hold of Noah's arms and struggling under his hold. But Noah was bigger, and he pushed his forearm against the detective's throat. "I'm a police officer," he choked out when he knew he couldn't fight Noah off. "This is enough to land you in jail."

Noah's eyes narrowed. "I know what you are doing, and you need to back off."

"What are you talking about?" Boone snapped.

"Cora, the case, the whole thing," Noah growled. "You're sticking your nose where you don't belong."

The detective frowned. "What do you know about my case?"

Noah pushed harder. "I said back off." Then he pushed himself off the wall and backed away from Boone, who reached up and rubbed at his neck where Noah had applied pressure. "Things will get a lot worse if you keep trying to make them better."

Noah turned and ran; he could feel Boone staring after him. He moved into the shadows and watched as the detective turned and headed to his car. He seemed shaken, even if he tried to hide it. Good. Noah had intimidated him.

When the detective was gone, Noah left as well.

Slowly, his anger began to dissipate, and he took several calming breaths. When he was a fair distance away from the hotel, his phone rang. He was quick to answer it with a simple "Hello."

"Towhee," the female voice responded.

"Flying low," Noah said, the code phrase that Caroline had given him.

"Fly north," Caroline said. "You know where to meet."

"When?" Noah asked, thinking about the trek he'd have to take across the river to Gatineau to meet Caroline at their predetermined location.

"Tomorrow, dusk."

"Okay."

The call ended. Noah pulled the phone from his ear and tucked it away. Then he started down the street. Back to the motel to sleep, then an early morning. Caroline said she'd only call if she found something. Noah hoped it was something that could bring the whole drug conspiracy to an end and even better if he could end the man himself.

Chapter Twenty-Two

BLAINE ROCHE

For four days, Blaine visited the addresses that Mel had curated. His search took him from Toronto to just outside of Ottawa, following Highway 401 and making each stop along the way. Much to his chagrin, he found the houses occupied by residents other than Alison. With only one left on his list, leading him to the center of downtown Ottawa, he'd crashed for the night in a dingy motel outside the city. He'd been sleeping in his car since the discovery of the addresses, and feeling grungy, sleep-deprived, and defeated, Blaine could think of nothing but rest.

The shrill ring of his phone jolted him out of a dreamless sleep. Groggy, he slapped it, trying to silence the incessant alarm. But the ringing didn't stop.

He reached for it and saw the psychiatric hospital's number on the screen. Blaine shook himself out of sleep, unsure what to expect from the strange call.

"Hello?" Had something happened to Patsy? How did they know how to reach him?

"You're an absolute idiot," the voice hissed.

Blaine recognized Mel's voice immediately. The tone, the annoyance, the inflection. He'd known her for years. They had been intimate. This was a voice he'd never forget.

"Mel?" he asked cautiously.

"Of course it's me." The words came out sharp, and Blaine imagined her teeth were clenched with irritation after she spoke.

"Why are you calling me?" Blaine fell back on the bed and glanced at the time. It was early, barely 6 a.m.

"Because you're messing everything up!" Mel's voice rose with frustration. "I didn't think you'd actually be stupid enough to go after Alison."

Blaine rubbed his eyes, unable to make sense of what she was talking about. Thankfully, Mel continued before he could ask.

"When Jenny showed up to visit, she told me everything," Mel snapped. "That you drilled her on questions about Alison and made it very clear you intended to find her."

Jenny would have spilled his secrets days ago. Perhaps he should have expected the call.

"Don't you want me to?"

Mel groaned with frustration. "Of course not. Alison can't give you anything more than what you already have."

Blaine didn't answer her. How could Melanie have any insight into what he'd found or what his plan was? She'd hidden this information and research about Alison from him their entire relationship.

"Don't do something stupid." Mel's voice softened. "You know Detective Hot Shot is on your trail. You're going to get caught if you don't stay away from her."

"I've been fine so far." Blaine frowned. He'd been on the run from Boone since that night at his farmhouse months ago. Since then, the man hadn't even come close to trailing him. Blaine was good at hiding. He'd been hiding in one way or another his whole life.

"Blaine, you're not listening," Mel pleaded with him in an unfamiliar way. It wasn't like her to be gentle, concerned. There was an edge of worry in her tone that made Blaine stop and consider her suggestion.

"I haven't seen her in years," Blaine said softly. He'd been waiting to find her. Waiting until it was safe. But safety never came. The drug was never discovered. This was his only chance to make it right. Alison had promised this time would come. Why not now?

"I know," Mel said. "And I know how much you loved her. But if you do this. If you go after them . . ."

Her voice trailed off. Blaine didn't need her to tell him what would happen if he went after the people behind this drug and failed. He already knew what would happen. It had been happening since the trials had been forged. Anyone who tried to bring light to the drug was dealt with, but Blaine couldn't just let it go.

"I'm not scared of what could happen," Blaine said gently. "I can't keep doing nothing."

Mel didn't answer him.

"There are more like you, Melanie," Blaine said. "More like Patsy. Like I tried to help you, Alison has been trying to help them. The truth needs to come out before this goes too far. Before anyone else's life is threatened."

"They have already threatened your life," Mel said. "That's why you found me in the first place. You are in danger from more than just that hotshot. You know that the cops finding you would be a better outcome than what happens if you fail."

Blaine closed his eyes. "You're right. But I also know what will happen if I don't try. And that isn't something I'm willing to risk."

"Then you really are an idiot." Mel's hard voice returned.

"Mel—"

"Don't say I didn't warn you." The call ended before he could challenge her again and Blaine was left alone in the silence of his motel room.

He placed the phone back on the bedside table and placed a hand over his eyes. Light trickled through the curtained windows. He wouldn't be able to get any more rest. Blaine had never been good at sleeping in anyway. Except when he had someone worth staying in bed with.

For a moment, his heart hurt. Hearing her voice, whether critical or caring, always made him twist with confusion. Was she Patsy, or was she the Melanie he'd gotten to know? Or was she somehow a combination of the two? Blaine wasn't sure. All he knew was that he'd fallen in love with whoever Mel was and it was hard to imagine a life without her in it.

Blaine knew there was no life with Melanie, no matter what the outcome. Whoever she was now wasn't the woman he'd been with. Whoever she was now was different enough. Blaine was different too. Revenge always changed people.

He'd been so willing to forget everything and have a life with Mel, despite the complications, despite her constant shifting. He'd been willing to find a way to make it work. He would have done whatever Mel asked of him.

But she couldn't cope with being two people at once. Her rigid exterior couldn't handle the meek, frightened woman she'd buried beneath and without help, Mel caved to her confusing desires. She'd rescued Patsy from their life of misery, but she'd sentenced Blaine to a life without her.

Blaine pushed himself from the bed and headed into the bathroom.

He couldn't deny the things Mel had told him. Finding Alison would mean trouble. Blaine didn't know how she'd been spending their years apart. Blaine didn't know if she'd been able to hide like he had, or if she was even on anyone's radar.

A part of him knew that even if he found her, Blaine couldn't stay with her long. Together, they gave way to their location, their plans. Together, they were recognizable by the people they were trying to avoid.

He stepped into the shower and let the warm water cascade down his body. Blaine could go on without seeing Alison. He could choose to stay away and continue his search to find Parsons. But even as he thought this, the idea of seeing Alison again tugged at his heart. It had been so long since he'd seen her. Since he'd hugged her. It had been so long since he'd had a family.

Even though his mind told him there was danger in the two of them together, he couldn't let the possibility go. He didn't know when he'd get another chance to tell her how much he loved her. How much he missed her and the life they'd had before all the bad happened. When they'd been nothing but carefree siblings, dreaming about the lives they would have together.

No, Blaine couldn't deny himself this one luxury. This one chance. He had to take it. He might never have it again.

Chapter Twenty-Three

CORA PORTER

C ora stumbled through the precinct doors. It had been an exhausting morning with Lyssa. Nothing would go right. She didn't want to get dressed. She didn't like the lunch Cora had packed. She didn't want to go to school. She didn't want Nana to pick her up at the end of the day.

All she wanted was Isaac. The one thing Cora couldn't deliver.

There'd been no word on her ex and his whereabouts for five days. The police and the investigators were coming up blank. Cora was getting more concerned by the hour. He'd only ever disappeared like this once in her memories of him, when he'd been on a particularly bad bender.

They'd been living together at the time. Lyssa was barely a year old and one night Isaac left his infant daughter alone in the house and disappeared. Cora had returned only moments later, thankful that Lyssa hadn't been abandoned for long. She'd been angry with Isaac, ready to reprimand him when he dared show his face back at the house, but he didn't come home. For days, Cora agonized over his whereabouts, worried, like she often was, that he'd become one of the many John Does who passed through the coroner.

When he turned up five days later looking haggard and bruised, Cora's anger had long since dissipated. She didn't yell, but she did give him an ultimatum. Get help, get clean, or don't be a part of Lyssa's life any longer.

At that point, Isaac hadn't cared much for his daughter and he left their home without a word. Cora used police resources to keep tabs on him, using street informants as a set of eyes on her troubled ex. While she hated Isaac for his carelessness and his endangerment of their daughter when he'd acted recklessly, Cora knew the man Isaac was before the alcohol changed him. She only hoped that man still existed.

A year later, when he finally sought help, Cora slowly allowed him to be a part of their daughter's life again. Things seemed better for a time, but in the past several months, he'd fallen off the wagon again. While he denied it vehemently, Cora knew better. She'd lived through this once and she wouldn't put her daughter in harm's way. Lyssa was old enough to understand and remember the trauma.

"Are you alright?" Ryan asked as he approached her.

Cora pushed the thoughts of Isaac and his whereabouts away. She'd done all she could to try to find him.

"I'm fine," Cora said. "It's just been a tough morning."

"I'm sorry. I get that." Ryan reached up and scratched at his chin in a way that said he wasn't finished talking.

"Are you okay?" Cora asked, studying his concerned expression and wondering what could be plaguing him this early in the morning.

"Something happened last night."

Cora frowned. "With the case?"

"Maybe." Ryan looked at the floor between them. "I was approached, handled, and threatened after I left the hotel last night."

"What?" Cora's heart began to race. "By who?"

Ryan shook his head. "I don't know. I'd never seen him before. He followed me from the hotel and pushed me up against a wall. He told me to back off the case, to back off *you*."

"Why?"

"He said I was sticking my nose where it didn't belong." Ryan shook his head again. "It was weird. He left before I could do anything." He reached up, running a hand along his collarbone.

Cora's stomach flip-flopped. The outburst sounded familiar—too familiar.

"Were there any defining features about him?" Cora pressed. "A scar?"

Ryan frowned. "I hate to say it, but I don't know. He was tall, with long, dark hair. I think his eyes were brown, but the lighting was so terrible, I can't say for sure." Ryan let out a sarcastic chuckle. "Some detective I am."

"He caught you off guard," Cora said, reaching out and touching Ryan's arm. "It happens to the best of us."

Ryan offered a curt nod but said nothing more on the subject. "Hunter and I were just going over Rickie's file. They're pushing for a quick trial. Will you join us?"

Cora's mind was elsewhere, focused on the assault Ryan had experienced and the words his attacker had spoken.

"Actually no," Cora said, dropping her hand to her side. "I completely forgot; I have to drop off Lyssa's school project. I came by just to quickly check in with the lab, but they seem fine."

She hadn't even had a chance to check on her workload, but she couldn't think about that now.

"You'll be back after?"

"Yes." Cora nodded. "I shouldn't be too long."

"Sounds good." Ryan turned and headed back toward Aidan's office and Cora turned on her heel.

Back in her car, it took all she had in her not to speed across town to Isaac's apartment.

When she arrived, the place was the same as it had been when she found Lyssa here alone several days ago.

If he hadn't been home, where had he been? For a moment, an image of him lying in the gutter with broken glass all around him popped in her mind. She closed her eyes and willed it away, refusing to think that he could be dead and still not found.

Cora remembered how, when another student back in college had asked her out for coffee, Isaac had attacked the man. She'd thought the invitation had been innocent, about class. When Isaac found out, though, he flew off the handle. He'd never been particularly level-headed, but the anger that came out of him when he'd confronted her classmate had scared the man off from ever speaking to Cora again. Thankfully, the class had ended a few months later and she never saw him again.

He'd had a similar reaction after Cora slept with Aidan for the first time. She'd kept Aidan at arm's length because of it, or so she told herself.

What Ryan had described seemed too much like Isaac's previous outbursts, but how would Isaac know about her relationship with Ryan? Had he been watching her? If he had, why hadn't he come forward? Cora's mind spun with the confusing possibilities.

There were dishes in the kitchen sink, the same ones that had been there when she picked up Lyssa days ago. The kitchen held a distinctive smell—rotten and dirty—and Cora scrunched her nose, moving into the next room.

It was stifling in the apartment, the air heavy, and Cora imagined no one had been through it in days. The bed was unmade and Lyssa's lone pop can still sat in the center of the coffee table. Cora moved to throw it out, but then she hesitated. The cop in her told her to leave everything as she found it.

In the bathroom, she opened the cabinet behind the mirror and stopped. Staring her in the face was an orange bottle of pills with Isaac's name written on the prescription. *Isaac Simon Kirby.* She reached for the bottle and slowly turned it in her hand, fearful of what it contained. Solydexran was written clearly on the label.

A pit formed in her stomach as she pocketed the pills. Could this mean Isaac had an alter? It was one of the possibilities that she hadn't allowed herself to consider. She could swear Isaac hadn't mentioned being on any medication recently, but maybe he'd chosen to keep her in the dark. Still, if there was another that lived inside of him, how could Cora not have known?

Before leaving his apartment, Cora took the lone framed photo from the mantel. It was Isaac and Lyssa grinning like fools as he took a selfie of them. She'd show Ryan the photo and see if he recognized Isaac as the man who'd approached him.

Cora was almost certain it was.

Chapter Twenty-Four

BLAINE ROCHE

The house was dark when Blaine pulled up out front. It wasn't unlike Alison to be incognito, especially after everything they'd been through, but as he approached the front steps, Blaine paused. He rounded the corner and fingered the remnants of yellow tape that rippled in the wind.

The police had been here. This had been a crime scene. Blaine's chest constricted. Had the police taken her?

Blaine went to the front door and tested the handle. The door swung open with a gentle creak and he was hit with the musty smell of an unaired house. The heat inside was sweltering and Blaine had no doubt that mildew or mold would start to form. Whoever actually owned this property should be informed.

The house was barren, other than some old, tattered furniture. Blaine paid little attention to the sitting room or kitchen, knowing Alison tended to hide her secrets in her bedroom, a habit brought on from childhood when they were in the system and Alison rarely had any space to herself. She was notorious for hiding her things from the other foster children.

That had kept up until the adoption. Her mothers had been kind, loving women and Alison had started to open up and come out of the shell she'd pushed herself into. She'd flourished and soon the hiding she used to practice was a thing of the past.

But Blaine knew one thing about Alison that never went away. She was a survivor and that survival instinct would resurface at a moment's notice.

Blaine descended the stairs to the lower level of the house. An odd design for bedrooms, but Blaine found what looked like the primary room easily. Inside, the closet doors had been left open and a false back tossed aside. It was clear the police had come through here and had taken little care for covering their tracks.

He took an inventory of the bedroom before deciding to follow the tunnel. It was dark and soon Blaine pulled out his phone, using the flashlight to illuminate the narrow corridor. The stone walls were aged and dirty and a few wooden steps led him down into the darkness. Cobwebs occupied every corner or nook that Blaine could see. His skin crawled as if he could feel them on him. He'd never really cared for bugs.

He remembered a time when Alison had chased him around the yard. They'd been young, before tragedy struck their quiet little family. Before their world came crashing down around them. Alison had found a particularly large spider hiding in the depths of their cellar. She'd caught it quickly and brought it to show her parents. Dad had expressed joy at their brave daughter. The look of disdain he held for Blaine when he recoiled from the creature was something Blaine never forgot.

What he wouldn't give to see his father's disappointment once more. While Blaine had wished as a young child that he could have a different family, come from a different home, have a father who loved him and wasn't hard on him, he hadn't realized what he truly had. What was lost the moment they vanished and never returned.

Blaine later learned the truth; his mother had been terminally ill, which accounted for her declining health and his father's protectiveness. Soon after she succumbed to her disease, his father threw himself off the city bridge, unwilling to raise unruly children and face the world alone. Blaine learned then that the strength he'd always thought he'd seen in his father had been a front.

He pushed the memory of his troubled childhood aside when the tunnel seemed to lighten. At the end was a cracked wooden doorway, which Blaine pushed out into the open air. So peculiar.

The city bustled behind him, but an outstretched field in front lay not far off, with a dense forest past it. To his left was the freeway, where cars whipped by at breakneck speed. To his right was a river that flowed downwards, disappearing into the field and then the forest.

He stood for a moment, considering his options. Alison had found her way here, then what? Had she met a car to take her out of the city? Had she trudged into the forest looking for shelter, or had she followed the river? Blaine opted for the latter and moved towards the flowing water but not before turning back and looking at the tunnel.

The entrance was shrouded with bushy ferns that hid the moss-covered doorway from view. It certainly wasn't impossible to locate, but unless one was looking for it, it was likely they'd miss it entirely.

A large rock jutted out from the side of the hill that held the tunnel. A message had been scraped into the stone. Had Alison left it for Blaine to find? He reached up and ran his fingers over the lines. They were jagged and looked like simple scratches. They would appear as natural markings to the police, but to Blaine, they told a story.

Three lines parallel to the river, to indicate the route that she had taken, as Blaine suspected. Then two lines horizontal to indicate she'd stopped. There was a partial triangle further from the lines, but clear enough to tell Blaine that it was part of the message.

Follow the river until the natural break, then stop and look east. It was vague, and Blaine wasn't certain what he would find, but he had no other options. It seemed they both were on the run from the police now, though what Alison's involvement was still perplexed him.

He gently traced the markings and thought about seeing his sister again. Would she be happy to see him? Blaine was certain she would. Alison had been leaving him clues, ones that only he would understand. She must be as lonely as he was.

Blaine began down the river, listening to the gentle flow of the water. It was peaceful and quiet, despite the freeway only a short distance away. The sun had begun to dip below the buildings behind him, casting the area in a gentle glow. He hoped he'd reach the natural stop before he was completely immersed in darkness.

By the time the river forked and flowed in two opposing directions, Blaine began to lose hope. The sun had long gone down and the moon lit up the surrounding area. To his left, a vast forest hid the freeway from view and Blaine had to stay close to the edge of the riverbed to ensure the moon would light his path. He'd already heard too many noises from the darkened trees to know he didn't want to come face-to-face with any creatures that might be hiding there, big or small.

He let out a long breath and glanced around. He couldn't see much, but he knew from Alison's drawing that he needed to look east, which also meant crossing the wide river.

Blaine shone his phone's light along the moving water, looking for any rocks or debris that could act as a bridge. For a moment, he wished he'd thought of crossing the river further south, back the way he'd come.

He tested a large boulder and hopped across the water, landing on the opposite bank. He surveyed his surroundings again, still unsure what he was looking for. Then he climbed a slight hill and found it. A tiny log cabin sat nestled among the tall reeds that encircled the area. Only one window was visible from where Blaine stood and although the blinds were drawn, there was clear light behind it. Someone was likely home.

Blaine trudged towards the cabin. It didn't give way to any noise inside the tiny home, but Blaine didn't worry. Alison had led him here and he could trust her. He lifted his fist and knocked.

Chapter Twenty-Five

NOAH BAKER

N oah waited in the darkness of the alleyway, unsure where Caroline was. He'd arrived exactly where she'd indicated. The sun had already begun to dip below the tall buildings surrounding him, still, he'd seen no sign of her. His skin began to prickle with unease. With everything Caroline had told him, Noah worried about being spotted with her. Were people other than the authorities searching from them, like Caroline had implied?

When he was about to give up hope and venture back out into the busy street, someone stepped into the alleyway. Noah moved back, looking for an escape, until the figure pushed back her hood and revealed Caroline's red hair. It glistened under the lone, dim light at the alleyway entrance.

He released a breath. "You came."

"Of course," she said softly, though her voice was rushed. "I found something I think you'll want."

She reached into her pocket and withdrew a folded piece of paper, which she promptly pressed into Noah's hand.

"What is this?" he asked as he unfolded the sheet. It was an address.

"You remember what I told you about why the drug was pushed to market?" Caroline's voice remained low.

Noah hesitated, hearing chatter and laughter at the mouth of the alleyway. Soon a group of young women sauntered by, but they didn't look in.

"Yes." Noah thought back to the conversation about Julie and the woman, Vivian. He remembered what his research had told him and how beautiful the young woman had been. He thought about what Caroline had asked him to do and Noah still struggled to see how he would execute her task.

Caroline pointed at the paper he still held. "That is where you can find her."

Noah frowned at the thought. There was so much he wanted to know about Solydexran and Grace. More so, he wanted to know about Julie and her involvement in the corruption.

Noah had never been a particularly warm person, but he couldn't understand how someone could be involved in a corporation that abducted people due to something they had caused. It was callous and so unlike Julie. Noah may have only dated her for a short period of time, but she'd been kind, genuine. The idea that she was going to report Grace, twisted the innocent image he held of her.

"I'm not sure," Noah said. Caroline wanted this man—Dylan Parsons—to suffer as she had. To have the thing he loved most taken from him.

Caroline's usually soft expression hardened. "What do you mean, you're not sure? They have ruined lives. Many of them. There is no justice in our legal system. There is only justice in death. A life for a life."

Noah frowned, looking over the address once more. He didn't wish to bring harm to someone like Vivian. He wasn't certain she deserved it and until it was proven otherwise, he couldn't imagine himself a murderer despite all that had happened with Julie.

Noah met Caroline's hard eyes and nodded. "No, you're right."

Caroline's shoulders relaxed and relief washed over her face. "Good."

He had no intention of fulfilling Caroline's wishes, not until he knew more. Noah had only agreed to help in the belief that in finding this woman, these people, he could learn the whole truth about Grace and the drug. Only then would he do what was necessary. First, he had a plan of his own.

Caroline glanced over her shoulder and drew her hood. "I have to go."

"Where can I find you?" Noah asked.

"You can't."

"But—"

Caroline cut him off. "We must part now. If we meet again, well . . . fate will decide that. For now, I have given you all I can."

She exited the alleyway, leaving Noah alone looking at the address in his hand. He waited a moment before following her steps and heading for the library. He'd look up the address and see where Caroline was sending him. It was in his city, so if he was lucky, she wouldn't be far.

Chapter Twenty-Six

BLAINE ROCHE

The door to the cabin swung open to reveal an elderly woman. Her paper-thin skin drooped at the sides of her lips and eyes. However, after giving Blaine a once-over, her dark eyes lit up and a smile broke through.

"We've been waiting for you." The woman stepped aside and allowed Blaine to enter. "You've taken longer than anticipated."

He hesitated at the threshold, unsure if he should follow the unknown woman's invitation. She simply continued to smile at him.

"She's in the kitchen," the woman said. "She's only just returned."

Blaine frowned but took a careful step through the front door, as if he might be struck down as soon as his feet hit the floor. When nothing happened, he continued through. The house was quaint, nothing much to look at. Blaine wondered how this woman survived out here alone. There hadn't been a road that one could take to her house, at least not that he'd been able to see. She claimed someone had just returned, so there had to be a way in and out. Still, she seemed isolated. Perhaps that was the appeal.

The furniture in the foyer was plain. A small love seat rested in the far corner and a plush chair sat by a lit fire. Both pieces were beige and faded with age. An aged box TV sat in the left corner opposite the chair. A style Blaine hadn't seen since his early teens.

"This way." The older woman hobbled past him towards an open door. It gave way to a small kitchen with a wood-burning stove and a rounded table. An old rotary phone hung on the wall.

Blaine stopped when he locked eyes with his sister. His heart began to thump at an unusual pace. Her dark eyes were tired, more tired than they'd been all those years ago. But beyond that, she hadn't changed much. She was still the short, stout sister he'd loved. Sturdy, their father had always said. She'd dyed her hair a terrible fake red and it must have been some time since she'd last treated it, as her dark roots were showing through. He thought it was a bad choice, but he knew she'd been hiding more than he had in these years past. She'd been the unlucky one.

"Thank god," Alison whispered. She pushed herself from the table and approached Blaine slowly, as if trying not to spook him. When she was within arm's reach, Blaine didn't hesitate. He wrapped his arms around her and pulled her close, deeply inhaling her lavender scent. He'd missed it in their years of separation. Once, it had been a scent of comfort.

Soon, her body began to tremble and Blaine knew that tears flowed freely from his sister's eyes. His own eyes welled. They were together again. The only family they had left.

Blaine allowed his hold on Alison to loosen and she stepped back, reaching up and wiping away the tears that streaked her face.

"I almost can't believe it," Alison whispered. "I never thought I'd see you again."

Blaine nodded, at a loss for words. He felt like he'd been searching for Alison for so long. Even when they parted, after the danger and the bad, he'd never stopped looking out for her. They'd agreed all those years ago that it was safer to be apart, that they could help people if they hid from the world. Blaine had never been as scared as Alison when it came to those who wanted to hurt them, but he was safer than she was. No one knew he existed.

"Greta," Alison said to the elderly woman. "Do you mind giving us a moment?"

Greta smiled and exited the kitchen without a word. Alison motioned to the table, inviting Blaine to sit across from her.

"Are you okay?" she asked.

Blaine shrugged. "I mean, as okay as I think either of us can be at this point." He paused. "The police have been through your house."

"I know," Alison said. "I knew they were coming. The moment they arrested Rickie Hastings, my time in this city was done."

"Aren't you worried about them finding you here?" It wasn't like the cottage was impossible to find.

"We'll know if they're coming." Alison shrugged, then pointed at a device on the kitchen counter. It looked like an old police scanner.

Blaine frowned but didn't answer.

"I understand you've experienced the same—the cops coming to your house, looking for the ones you've helped." She didn't say it, but Blaine suspected Alison had kept tabs on him over the years. She'd never been one to let him too far out of her sights. Big sisters were like that.

For a moment, Blaine was bitter that she'd never come to find him, like she once promised she would. But as quickly as the thought came, he pushed it away. There were too many reasons that had kept them separated over the years.

"Something like that."

Alison nodded. "Did she ever get help? Patsy?"

Blaine's throat tightened at the mention of his once-lover. "I couldn't save her."

"You were never meant to save her." Alison offered a sad smile. "You did all you could. At least *they* didn't get her."

"The police did get her," Blaine said, confused by who Alison was referring to.

"Oh, you were always so naïve. Being in police custody is the best place for Patsy. They can help her. They can keep her safe, little mouse."

Blaine flinched at hearing his old nickname pass through Alison's lips. It was one she had coined for him in the early years of their family. Blaine had been so meek and quiet compared to Alison. She used to joke that as a baby, he wouldn't coo, but squeak. Blaine wasn't certain how true the story was, but for many years, Alison called him nothing else. He'd nearly forgotten.

"Who are they keeping her safe from?" He had a good guess. The same man he was looking for. The one who'd ordered every bad thing that had happened. The drugs, the murders, the disappearances. He was the driving force behind it all.

"It got bad after you left," Alison said. "They started taking people. Anyone who they found was afflicted, anyone who could give Solydexran a bad name."

"Taking them where?"

Alison shook her head. "I don't know. I found a young woman several years ago who was suffering badly. It was more than just one other personality that lived within her and they battled. I tried to help her, to keep her with me, but whenever a new person came out, she would leave. I kept an eye on her, even when she wasn't the one that I'd been close with. Just to make sure she was okay, you know?"

Blaine nodded. He did know. He'd done the same with Mel over the two years they'd been together, and he always knew when she returned to Fraser. He'd tried too hard to stop her.

"Then, one day, she was picked up on the side of the road by an unmarked van. Just pulled up beside her and brought her in. She went willingly, so who knows what they told her. I tried to follow them, but I lost it. I never saw her again after that. I went by her apartment and it was like she'd never lived there. It was then I realized that I was not the only one on the lookout for the afflicted."

Blaine wondered if the company kept tabs on every Solydexran user. Though considering how widespread the drug was and the way Dr. Miranda Konch had been paid off, Blaine doubted that they'd be able to track them all. After all, the drug had provided more good than bad in the original trials. Maybe this was their way of cleaning up their own mess. At the expense of others.

"You're saying there is some huge conspiracy that traps and possibly kills those who have suffered from the effects of Solydexran," Blaine said. The idea sounded so farfetched. It was true the reports had been forged, it was true there was a darkness behind this drug that had forced him and Alison to separate and hide, but to be abducting people, just to keep the drug on the market? Just to avoid the scandals? Blaine wasn't sure he could believe that.

"That's exactly what I'm saying." Alison's tone was firm, authoritative. "There is something bigger going on here. There always has been. It's no coincidence what happened all those years ago. You know that better than anyone."

Blaine did, but he'd tried hard to suppress the memories. The strange phone calls, the feelings of being followed. The random break-ins.

They'd run when whoever hunted them came too close. They'd been running ever since, hiding, lying, anything to keep one step ahead of them.

"It just seems like a lot for a drug," Blaine said.

Alison shook her head. "It's big money. It's Big Pharma. Could you imagine the implications if this all surfaced now? ACE would be done. There's no coming back from this."

"But it's coming out," Blaine said. "Whether they want it to or not." What had happened with his girls couldn't just be denied. That detective—Boone—wouldn't allow his evidence to be swept under the rug, even if it seemed like the case had been.

Alison let out a sarcastic laugh. "Because someone figured it out? Didn't you figure it out all those years ago? Didn't we try to stop it? Look where it got us. What do you think is going to happen to a low-level detective who questions a money-making corporation? You know this is beyond corrupt."

Blaine didn't answer, as he couldn't match his sister's cynicism. She thought him naïve, as she always had, but he knew more about this than she realized. He knew about ACE and about Vivian. He knew about the dangers of being involved with them—and of opposing them. He'd come so close to losing it all before he ran, but he'd also seen Boone at work. He'd seen the level of care and caution the experienced detective brought to his job. Blaine knew the man was searching for him, but he also knew that Boone cared about the girls he'd found. He knew something bigger was going on, and he wanted to stop it.

This was so beyond a drug that had helped one young woman and hindered others. This was a crime.

"They're looking for both of us," Alison said when Blaine did not respond. "They'll figure you out eventually. All of it. And our arrest—well, it's only a matter of time before they pull us into the depths of this conspiracy. We don't have the evidence to prove any wrongdoing."

Blaine shifted in his chair. That wasn't entirely true. He'd left the research for Boone to find. He'd made sure the police had all the falsified details on the Solydexran trials. The evidence was out there now; he was certain it was just a matter of time.

"What will you do?" Blaine asked.

Alison let out a long breath. "I should leave, but I can't yet. There's someone else who I've been helping. He's in danger."

"Another afflicted?"

Alison nodded. "His name is Isaac. He got too close to one of ACE's employees and she paid dearly for it. Now he's out for revenge."

"What did you tell him?"

Alison looked down.

"He doesn't know, does he?" Blaine had kept the secret from his girls for a long time. He knew the burden, but sometimes revealing the truth too soon was worse.

Alison shook her head. "I didn't know how to tell him. His alter, Noah, is the one I've met most recently. He doesn't know that there's another living inside him."

"What did you do?"

Again, Alison looked away from Blaine's accusatory gaze.

"He was so angry . . ." Her voice was quiet. "I saw an opportunity."

"To do what?"

"I sent him after Vivian." Alison whispered the words, and Blaine stiffened.

"Why would you do that?"

When Alison dared to look at him again, her eyes were shining with tears. "Because Parsons deserves to know what it's like when your life and loved ones are threatened or taken from you."

Blaine's eyes widened. "You ordered a hit on an innocent woman? This isn't like you."

"You don't know what I'm like," Alison said. "What I've seen. I can't bear the idea of you going after him. I can't allow you to get that close to them again. After what happened . . . I could actually lose you this time."

"That was stupid, Alison. Even for you. You sent someone who has no idea what is going on inside them to fight our battle? Are you so afraid of them?"

"Of course I'm afraid!" Her voice rose. "Why aren't you? You've seen what they do to people who oppose them? We're lucky we made it out alive."

Blaine's chest tightened as he thought back to the release of the drug and the failed trials. Alison wasn't wrong. They were lucky when others hadn't been so, but this was *their* fight, no one else's. This had always been their cross to bear. Their failure to stop. It wasn't fair to put it on someone who'd needlessly suffered.

"I don't want to hurt you," Blaine said slowly. "But you must realize that by asking this man to avenge us, to try and fix this, you're as bad as they are. You're using him and he doesn't even know it."

Alison's face crumpled with sadness. "That is not true."

"It is," Blaine said, though he kept his tone gentle. "You know it is. And worse, you're not sorry."

Alison closed her eyes.

Blaine's breathing hitched as he considered his sister's actions. Did Alison know anything of this man, Isaac? Did he have a family? Her endangerment of another, especially one harmed by the drug, was so out of character that Blaine wasn't sure how to respond to it.

Finally, he said, "I need you to give me everything you gave him."

"Little mouse, no—"

"This was always going to be my fight." Blaine stood. "I won't let someone else go down for something I intend to fix."

Alison stood to meet him. "I don't want to lose you."

"Maybe you're supposed to," Blaine said simply. "Maybe all those years ago, you should have let this go. Let me go."

Alison's eyes grew wide. "How can you say that?"

"Because I never wanted you to have this life," Blaine said. "Neither of us did. Yet here you are. Now tell me what you know and I'll go."

Alison's shoulders slumped in defeat. "I'll tell you, but please stay the night. We're safe here for now."

Blaine nodded and followed his sister from the kitchen. Regret boiled up inside him as he saw how defeated and exhausted she was. It was time this ended, one way or another. The truth needed to come out. Even if it meant exposing himself to the danger he'd been running from for the last decade.

Chapter Twenty-Seven

CORA PORTER

Cora's knuckles ached as she rapped on Ryan's hotel room door. She'd returned to the precinct with Isaac's photo, only to learn that Ryan had left without a word. Cora had tried calling and texting, then calling the hotel, but without any luck.

Before she could investigate it further, she was interrupted by a call from Lyssa's school. Her daughter had gotten into a fight with another child. There was scratching, crying, hair pulling. An absolute mess. When Cora retrieved Lyssa and then dropped her off at her parents, as originally planned, her seven-year-old wouldn't say two words to her. Cora was getting desperate. She needed to find Isaac. She and Lyssa needed an answer.

"Ryan?" Cora called, banging on the door again.

When the door finally swung open, Ryan stood before her bare-chested with a towel wrapped around his waist. His damp hair stuck out in every direction and droplets of water rolled down his worried face.

"Jeez, Cora, are you okay?"

Heat shot up her neck. What had she been thinking? She'd come over frantic, banging down his door like a lunatic.

"I am so sorry." Cora's eyes were so wide and crazed, it felt like they were trying to jump out of her skull. "I don't know what I was thinking."

"It's okay." Ryan's voice was gentle. He stepped aside, allowing her space to enter.

Still, Cora hesitated.

"C'mon," he coaxed. Ryan reached out and took her hand, gently guiding her further into the room. When the door close behind him, he motioned to the bathroom. "Can you give me one minute?"

Cora nodded and sat on the edge of the king-sized bed.

Ryan turned into the bathroom and exited a minute later, dressed and with his hair combed back. He gave her a playful smile.

"All ready now." Ryan settled onto the bed next to her. "Now, tell me what has you so upset."

Cora lowered her eyes and let out a steady breath before reaching into her pocket and passing him the folded photo of Isaac and Lyssa.

Ryan's thick eyebrows folded with concentration as he looked over the picture. "This is him," he said when he looked up at her. "The guy that approached me the other night. He looks a little different, absolutely, but it's him."

Cora's shoulders slumped forward. The idea started to form in her head. "I think Isaac may have an alter." The words came out so quietly, she wasn't sure she'd said them.

"Isaac . . ." Ryan said slowly.

"Lyssa's dad."

Ryan glanced back at the photo. He ran a thumb across the side of the picture, which showed a younger Lyssa smiling brightly.

"This is your daughter." It wasn't a question, simply a fact. "She's beautiful."

Cora nodded her thanks as she took the photo from Ryan's hands. Sadness passed over her as she looked into Isaac's once-beautiful eyes. He'd had his bad days, Cora knew that. He'd suffered panic attacks since he was young. Did he turn to Solydexran in hopes to be the father that Cora so often pressured him to be? Could this partly be her fault?

"Hey.," Ryan's gentle voice broke through her downward spiral and he touched her arm. "What's going on? Why do you think he has an alter?"

Cora fished out the bottle of Solydexran from her purse and placed it in Ryan's hand. "I found these in his apartment."

Ryan flipped the bottle around in his hand, reading the label.

"The confrontation you described," Cora said. "It's happened before. Isaac could be jealous."

"You think your ex held me up out of jealousy?" Ryan asked.

Cora shook her head. "No, I think a part of him held you up, but I don't know why."

"This doesn't necessarily mean he has an alter." Ryan rotated the bottle of pills. "Do you know if he's ever suffered from any dissociation?"

Cora shook her head. "Not that I've ever seen. Other than his drinking and drug use, Isaac always seemed so normal."

"We should make an appointment with the Dr. Stephanie Kwon listed here. She might have some insights," Ryan suggested.

Cora had considered this, but without a warrant, Dr. Kwon wouldn't tell them anything.

"I think him having an alter would make sense," Cora said. "His unexplained disappearances, his untouched apartment. Maybe it wasn't him that held you up, but someone who lives inside of him."

Ryan didn't look convinced, but it didn't stop Cora from blaming herself. She leaned forward and placed her face in her hands, forcing her rapid heartbeat to slow.

"I told Isaac that he could only be in Lyssa's life if he got his shit together. What if he started taking this medication as an attempt to do that?" She looked up at Ryan. "I basically sealed his fate with an ultimatum."

"Whoa, whoa, whoa," Ryan said. "You're jumping to conclusions. You don't know what has happened with Isaac or why he started taking this medication." Ryan placed his arm across Cora's shoulders, and she leaned into him. "This is not your fault. This is the farthest thing from your fault, okay? We'll talk to the doctor and see what she says. If Isaac is suffering like we've seen others suffer, then we just have to find him and get him help."

Cora rested her head on his shoulder, running through the scenario in her head. It seemed to explain so much. Isaac's strange disappearances, his lies. For all Cora knew, Isaac suffered like she'd seen with Rickie and Grace. Perhaps Isaac didn't know that another lived inside him. For all he knew, the truths he told were the only truths.

Cora straightened. "What if we show Rickie the photo of Isaac and Lyssa?"

"What?" Ryan frowned.

"Maybe, like the girls in your case, they've met each other." Cora had to admit that two random people having coincidentally met in a city as large as theirs did seem farfetched, but at this point, what did they have to lose?

"I guess it's possible," Ryan said. "Especially if we think someone like Alison is bringing these people together."

Cora stood, ready to burst into the detention center and demand to see Rickie, but as if reading her mind, Ryan reached up and pulled her back to the edge of the bed. "We'll have to wait until morning."

She chewed on her lower lip, certain she couldn't get any rest or push this idea from her mind for an entire evening, but she also knew Ryan was right. They couldn't pull Rickie into questioning now. Besides, Rickie might prove to be as clueless as he'd ever been. It was really Grace they needed to speak to.

"You're right." Cora allowed her stiff shoulders to relax, and she shrugged off her jacket.

"Did you still want to stay?" Ryan asked, his tone hopeful.

"Of course," Cora said. She'd made the plan to have Lyssa stay with her parents, as going home would only make her more anxious and she'd have no distraction. "But can we stay in, order room service? I don't think I can handle a busy restaurant right now."

"Deal." Ryan stood to fetch the menu.

Chapter Twenty-Eight

BLAINE ROCHE

"*What* are you doing here?" Alison snapped. Her eyes were wide and wild. Blaine had never seen her look this way before.

He'd returned to her home only a few minutes before, expecting to have a quiet dinner with his only remaining family. Something he'd grown used to over the years. It had been difficult when he'd been on his own.

But now, something was wrong.

"I told you I was coming," Blaine said. Her house was a mess, with items strewn about like she'd been looking for something. Then he saw it. His suitcase by the door. Hers lay open in the main room, half-filled. She was leaving, but where?

Alison shook her head as if his answer was foolish. "You have to leave, now!"

"Why?" Blaine's heart began to race. Where was he supposed to go? She'd been taking care of him for the past two years. She was the only life he knew now. He didn't want to be alone again.

"Because I can't take care of you anymore," she snapped. "You've mooched off me long enough. You need to get out."

Blaine stepped back. He hadn't mooched at all. He'd brought his own money and he helped around the house. Other than keeping a roof over his head, Alison's care had been little. He'd hardly been a burden.

"But I—"

"No." Alison cut him off. "Enough is enough. You need to leave now."

Blaine studied her for a moment. The quick rise and fall of her chest. The way her eyes bulged in anger—no, fear. She wasn't mad. She was scared. But why?

"Let me help you." Blaine stepped closer to her, and she immediately recoiled.

"You can't help me." Alison pushed him towards the door. "And even if you could. I don't want it. You have to go. Don't call me. I'll call you, when I know I can."

"Alison," Blaine said. "What's happening?" He tried so hard to keep his voice calm and steady, but the fear radiating from his older sister shook him to his core. She was the brave one. She was the strong one. Something had broken her.

She stepped closer to him and thrust a folded letter into his hands. "Just run. You need to save yourself. I'm too dangerous to be with now." Alison gave him one last gentle push out the door, then threw his bag of luggage out with him and slammed the door in his face before Blaine had a chance to respond.

Slowly, he unfolded the letter and read the words written there. His body went cold. She was right. It was no longer safe. He picked up the bag she'd thrown at him and turned to go. He had no choice now. He had to run.

The memory vanished as quickly as it came. Blaine stared into the flames dancing in the fireplace. For a moment, he thought it odd that the memory had come to him now. Maybe seeing Alison had triggered the reminder of how their once-perfect sibling relationship had ended.

Before Blaine was kicked out, Alison had been dating a married man who had no regards for her feelings. She allowed him to treat her poorly, because he was wealthy and he could take care of her. That was all Alison had ever wanted.

When he inevitably ditched her, which Blaine had always known he would, Alison crumbled. It was strange now, sitting with her and knowing more about how their troubles all began.

"What are you thinking about?" Alison asked, eyeing him carefully. "You have that look about you."

Blaine offered a small smile. "The last time we saw each other, actually."

Alison visibly stiffened at the mention. "Why?"

"I don't know," Blaine said. "I guess because I'm seeing you again now."

"That was a long time ago. Things are different now."

"Different, but more dangerous."

Alison shrugged, as if the danger didn't worry her anymore. Blaine knew it was an act. A wall built up over years of fear and pain. He knew the feeling too well.

"But now we have a purpose," Blaine said.

She nodded but didn't speak again on it.

When they'd been silent for a time, Blaine shifted and turned towards his sister. "I want to ask you about Patsy."

Again, Alison nodded, like she'd known this was coming. "Of course, you do. Go ahead."

"Why did you stop helping her?" Blaine demanded. "When I met Mel, she was a total mess." He still remembered the way she'd looked at him that first night in the bar, when she'd been cold and closed off. He almost laughed at the thought. Mel was always cold and closed off, even after her walls started to crumble for him.

A hint of sadness crossed Alison's face. "I'm ashamed to say that I thought there were others who needed me more."

"Isaac?" Blaine offered.

"Him," Alison agreed. "And others. Ottawa has been a cesspool of the afflicted. When I discovered that people were being taken, I sort of forgot about Patsy and her trials. Besides, Toronto was too far away for me."

Blaine didn't like her answer, but he knew it to be true. Alison would never let Parsons out of her sight if she could help it.

"Was she the first?" Blaine asked.

Alison shook her head. "I focused on the people I knew from the trials. The ones I could find, that hadn't been conveniently covered up. I worked with them. Encouraged them to give up the medication if they were still using. I tried to find a solution."

"Did you succeed at all?" Blaine tried to keep the bitterness out of his tone.

A strained look appeared on Alison's face and she didn't answer the question. Blaine didn't press her.

"How did you find out about me and Patsy?" Alison asked.

Blaine gave a short laugh. "From Melanie of all people. She sent me to the private care centre in Kingston where you were both treated. A young boy there mentioned your constant visits."

"I felt for her," Alison said. "Before the shifts even became a problem. She was so broken."

That, Blaine understood.

"When we first met, she was so kind. She denied any wrongdoing by that monster of a husband." Alison's expression tightened.

Blaine grimaced, though Fraser had gotten what was coming to him after all the years of abuse.

"I just wanted to help her," Alison said. "Give her someone to talk to. Then, one day, I met Melanie. The hospital thought she was having a mental breakdown, but when I learned about the Solydexran, I knew the truth. I told her sister to remove the pills from the house each time they saw each other, but it didn't stop her from getting a new prescription filled whenever Patsy thought she needed it." Alison shook her head. "I wish I had done more."

Blaine looked away because he felt the same. He stood, as he had nothing else to say on the topic and reached for the file Miranda Konch had given him. When he lowered himself back on the couch, he passed the information to Alison.

"This is from the doctor who treated Patsy," Blaine explained. "Three of her patients suffered side effects and her practice is almost destitute from the fallout. I got her to pass along any other names she could. Those are them."

"Other users?" Alison asked, flipping open the folder and scanning the contents.

"Yes," Blaine said. "I thought you might know best how to handle them."

For a moment Alison scanned the words on the page in front of her. Then she flipped the folder shut. "Thank you."

They sat in silence for a moment before Blaine spoke again. "I was angry at you, all those years ago."

Alison nodded, like she knew it to be true.

"I didn't understand why you pushed me away," Blaine said. "Despite what happened. You promised you'd always be there for me. You promised we'd stay together."

"I've broken a lot of promises over the years," Alison said as she tore her eyes away from Blaine, shame written on her face. "I was naïve. I thought I could fix everything. I thought he would listen to me."

"It took me a while to understand that," he said. "For a long time, I didn't forgive you for pushing me out. I understood why. But I never thought you made the right choice."

"And now?" Alison asked.

"I'm still not sure you did," he said simply. He wondered if their lives could have been different. If instead of running and hiding and being apart, they could have both gone to the Roche farm. Perhaps they could have found their own safety, hidden in plain sight. They'd been doing just that all along. Maybe, if Blaine had taken Alison out of Ottawa, maybe then this wouldn't have been their lives. Their problem. Even as he thought it, though, he knew it would have always been a mess they'd be tied up in. There was no way he and Alison could have left all this behind.

"But?" she prompted, as if she knew something else would follow.

"But, if you hadn't, then who knows what would have happened to my girls?" Blaine said. "Who knows what would have happened to us?"

Alison nodded but didn't answer.

Blaine reached out and grasped his sister's hand. "I'm glad you kept some of your promises."

"I kept as many as I could."

They sat for another moment in the quiet, listening to the fireplace crackle and settle as new wood caught flame. Then Alison stood.

"I'm going to help Greta with dinner. I'm sure you're hungry."
Blaine nodded his thanks and watched his sister go.

Chapter Twenty-Nine

BLAINE ROCHE

A fter dinner, Blaine lay on the short beige couch and stared at the cracked ceiling. He couldn't truly describe what he was feeling. Relief at seeing Alison and knowing she was still alive, anger that they'd been apart for so long—when it seemed she'd known exactly where he was the whole time, sadness thinking of the woman he'd lost and how she too had been close with Alison. Perhaps in another life, Blaine and Patsy would have been together. That was a life Blaine often forced himself to forget.

Alison emerged from the kitchen holding two cups of steaming tea. "I thought you might want a night cap."

She placed the cup on the coffee table between them and settled into the armchair.

Blaine sat up and reached for the discarded cup. He blew on the steaming liquid and inhaled the scent of peppermint. Alison's specialty. She made it from fresh mint leaves. He set it back down, as it was too hot to sip. But Alison continued to clutch her cup between her hands.

"I'm sorry," Alison said, though Blaine wasn't sure what she was apologizing for. His expression must have said so, as she continued, "I never thought I'd put another person in harm's way. And honestly, I didn't think of the consequences until you looked at me like that earlier."

Blaine glanced away, unsure what to say. Alison's choice to get one of the afflicted mixed up in their problems surprised him. Blaine hadn't meant to hurt her feelings, but the act went against everything they'd ever done for the people they'd inadvertently hurt.

"Why don't you tell me about him?" Blaine asked. "You said his name was Isaac?"

Alison nodded. "I met him a long time ago. Around the time I met Patsy. I discovered he was a new user because a friend tipped me off. But Isaac was fine. Sure, he had some anxiety issues and I could tell the drug wasn't helping him in the way it had others, but no alters had surfaced, at least none that I could see."

"Why did you help him?"

"I wanted to convince him to get off the drug." Alison sipped her tea slowly. "I could tell where it was headed and I believed I could help him. And for a time, it seems, I did."

"But you said an alter eventually surfaced," Blaine said. "Did he stay on the drug?"

"I don't know," Alison said. "When he showed up at my door after everything that happened with Julie Kanner, I realized who he was. Grace, that woman I was helping, had told me about a man she'd fallen for. One she believed was afflicted like her. She had wanted me to meet him but could never convince Noah to come to my place. When he arrived after Julie's death and introduced himself, I knew it was Isaac immediately, though it had been years since I'd seen him. I invited him in and when I realized he didn't recognize me or know the truth, I saw an opportunity."

Alison looked away, ashamed. They'd covered her lies earlier in the evening, and Blaine didn't need her to repeat them.

"That woman, Julie. I'd learned from Grace that she had a jealous streak. When I looked into Julie, I realized she was tied to ACE."

Blaine nodded. "An employee." He remembered the quick search he'd done after discovering the article in the *Ottawa Citizen*.

"That's not all," Alison explained. "As I learned more, I discovered she was Dylan's niece and likely had a vested interest in the company's success."

"She was reporting those afflicted?" Blaine still couldn't wrap his head around the conspiracy that people were vanishing. The whole operation made it seem like they were in some crazed thriller movie. It seemed impossible that a company's reach could be so far, that no one would notice loved ones disappearing.

"I believe she intended to."

"Then she died?" Blaine looked down at the cup on the table in front of him and reached for it, hopeful it would have cooled enough to sip. His head was spinning with the information she'd shared since his arrival. The murder of a young woman, the alters tied into it. It made him shiver with familiarity. It was all too similar to what had happened with his girls. A preventable murder, caused by a corrupt drug.

Alison didn't answer his inquiry, but he didn't need her too. The murder was old news now. He'd seen the papers. The reports of the murder, the photo of the man—Rickie—who was responsible. Alison had explained that she knew him as Grace and that she alone was guilty of the crime.

"Did you tell them?" Blaine asked. "About Julie and who you thought she was?"

Alison pressed her lips together in a way that told Blaine she didn't want to elaborate. She'd confessed to heinous practices already and Blaine still grappled with the fact that she'd put another in a dangerous place, but something told him the secrets weren't done. They were never done when it came to Alison.

She'd been a vault of secrets since they were kids and she always held it over his head. The older sister. The one in charge. The designated secret keeper.

Alison believed she did it for his own good. She protected him from things that he didn't need to know. In truth, she was protecting herself. Keeping her brother at arm's length from her own mistakes and the choices she'd made. In some ways, she'd started all of this. Blaine knew she struggled with that regret sometimes.

Still, they weren't kids anymore and this wasn't a game. People's lives were in danger and even if she'd meant well, Alison had helped put some of them there.

"Alison," Blaine said. "Did you tell them?"

"I told Grace." She said it so softly, it took a moment for Blaine to register her words.

He didn't answer right away. He wasn't sure what to say. She'd effectively put the weapon in the alter's hand. She'd fanned the flames.

"I know what you're thinking," Alison said. "But I trusted Grace. We'd been close and she was kind, gentle. I couldn't predict what she would do."

Blaine looked away from his sister so she wouldn't see the pity that filled his eyes. He understood the closeness she'd felt to the alter. It was a closeness he'd had with Melanie. A trust. Love. Blaine had been certain that their love was enough, that she cared for him enough, but he'd been wrong.

"No matter who we believe these people to be," Blaine said, "they're very sick. They're mentally unwell. These alters are not our friends. They cannot care for us. They cannot give us what we seek out from other people. They are ill and that is the bottom line."

"Don't you think I know that?" Alison snapped.

"Do you?"

"Of course, I do. I made a mistake."

It had been more than one mistake. Blaine looked away, unwilling to reveal his thoughts with a single look. The woman—Julie—was dead because of Alison. Because she trusted someone who was unwell with a dangerous secret. It was naïve. Foolish. And exactly what Blaine had done with Melanie.

His stiff shoulders softened and he looked back at his older sister with sad eyes. "I'm sorry. I know how lonely this can be. I know how easy it is to fall for the people you're trying to help."

Alison's hardened expression melted away and she simply nodded.

Blaine sipped his tea and let Alison's warm peppermint drink take him back to sunny August afternoons on her porch or cool fall evenings by the fireplace. He let the sweet flavour envelope him in lost memories and a past that seemed impossibly far away. Back then, they could never have predicted where they would be now.

"Little mouse, I need you to know something," Alison said. "Noah, Isaac, whoever he is—well, I felt terrible after I sent him off on a revenge path that would likely get him killed. I felt terrible that I'd never told him the truth. So, I left something behind in my apartment. A note. I stuck it inside a figurine that I made sure to point out to him when he first visited. I don't think the cops would have touched it. It wouldn't have looked like anything more than an old decoration. I hoped one day he'd find it and he'd learn the truth."

Blaine grimaced at the cryptic ways in which Alison tried to share the truth. She'd never been one to be forthright. It always needed to be shared in subtle ways so she could deny any involvement. Exactly like their secret room and the box of knick-knacks Blaine carried.

"I understand," he said. "We will fix this."

Alison looked at him with tired eyes. "We've been trying to fix this for years."

"I know, but this time, we have to believe that something will be done." Blaine hadn't lost hope yet. He still believed that Boone would do anything he could to bring to light the research he'd found in Blaine's old house. He had to believe it—otherwise everything he'd ever done would be for nothing.

Chapter Thirty

NOAH BAKER

Noah had to take two buses before he was standing outside Vivian Parsons's townhome. The subdivision was gated and he found himself crawling through bushes and darting around trees to avoid being caught by the security camera at the top of the entrance gate.

Those types of gates only kept vehicles out. They didn't stop the desperate people on foot from finding a way through unnoticed.

This area was ritzy—and far from Noah's taste. The manicured lawns were all immaculate, with grass cut to the exact same height. The concrete sidewalks were swept clean and free of bird droppings or discarded gum. Noah imagined there was a by-law officer on call waiting to reprimand any wayward gum spitters with a hefty fine.

The rows of houses were cookie-cutter, with matching doors, windows, and colourful gardens, as if none were able to step outside the expected look of the neighbourhood. It felt rigid and controlled, two things that put Noah on edge.

He'd seen her only once, through the front window. Her long, flowing hair swayed as she moved. He stayed out of sight while he watched her. She seemed to be dancing around the room. Noah had been mesmerized by her beauty. He found himself wondering what she was listening to. What made her so joyful in a world so filled with hate and discomfort.

He wanted to know her, understand her. He wanted to feel her joy and let it warm him. He hadn't known such joy since before Julie's untimely murder.

His thoughts quieted when he saw her front door swing open. Vivian stepped out dressed in a long black dress that reached her ankles. She wore a pair of black high heels and Noah imagined the toned legs beneath and her buttocks, firm and plump. He shook his head as she turned her head toward him. Nerves swirled around inside him. Had he been caught already? But Vivian seemed to look past him and soon her eyes found the ground in front of her as she made her way down the sidewalk. He waited for her to get into a car, waited to lose her entirely, but she didn't.

Instead, she lifted her purse strap over her left shoulder and began walking towards the entrance gates. Noah fell into a slow step behind her, keeping his distance. He didn't look like he belonged here and he couldn't have anyone catch him. But even as he knew this, he was unable to keep himself from following her. His eyes were trained to the gentle sway of her hips and the way the cool wind tousled her curled hair. No wonder she could captivate an audience.

Her beauty alone made him consider abandoning Caroline's request and his desire to hurt those who had harmed Grace. Seeing Vivian made him wonder if the drug could really be all bad. If it really was worth the life of others so this angelic woman could have a life of peace.

As they neared the front gate, Noah stepped off the path and went back through the trees the way that he'd come. He kept an eye on Vivian from a distance, seeing her smile and wave at the gate attendant and soon she continued down the street towards a waiting car.

Noah stayed back, knowing he wouldn't be able to follow where Vivian went in the car, but he made note of the make and model—Chevy Cruze, black. How extraordinarily basic. It seemed out a character for someone like her.

Vivian hesitated before climbing into the passenger side. The joyful smile that she'd offered the attendant had vanished and a look of worry had melted in place. She glanced around quickly, as if making sure no one was watching her. Then when satisfied, she slipped into the car, pulling the door shut behind her.

Noah watched the black car disappear down the street. Why wouldn't they have picked her up at the gate, or better yet, at her house?

All feelings he'd felt about Vivian and the necessary sacrifices to give her a wonderful life were paused. Clearly, she was hiding something too.

Chapter Thirty-One

CORA PORTER

The next day, Cora stood outside the visitation room while Ryan and Aidan spoke to Rickie. He'd been in disbelief at first, but slowly seemed to thaw to the idea that there was something inside him that could assist the detectives. Still, Grace refused to make an appearance. Cora wondered if having Rickie clear of the drug had made him more lucid and less likely to fall prey to Grace's control. Whatever the cause, without her, Cora feared they'd never get a straight answer.

When questioning seemed unable to provoke Grace's arrival, Ryan did as they'd agreed and slipped the photo of Isaac and Lyssa across the table for Rickie to review. "Do you know this man or his child?"

At first, there was no reaction, but soon, Rickie's confused and disinterested persona melted away and he burst into tears.

Cora jumped at the sound, watching the man crumble before the two detectives and weep into his folded arms.

"He lied to me!" Rickie wailed. "Why would he lie to me?"

"Who lied?" Aidan demanded, tapping the table and trying to get Rickie's attention. "This man here?" He pointed to the photo. Aidan had been resistant when Cora told him the plan, annoyed that Isaac was coming up at all, but when Cora told him what had happened to

Ryan—as much as Aidan hated the idea of Cora and Ryan, he knew Isaac's signature anger from experience.

"I didn't know," Rickie whimpered, looking at the photo with teary eyes. "He had a daughter? How could he have had a daughter?"

Cora leaned forward, watching Rickie's reaction closely.

Ryan stepped around the table and placed his hand on the man's shoulder. The touch, though unprofessional and unprecedented, seemed tender and caring as he gently rubbed circles on his back.

"It's okay," Ryan said softly, continuing the gentle movements. "Can you tell us who this is?"

When Rickie spoke again, that same feminine Southern voice came out, the one from the previous interviews. Grace had surfaced.

"That's my Noah," Grace sniffed. "He never told me he had a family."

Ryan's hand dropped to his side and he rounded the table and lowered himself to the chair so he could be level with Grace.

"This man," Ryan said, pointing to the photograph. "His name is Isaac. He was also on Solydexran."

"I know," Grace said. "I mean, I know about the drugs. I didn't really know who he was."

"How did you know about the drugs?" Ryan glanced toward where Cora stood, watching.

"I found them," Grace said. "I threw them away. To be honest, they were prescribed to someone who wasn't my Noah. But I didn't want to know that he wasn't who I thought he was. Just as I'd hoped he'd never really know who I was. Or who I could be."

There was a sadness in her tone that made Cora's heart ache. She understood that desire to keep secrets hidden. She understood wanting someone to be something that they weren't. Most of all, she understood that when it came to Isaac.

"She was going to help us," Grace said. "Caroline. It's all my fault that she didn't get a chance to."

"Because of Julie."

Grace nodded. "That wicked woman had no idea what they would have done to us."

"What who would have done?" Aidan asked, standing behind where Ryan sat.

The woman looked up at Aidan, eyes damp with fresh tears. There was no fear in her eyes, just a sadness, pity. "You think that we are the problem. Or that people like Caroline don't know what they've gotten involved in. But the truth is far more dangerous than us or her. People like me didn't just start happening. Don't you wonder why you're only finding out about all this now?"

Grace shifted her gaze back to Ryan's. "You know there is more going on here."

"What do you know?" Ryan asked.

"Not enough to solve it for you."

Cora frowned at Grace's words. Ryan had said there was a conspiracy and it was easy to see that there was some nefarious business at play. A dead, or not dead, doctor from a drug trial that had been forged. People with split personalities popping up in densely populated areas tied together by a strange anxiety drug.

But they were here to solve a murder. Why had Julie Kanner been murdered and who did it? Did it matter if the why was bigger than the who? It wasn't their job to uncover a whole conspiracy from a small strangulation case. Or was it? Cora couldn't be sure anymore.

Her head began to spin. Isaac was tied into all of this. It *was* bigger than a whodunit. This was about her family. About Lyssa.

Ryan exited the visitation room looking stressed. His lips strained at the sides as his frown drooped low.

"This only confirms our suspicions." Cora thought back to their conversations about Blaine and Alison and how they perhaps were acting as dark angels to all those affected.

"It does." Ryan nodded.

Aidan exited the room. "You know what's next."

Cora closed her eyes for a moment. Grace had confirmed it. Isaac was tied to this crime. The missing boyfriend and possible accomplice. It was time to bring him in—if they could find him. When she opened her eyes and met Aidan's gaze she nodded. "I know. Issue the arrest warrant."

Aidan gave a curt nod, then strode out of the room. Cora couldn't help but notice that his steps were almost gleeful.

Chapter Thirty-Two

NOAH BAKER

Noah entered the university lecture hall, trying to seem like he belonged. He didn't look anything like the disgruntled or hungover students who piled in to hear her speak, but no one seemed to pay him any attention. After all, anyone could attend university these days, as long as they had the funds to do so. The joy of higher education.

He found a seat in the back. The hall could hold at least a couple hundred people. It was the kind made for required first-year classes that as such had a lot of demand. On the stage was a podium, and behind it a large screen. Vivian was set to speak to the attendees in a matter of minutes, yet people were still filing in slowly.

Noah still had a mix of emotions when it came to the beautiful young woman. He'd kept an eye on her for three days, seeing her meet the person in the Chevy Cruze twice more. Each time, she met them down the road from her house. Noah hadn't been able to get close enough yet to see the driver.

He was still enamoured with her beauty and struggled to see the danger she posed. Why had Caroline been so frightened by this woman and the company she kept? Noah had yet to see anything nefarious about her. In fact, she seemed perfectly ordinary.

This was the first chance he'd had to see her speak in person and he hoped it would be an eye-opening experience. Perhaps she could help him better understand why this drug had been made for her and why there'd been such a huge cover up. How did she tie into this farfetched conspiracy?

Someone approached the microphone on the podium and called out to the crowd. The incessant chatter of bright-eyed university students quickly quieted and the gentleman introduced their guest speaker—Vivian Parsons.

Her entrance on the stage was welcomed with a round of loud applause and a few whoops. Noah imagined they were from the men in the audience when they saw how gorgeous their guest speaker was. People straightened and leaned forward when they saw her. She was captivating—and she hadn't yet spoken a word.

"Welcome." Vivian's clear but soft voice sounded through the lecture hall speakers. "Thank you all for joining me today. I am here to talk to you about mental health, anxiety, and how you can still live a fulfilling life despite the ailments you may face."

When the lecture ended, Noah was quick to leave his seat. He'd hung on her every word and truly did feel that she was a success story. Despite his vested interest in her and the wavering feelings he had, he needed to know more.

Outside the lecture building, he waited until she emerged. She was surrounded by several people, but Noah wouldn't miss his chance. He fell into step behind the crew and called to her.

"Miss Parsons. A word, please?"

Vivian whirled around to face him. "Yes?"

The people surrounding her stopped as well, eyeing Noah with suspicion.

"Alone, please?" Noah tried to appear desperate, like her advice might be the thing to save him. It seemed to work, because Vivian turned to her followers and shooed them away.

They stepped out of earshot but never took their eyes off the pair.

"Are you okay?" Vivian stepped closer to Noah and he inhaled her scent, a beautiful spring breeze with a hint of honey and lilac.

"I'm fine," Noah said. "But I had a couple questions."

"About the lecture?" Vivian's head tilted to the side as she regarded him.

"No," Noah said. "About a woman named Julie."

Vivian's features contorted into a confused frowned that looked out of place on her face. As if the expression were not truly her own.

"Julie Kanner," Noah said.

Vivian's confusion vanished and she took an uneasy step back. "I don't know what happened."

"I don't care what happened," Noah said. He already knew enough about Julie's death. He didn't need answers. He had those answers. *He* was that answer. "I have to know about the drug. About the people affected. About the ones you're taking."

Vivian's eyes widened. "What are you talking about?"

"This drug that you claim has saved your life is ruining the lives of others," Noah said. "What are you doing with them to hide the truth? Why did Julie want to harm one?"

Vivian's chest rose and fell with hurried breaths as her eyes darted from side to side. "I don't know what you're talking about. This drug helps people. It's helped so many people."

Noah frowned. Was she completely unaware of the effects Solydexran could have on others?

"You really don't know?" Noah asked, feeling defeated. Why had Caroline sent him here if Vivian didn't have all the answers? What was the point of Julie's death if she wasn't the driving force behind Solydexran's nefarious consequences?

For a moment, Vivian didn't respond. Then, in a hushed voice, she said, "What do you know?"

"Solydexran is not all good," Noah said. "It affects some people poorly. For some, it ruins their lives. Someone is trying hard to keep this away from the public."

"Ms. Parsons." A man in a suit approached from behind her. "Are you okay?" He glared at Noah. From the earpiece and bulky arms, Noah imaged he was a bodyguard.

"I'm fine," Vivian said between huffed breaths. It was clear she was distraught by what Noah had told her. How could she be so blinded to what was happening?

"Come with me." The man moved to take her arm, but Vivian moved away from him.

"Just one minute." Vivian stepped closer to Noah and reached for his hand. "Thank you for attending the lecture today. I am so happy to hear that Solydexran has made your life better too. Call me if you ever need to discuss anything. My personal number is on the back."

For a moment, Noah's confusion at her words made him frown. But as she pulled away, Noah realized she'd tucked a card into his hand. He shoved it into his pocket.

"Of course," he said, his voice uneasy. "Thank you."

Vivian turned without another word and allowed the bodyguard to lead her away. Noah didn't dare look at what she'd slipped him before her car was out of view.

Slowly, he pulled his hand out of his pocket and looked at the card. It was a blue and white business card with *Vivian Parsons* scrawled across the front in cursive writing. Her contact information was included and a small bit of text encouraged him to connect with Vivian on her website.

He flipped the card over to find a number written in blue ink. Frowning, he pushed the card back into his pocket and resolved to give her a call if only to know why she'd given it to him. She'd seemed so confused by their conversation, so why did she want him to reach out?

His neck prickled as if he was being watched, and Noah glanced around. A man stood in the nearby parking lot, leaning against his car. His arms were crossed over his chest and he wore sunglasses. Noah couldn't be sure, but it felt like the man was staring right at him.

As Noah turned to leave, he realized the man had been leaning against a black Chevy Cruze.

Chapter Thirty-Three

BLAINE ROCHE

B laine watched from a short distance as the man approached Vivian Parsons. Blaine had noticed him when he'd first entered the lecture hall. He'd seen him cower in the back, desperation on his face. Blaine barely listened to a word Vivian said during her presentation. He'd heard it all before. She'd been paraded from campus to campus over the years so she could talk to overwhelmed first-year students in an attempt to show them that a medicated life—if necessary—was still a full life. It was another part of the brainwashing ACE Pharmaceuticals had started.

The conversation between the unknown man and Vivian had struck Blaine as odd. She was the poster child, but she seemed to know nothing about the forged trials or about the victims who had suffered needlessly. Blaine hadn't expected that. He'd always been certain that she'd been involved. Could she really be unaware of the shady practices her father's company had adopted, all in the name of saving her?

Still, Blaine hesitated when he saw what looked like a card pass between Vivian and the man. He also couldn't help but notice the other man who waited a ways off, leaning against his car, watching the exchange. Perhaps there was more to Vivian than Blaine gave her credit for.

Yet she was likely a dead end and Blaine knew where to go next. Dylan Parsons had started all of this for his troubled daughter. Blaine didn't doubt he had the capabilities to harm others, as Alison had implied.

Blaine climbed into his waiting car and followed the instructions Alison had passed on to her assailant—Noah—and soon he found himself parked not far from the CEO's mansion.

Blaine pulled a cap over his head as he approached the gated home. It spanned much of the property, blocking out the setting sun. Blaine scanned the tall iron fence. It would be a pain to get through. What was he hoping for, really? The truth, of course—that had never been a question. Also revenge, but what did that mean? Blaine had never been an aggressive person. It made his work with Melanie ideal, as despite the assholes she would get involved in, he was able to remain calm and handle the situations with tact. It kept their cover hidden. The only times he couldn't handle it was when Fraser had attacked, or when that poor innocent woman, Jess, had been brutally raped.

Blaine didn't know the right answer for his revenge. Would Parsons's death be enough to soothe the monsters that had been buried inside him all these years? Would Parsons's death be the thing that allowed Blaine and Alison their freedom? Would it save those who had already suffered or suffered unknowingly?

It seemed impossible that a single death could solve all the bad, but Blaine knew the truth. Given that ACE Pharmaceuticals had been floundering and the effect Solydexran had on his only child, Parsons had been desperate when the trials had failed. He'd buried so much money into something he'd been sure was the perfect solution. Without all of that . . . Parsons was nothing.

Blaine turned his head away from the security camera that sat atop the entrance gate. He didn't need his likeness caught on camera or that pesky detective coming after him. Despite his belief that Detective Boone would help unravel the mystery behind Solydexran, he also believed that Boone was still too focused on Blaine and his secrets to see the bigger picture.

As Jenny had said, Blaine had aided and abetted Patsy's crimes. It was enough to land him in prison or at least with an obstruction charge.

As Blaine continued to follow the fence line, he realized he was not the only one casing the CEO's property. The man he'd seen speaking with Vivian at the university campus was there as well. He hadn't yet noticed Blaine, or if he had, he didn't give it away. He simply stood several feet away, staring up at the building.

Blaine hesitated, unsure if he should approach him.

Before Blaine could make a decision, the man turned to face him. His expression did not seem surprised or concerned.

"What are you doing here?" the man asked, his tone cold accusing.

"I would ask you the same thing." Blaine glanced up at the large house that now shrouded both of them in shadow.

The man didn't answer him, instead following his gaze to the house. "He's near dead, I hear."

"Who?" Blaine asked.

"That CEO," the man said. "That's why you've come right? He's hurt you too?"

Blaine frowned, unsure what to say.

"His drug ruined my girlfriend and killed a former one." The man shook his head. "I don't know what I hoped for, coming here."

Blaine could understand that feeling.

"I mean, if he's nearly dead . . ." The man shrugged. "What else I can do?"

Blaine realized then that he was looking at the man that Alison had hoped to use as a would-be assassin, Noah. He took a step towards him but stopped when he heard sirens sound in the distance. His hair stood on end.

Noah stiffened, turned, and ran away without another word. Blaine knew he should follow him, but he was more interested in the words he'd spoken. Could Dylan Parsons really be on his death bed? What then? The papers had implied he was recovering, but perhaps that was just another cover-up.

The sounds of sirens grew closer and Blaine forced himself to step away from the house. It would do no one any good if he got caught today. He didn't have enough evidence yet to uncover all the wrongdoings.

Blaine headed back the way he'd come, but then the gates swung open and several police cruisers rushed through. To Blaine's relief, the gates closed behind them and he was quick to slip by.

He risked a glance back to see one of the officers climb out of the passenger side of the cruiser. His slicked-back hair and stature were familiar. Detective Ryan Boone.

As if sensing his gaze, Boone looked up from car and met eyes with Blaine. For a moment, the two men simply stared at one another, as if unsure how to react, as if they'd never actually expected to be this close.

"Hey!" Boone yelled. He glanced back at the blond officer who had just climbed out of the driver's side. "That's him."

Blaine didn't wait another moment before dashing back to his car. He didn't allow himself a pause for a breath until he brought his car to a stop several miles from the house. Even then, he thanked his lucky stars that the gates had sealed the police cruisers behind a barricade, offering him a chance to escape.

They were getting close.

Chapter Thirty-Four

CORA PORTER

Cora ended the call. Ryan had been frantic in a way she'd never heard before. He'd finally found Blaine after months of searching and the man had *just* slipped through his grasp.

The last several hours had been a whirlwind. The warrant for Isaac's arrest had been issued two days earlier and an APB had been sent out to all neighbouring forces to be on the lookout for a man of his description. The first sighting had been at a university nearby, though Cora couldn't imagine what Isaac would have been doing there.

It was still so strange for her to think about Isaac's alter like the other cases she and Ryan had seen. That Isaac could be afflicted like Rickie was. That this man, Noah, could really be a part of the man Cora had fallen in love with all those years ago. That Isaac had this darkness inside him. Worse, that she'd helped push him into it when she was so adamant about his recovery. The idea still made Cora's heart twist with sadness and guilt.

"Mommy," Lyssa called from the sitting room. "When's dinner? I'm hungry."

Cora had forgotten all about dinner the moment the police had gone after Isaac. The sighting at the university was followed by an alert at the well-known Parsons residence in Kanata. Isaac had been caught on camera.

But as Ryan said, Isaac hadn't been the only one there.

"Knock, knock," a voice echoed through her front hallway. Cora froze for a moment before registering the singsong sound. Hadley.

"In here," Cora called from the kitchen. Hadley rounded the corner with Danny in tow. She carried two large brown paper bags in her arms. Cora immediately smiled. Chinese food.

"Thought you might be hungry," Hadley said.

Lyssa bounded into the kitchen. "Danny!" she squealed, taking the younger boy's hand. "Come see my castle." She pulled him into the sitting room and plopped him down in front of the fairy-tale castle she'd been playing with. "You can be the prince." She passed the prince doll to him and the two began their routine of make believe.

"How did you know?" Cora said, relief washed over her.

"Sawyer told me about Isaac." Hadley placed the bags down on the counter and began unloading their contents.

Cora nodded. She should have realized that Hadley would be by the moment she found out.

"I figured you'd be . . . distracted." Hadley flashed her a sympathetic smile.

"You know me well." Cora went to the cupboard and pulled out four plates. Then she went to the fridge and reached for the open bottle of Pinot Grigio, pouring two glasses and passing one to her friend.

"You okay?" Hadley asked.

"Yeah," Cora said. "I just got a call from Ryan."

Hadley raised her eyebrows in a suggestive manner as she sipped her wine.

"Not like that." Cora laughed, but it was short lived. "He found Isaac with a criminal he's on the lookout for. I'm just feeling a bit confused. Like why would Isaac be with him?"

Could Isaac's alter have something to do with Ryan's old case? Beyond the drug, Cora struggled to imagine how Isaac and Blaine could have met. Unless Alison had made it happen, wherever she was.

Cora's phone pinged with a message and she glanced at the screen.

Sorry. I just can't believe I lost him ... again.

"Is that him?" Hadley asked as she started making plates for the kids.

Cora glanced up from the text. "Yeah."

Ryan sounded defeated even through the text and Cora wished she could see him, help him. Anything. He'd agonized over losing Blaine so many months ago and again when his previous lead had been a dud. They felt no closer to solving the mystery behind Solydexran and Calvin Wright. If only they could bring him in and find out more.

"He's having a hard day." Cora put the phone aside and reached for one of the plates Hadley had put together. She glanced into the sitting room before lowering her voice. "I'm running out of things to tell Lyssa about Isaac."

Lyssa had a whirlwind of a week and yet she still yearned to see him. How could Cora explain to her seven-year-old daughter that her father was wanted as an accomplice for murder? Lyssa barely understood death, let alone the anger that went hand in hand with killing someone.

"I don't envy that," Hadley said, reaching for the other plate, then taking the one Cora held and stepping into the sitting room. "Dinner is ready."

Hadley placed the plates on the coffee table and called Lyssa and Danny over. "Now, I want to see every last bit gone before you go back to playing." She grabbed the remote and put on an episode of *Wild Kratts* before returning to her wine and Cora.

"That should keep them quiet for a bit," Hadley said with a smile.

"Thank you," Cora said, and she meant it. Before Hadley had arrived, she was feeling lost and disoriented. Hadley had a way of centering her.

"Anything girl." Hadley reached for another plate. "Now grab some food and let's eat."

Cora followed her as she loaded up her plate with chicken balls and chow mein. Then, they sat at the small kitchen table together and sipped their wine.

Cora zoned out for a moment, thinking again about the man she used to love and the ones who were hunting him. She worried about what would happen when they finally found Isaac. Would he be the Isaac she knew and would she be able to make him fully understand what had happened to him? Or would he be the confused and angry alter that seemed to be the character of Noah? The one Grace seemed so desperate to save?

A part of Cora wished she could call Grace and ask more about Noah. Cora wished she could ask for a moment alone with Rickie's alter and learn about the Isaac she knew. How was Noah different from the unreliable yet carefree, fun-loving Isaac she'd met in college? Did they have similar personalities? Did they have anything at all in common?

The other part of her wanted to confide in Hadley about all the details she'd learned. Everything she knew about Solydexran and the alter that lived in the man they'd grown up with. But she still couldn't share those details with a civilian, no matter how trustworthy she knew Hadley to be.

When neither had spoken in a while, Hadley reached out and gave one of Cora's hands a squeeze.

"I know you can't really tell me what's going on," Hadley said. "But you know I'm here for you right? Me, Sawyer, and Danny. We'd do anything for you and Lyssa."

Cora gave her friend a grateful smile. "I know."

Hadley pulled her hand away, and the women resumed their comfortable silence.

When they'd finished dinner, Hadley scooped up Danny and the two departed. Cora was quick to put on *Encanto*, knowing that Lyssa would be asleep within minutes. If there was something Cora loved most about her head-strong daughter, it was how she could never make it through a full movie without falling asleep.

Cora allowed her mind to drift back to Ryan as she busied herself cleaning the kitchen and putting away the leftovers that Hadley had refused to take.

In Ryan's case, the alters had been so different, a part of the women that was buried deep within them. Isaac had once been prone to rage blackouts; could that have been a part of Noah rearing its ugly head? What did it all mean now? He was clearly suffering the devastating side effects of the anxiety medication. What Cora didn't know was if Noah had always been a part of Isaac, or was something that had surfaced from the medication. Would Isaac ever go back to normal? Ryan hadn't really spoken much on the women after his case concluded, so Cora didn't know if they'd found a way to heal and level out, or if they were forever scarred by the results of the drugs.

Cora reached for her phone and texted Ryan back.

Don't be sorry. I know how important this is to you.

It was a moment before he answered her. He expressed a desire to see her but said he knew she was with Lyssa for the night. Cora for a moment resented Isaac for being a failed father. Parenting always came first, even if she wanted to comfort Ryan on his loss.

They agreed to meet for lunch tomorrow, when Lyssa was in school and Ryan had had the night to cool down. At least one thing could be gathered from their failure today: Blaine was close. So was Isaac and whatever had connected them wasn't the question. There were bigger things at play now. What did they want? And how far would they go to get it if Ryan and Aidan don't find them first?

Chapter Thirty-Five

NOAH BAKER

Noah flipped the business card in his palm, looking at the blue-inked numbers again. He'd asked the librarian at the public library if he could make a call. The disposable phone Caroline had given him had long stopped working.

The librarian was hesitant at first, but soon passed him the handheld and put distance between them. Still, Noah hadn't the courage to actually dial the number. What did Vivian want?

The previous afternoon, he'd followed her to the large estate that her family called home. He'd been wary of her request to call and wanted to see what more he could find out. It had been for nothing, of course. The police soon showed up and chased him off, but not before he spoke to another man who seemed to be eyeing the building.

The librarian now eyed him from the other side of the desk with clear irritation, so Noah quickly dialed the number, worried he'd lose his chance if he didn't. The slow ring through was torturous. Just when Noah thought the voicemail would pick up, Vivian's voice came through the receiver.

"Hello?"

"Uh, hi," Noah said, unsure how to start the conversation. "I met you yesterday. You said to call."

"Of course." Vivian's voice lowered. "Thank you. Are you able to meet me somewhere?"

"I don't have a car."

"That's no problem. Can you get to Confederation Park?"

"Yeah, no problem." The library was only a block or two away from the park. It would be a quick walk.

"Great." There was a shuffle of papers on the other end of the phone. When Vivian spoke again, she sounded farther away, like he'd been put on speaker phone. "I'll be there at 5 p.m. Come look for me." The call ended before Noah could ask any further details.

He placed the phone on the desk and nodded his thanks to the waiting librarian. The large clock on the wall told him he had an hour to kill before Vivian would arrive. With nothing else to do, Noah started his trek to the park.

He spotted her the moment she stepped into his range. Her identity wasn't shielded and she seemed to be walking around the park as if she were just having an early evening stroll, not meeting someone for a secret discussion.

Noah stood from the bench he'd made his home for the last hour and watched her approach. As she neared him, he realized she wasn't alone. A man dressed in a fine suit trailed a few paces behind her. She'd brought protection. Did she expect Noah to hurt her? For a moment, that annoyed him, but he pushed the idea from his mind. He was here for something bigger.

As they drew closer, Noah recognized him as the man who'd been leaning against the Cruze in the parking lot the previous day. Vivian's secret meeting.

"Hello?" Vivian asked tentatively. She cocked her head in the way a dog would when trying to understand their human's odd speech. The way she regarded Noah wasn't like a stranger, but like he was something foreign. It unnerved him.

"Hi," Noah said. He didn't know what to expect from this meeting. Vivian had seemed to know little to nothing about the effects of her famed drug. She seemed completely in the dark when it came to the disappearances. What information could she really offer?

Vivian continued her cautious approach and when she was close, she asked in a lowered tone, "Are you one of them?"

Noah frowned, unsure what she was asking. But as he searched her eyes, he realized the truth. Vivian knew more than she let on. She was asking if he was like Grace.

"No, but I knew one." Noah eyed the man behind Vivian, who stood only a few paces off. "You brought a friend."

"Don't worry about him," Vivian said, waving off Noah's comment. "Tell me what you know."

Noah frowned, keeping his mouth shut. He didn't trust her. Caroline had said there were people after him. Was this a mistake? She could be here to take him in, after discovering what he knew. Was she a part of the whole conspiracy?

Seeming to recognize his hesitancy, Vivian continued speaking. "You mentioned Julie earlier. She was my cousin."

Noah met her gaze. Vivian's brown eyes started to water.

"We grew up together," Vivian said. "Well, I guess as much as you can grow up together when you're five years apart." She waved to the bench Noah had abandoned when she'd arrived. "Can we sit?"

Noah complied, now curious about Vivian's intentions.

"When Julie died, I started getting strange messages." Vivian shook her head. "They didn't really make sense. They just accused my dad of wrongdoing. Said the drug was evil. I ignored it, at first. Then one of the messages made a serious claim. That a doctor involved in the drug creation had been murdered—Calvin Wright."

She looked down at her hands. "I knew him very well and I'd always been led to believe that he'd died in an accident. I started digging. Looking for anything I could find that supported what I knew. I didn't want to believe what the messages were saying. How could I? If I did, my entire life was a complete lie."

This was news to Noah. He hadn't heard anything about a doctor dying. Caroline hadn't mentioned anything about someone being involved in the creation of the medication and then dying. No, he only knew what Caroline had told him. That people were being taken.

"What do you know?" Vivian pushed. "Are these claims truthful?"

"I don't know about any doctor."

Vivian grabbed his arm. "You have to tell me. I'm drowning here. I have spent my entire adult life vouching for a drug that may have harmed people. No one will tell me the truth."

"What about your dad?" Noah asked. "You said he was involved."

Vivian released her hold on his arm and averted her eyes. "He's not well. He's barely coherent. He couldn't tell me the truth, even if he wanted to."

"I'm sorry," Noah said. "I don't know anything about a doctor."

Vivian's shoulders slumped with defeat. "Then why did you find me?"

"Because I needed answers," Noah said. "I wanted to know why you're abducting people and where you're hiding them."

"I don't know anything about abductions," Vivian said sadly. "How did you know Julie?"

Noah grimaced. "I dated her. Very briefly."

Vivian nodded along, as if she knew Julie had been dating someone and this was no surprise.

"But I fell in love with someone else," Noah said, unable to look Vivian in the eye when he said it. He still felt overwhelming guilt for bringing Grace into Julie's life. He still thought of Julie's eyes and the way they begged him to help her. How she'd looked away and accepted death when she realized Noah would not save her. It wasn't something he'd easily forget.

"But she wasn't who I thought she was," Noah explained. "I later learned that my girlfriend, Grace, was a user of Solydexran and suffered one of the terrible side effects. She lived in another's body alongside that personality."

Vivian's face lit with recognition. "An afflicted?"

"What?" Noah had heard that term first from Caroline when she was describing the people being taken. Vivian must have heard of them too.

"One of the messages mentioned people with side effects," Vivian explained. "She called them 'the afflicted.' She claimed they were being rounded up and hidden away, but that's impossible."

"Is it?" Noah challenged. "Because Julie seemed pretty certain that Grace was dangerous. And I believe that had she not died, she would have reported Grace and her issues to whoever was doing this."

Vivian placed her face in her hands and drew several steady breaths. Noah didn't rush her, allowing her all the time she needed to process his words. He didn't blame her for her disbelief. He'd felt the same way. The whole idea of a massive conspiracy was so far-fetched. But what explained all the strangeness surrounding the drug, if not some sort of conspiracy?

When Vivian straightened, she looked to Noah. "I don't know if what you're saying is true. Or if the claims I'm hearing are true. But I do know there is something dangerous going on. Enough that Julie was killed for it and possibly Calvin too."

Noah opened his mouth to ask about Calvin, but Vivian stood and spoke again. "You need to stay out of this."

"What?" Noah rose to meet her. "How can you say that?"

Vivian reached out and touched Noah's arm. "If what you're saying is true, then you shouldn't get involved. It's dangerous and I don't know what is truly happening. Who knows what could happen if whoever is doing this feels threatened?"

"My girlfriend has suffered because of your drug," Noah snapped. "Someone has to answer for this."

"And someone will," Vivian said. "But we have to be smart about it. They can't see it coming." She stood and Noah followed. "I don't need your theories anymore, I need facts. Evidence. Something I can bring forward to prove or disprove what I'm hearing. Getting in the way will only hurt you."

"I will do what I have to," Noah said. "I'm not just thinking about myself."

Vivian nodded. "I understand, but you have to know that if this drug has caused the suffering they are claiming, then I will never forgive myself and I will want nothing more than for the truth to come out."

"Thank you." Noah was unsure what else to say.

"Call me if you find anything else. But remember, I need hard evidence." Then she turned and walked back the way she came.

The man who'd come with her eyed Noah for another moment before turning and following her steps.

Noah lowered himself back to the bench, unable to determine his next move.

Chapter Thirty-Six

CORA PORTER

Cora's fingers drummed the table at the French Bistro while she waited for Ryan's arrival. He'd texted an apology for his tardiness, but Cora had found herself getting impatient. She'd been anxious to see him since waking up this morning. He hadn't been around the station when she'd reported to the lab and she hadn't seen him when she stepped out to go to her car. Cora felt in the dark with the investigation, desperate to learn more about Isaac and his actions.

When Ryan pushed through the double doors, his normally slicked hair looked dishevelled, with strands sticking out every which way. It looked like he hadn't slept much, or maybe he'd just rolled out of bed.

Ryan reached up and straightened his tie as he approached her, then ran a hand through his hair, trying to tame the rogue strands.

"Are you okay?" Cora asked as he pulled out the chair across from her.

He didn't answer immediately; instead, he waved down the server and requested a glass of scotch.

Cora raised an eyebrow at the request.

"Sorry," Ryan finally said. "I had a rough night."

"What happened?"

"Didn't sleep." He shrugged like it was a common occurrence. The server came by with the drink and looked expectantly at their menus. Ryan indicated that he needed another minute. "I keep going over yesterday and how we just missed him. I'm starting to feel like an absolute failure." He sipped the scotch and pressed his lips together as the liquid ran down his throat.

"Drinking in the middle of the day isn't about to help with feelings of failure." Cora didn't mean to sound judgemental, but it was hard not to when she thought of how alcohol affected the men in her lives. Aidan had a tendency to get angry and Isaac was a beast all his own when it came to his alcoholism.

Ryan glanced at his beverage and seemed to weigh his options. Still, he tipped it back with a loud "ah."

"I'm sorry," he said when he pushed the glass aside. "I've never handled my stress particularly well."

Who did? Cora certainly didn't make the best decisions when stress took over, but that didn't mean you should numb your senses, or so she believed.

Still, she shrugged off the comment and said nothing more on the subject of his drinking. She reached across the table and took his hand, which rested beside the now-empty glass. He locked eyes with her as she gave him a gentle squeeze.

It seemed to calm him, as his eyes softened and he smiled. "I'm sorry."

She shook her head. "What did you learn?"

Ryan let out a sigh. "That at least they're together."

Cora nodded. Two suspects together could be more easily identified, especially the likes of Blaine Roche and Isaac. They were opposites. If they were staying somewhere, then someone might have seen them and could call it in.

"How did he seem?" Cora asked the question so softly she wasn't sure Ryan had heard her. Or that he'd registered who she was talking about.

He grimaced. "I didn't get much of a look at him. But I worry that if he's with Roche, then perhaps his personality is more dominant than we once thought."

Cora had considered this too. If Isaac had resurfaced, why didn't he come home? Did that mean he hadn't in the past two weeks or that he was too scared of the unknown? Did he even know that they were looking for him? Did he think about her or Lyssa? There were too many questions about him and what he'd been through.

Ryan flipped his hand to grasp her fingers. He gently lifted them to his cheek. "I missed you."

Cora cracked a half smile. "It's only been a couple of days."

"It's been long enough."

She agreed. She'd been wishing Ryan had been able to come over the night before. Thankfully, her mother was stepping up once again to take Lyssa for another fun Nana sleepover. This time, Lyssa was far more excited.

"I'm free tonight," Cora said, though they'd already made the plans.

Ryan allowed her hand to drop away from his face, but his smile remained fixed. "Good."

"What else did you learn?" Cora asked, hoping to get some insights into the case. Aidan had been stingy with the details since their last off-duty interaction. He'd ignored her theories and avoided her at the station. It was the least they'd spoken in years. Cora didn't blame him, but she couldn't satisfy her insatiable need for information.

"If Roche is really going after the owners of the drug company, then he's in for a rude awakening." Ryan leaned back in his seat. "Dylan Parsons is on his death bed. Stage four lung cancer that has already spread to various parts of his body. Bedridden doesn't begin to describe him. He was barely lucid enough to answer questions."

"Why else would they be at the house if not for him?"

Ryan shrugged. "It sounds like Vivian Parsons, the daughter of the CEO, was approached outside a university after one of her scheduled presentations. The description she gave matches Isaac."

"Did she say why?"

"Apparently he questioned her about the drug and the side effects." Ryan grimaced. "She seemed completely unaware of the consequences we have run into."

Cora wasn't totally surprised. When Solydexran had first come across her desk, she'd done meticulous research into the drug and its history. Though it was a short history, Vivian was well acquainted with the drug. The poster child for the possibilities of a life on medication. An inspiration to college students who suffered from anxiety or those who had turned to medication for support. Why should she know about the harm that had come to others when it was clear the drug worked for her? After all, she wasn't the one who covered the trials. She would have been no more than a teenager.

"She was pretty choked up," Ryan said. "She refused to believe that she'd been lied to. She was convinced it was just a setup. Sadly, we couldn't get much out of her. The answers were evasive at best when I tried to get too detailed about the medication."

"And Roche?" Cora asked. "Did she know anything about him?"

Ryan shook his head. "They knew about Wright, of course, as he worked on their team. They shared their sympathies at what was a tragic accident when he passed away. I bet they have no idea how close they were to seeing a ghost again. But get this. When I asked about the Wrights, Vivian immediately assumed I meant Alison. Apparently, she had been Vivian's nanny for a couple years, before Calvin was even a part of the company."

"Seriously?" That was a detail Cora hadn't expected.

Ryan nodded. "We showed her a picture of Roche and she identified him as Calvin, she was shocked to find out he was still alive. She disputed the fact but had no other details she could provide."

Cora didn't pipe up when he said it. As she thought more about the tie between Calvin and Blaine, she began to doubt that they were truly one and the same. The death had been too solid and she couldn't find any documentation that implied any tampering. Faking a death wasn't flawless. There was usually some sort of trail, if you dug deep enough.

She'd brought it up to Ryan once since their time together, but he'd shut down the idea quickly. He couldn't see beyond what he already suspected. Blaine and Calvin were one and the same. A vengeful doctor. Cora was beginning to believe that the story was more complicated than that.

The server came by and they placed their orders. With no more details to share on the case, their conversation fell into an easy dialogue. Ryan asked about Lyssa and how she was doing without Isaac.

"It's been hard," Cora said honestly. "Isaac is a hero to Lyssa. Though I suppose that's my fault. I always wanted her to see him as the hero he should be. So, I covered up his mistakes over and over again."

"You two met young?" Ryan asked.

"In college," Cora said. "He was this hilarious, carefree guy. Like no one I'd met. Sure, the alcohol brought the worst out of him, but it did that to a lot of people we knew. It wasn't until he dove too deep to pull himself out, that it became a problem."

Ryan nodded, understanding on his face. "My wife was the same way."

Cora instinctively leaned forward at the mention of his dead wife. He'd mentioned her only a few times in their days together. Enough for her to know that Ryan had been married and his wife Lillian had died young. They'd wanted kids, but it hadn't been in the cards for them.

"Did she drink?" Cora asked, treading carefully. She knew the territory could be sensitive. Any addiction was.

Ryan looked down at the empty glass in his hand. "Yeah, it started after the pregnancies kept failing. She was so desperate to be a mom and she would have been the best mom. But she couldn't hold on to the baby. By the third miscarriage, the heartbreak was just too much for her. And the accident, well . . ."

Cora reached across the table and gripped his hand. Her womb ached at the idea of losing so many babies to complications she just couldn't control. It made her heart yearn to hold Lyssa in her arms and inhale the bubble-gum shampoo scent of her hair.

Ryan pulled his hand away and cleared his throat. "I'm sorry. I shouldn't put all this on you."

Their conversation fell silent as their meals were set in front of them.

"No," Cora said, continuing where they'd left off once the server was gone. "It's okay. These things are too hard to get through on our own."

"It's wild," Ryan said. "Even after all these years, I still think about Lillian and wonder if I could have done something different."

Cora only nodded, realizing there was nothing she could say to sway him. Plus, she couldn't deny that she didn't sometimes wonder the same thing about Isaac.

Ryan gave Cora a sad smile. "It's good to talk to you about this. Archer—my partner—never cared to hear much about her. He always found death hard."

"Yet he was a detective?" Cora gave a half laugh.

"Yeah," Ryan's voice oozed amusement. "I often joked about that."

"How's he doing?" Cora asked, realizing that it had been over two weeks that Ryan had been working with them. Did his partner miss him back in the city?

"Good," Ryan confirmed. "He's on leave for another week before he goes back into the station. They'll keep him on light work until I return." Ryan added as an afterthought, "Whenever that is."

Cora nodded. "We never really talked about how long you'd be here for."

"Even when I go home, I'm not very far."

She couldn't argue. He was only about a five-hour drive away. An hour by plane if she opted for that option. It wasn't close enough for an evening visit by any means, but with both having such busy lives, they would have always had obstacles to plan around. Besides, Cora wasn't totally ready to ask those questions. Was she really considering their future when their present was still so undefined?

"How long will you be here?" Cora asked.

Ryan shrugged. "I should have gone back already. But I put in a special request to stay longer. Roche is here and until he moves on, I need to be here too."

She nodded, hoping that when Ryan had to head home, he did so with Roche in custody. Though as their case continued to drag on, she was beginning to doubt how this could all really end. Her phone beeped with an email from the lab and she looked at the time. They'd been sitting across from one another for over an hour already.

Ryan seeming to read her mind, pulled out several bills and placed them under an empty glass. "Let's go." He stood and offered his hand, which Cora took willingly.

The feel of his hand wrapped around hers made warmth spread through her body. She wanted nothing more than to press against him and feel his arms embrace her in a cocoon of safety.

Out in the parking lot, they hesitated before going to their separate cars. Ryan tightened his grip and pulled her closer. Soon, she had exactly what she'd wished for. His strong arms held her against him for a moment and she rested her head against his chest. His suit jacket was soft and smelled like his warm cologne.

"I'm sorry I have to get back," Ryan said softly.

Cora pulled away slightly so she could look up at him. "I'll see you tonight."

He didn't respond. Instead, he dipped down and captured her lips in a firm kiss. Cora melted into his hold.

Chapter Thirty-Seven

BLAINE ROCHE

B laine approached the man slowly. He seemed sad and confused as he sat on a bench in the middle of the nearly empty park. Blaine recognized him. Whoever he was, this was definitely the man he'd seen at the CEO's house.

"Hey," Blaine said quietly as he came up behind him.

The man jumped but didn't run. Instead, he slowly turned to face Blaine. There was no recognition in his eyes—he just stared like a deer in headlights.

"What do you want?" he asked, his tone hesitant.

Blaine rounded the bench, standing in front of the man and giving him a once-over.

"I just . . ." Blaine trailed off, unsure what to say. "Were you in Kanata yesterday? Did you visit the Parsons estate?"

The man reached up and scratched at his cheek. "I honestly don't know where I've been for a few days." He glanced around them. "Or where I am now."

He looked rough, like he hadn't slept, and Blaine wondered if he'd been on this bench since the previous day. The scruff on his face was wild and ungroomed. His hair seemed matted and knotted, though it was pulled back to the base of his neck.

"I'm Blaine," he said carefully. "I think you may have known my sister, Alison."

The man frowned. "Alison . . ." He tested the name on his tongue as if he hadn't heard or said it in ages. For a moment Blaine worried that Alison may have met him under an alias, as they'd both done more than once in their lives.

Then the man nodded. "Alison Wright?"

"Yes." Blaine's shoulders relaxed.

"I remember her, sure," he said. "That was a long time ago."

Blaine frowned. That didn't match with Alison's tale of the man she'd been helping recently.

"I'm Isaac, by the way."

That confirmed Blaine's belief of who the man was, at the very least.

"Good to meet you." Blaine glanced over his shoulder. "May I?" He motioned to the bench. The sun had begun to set, and a darkness was starting to overtake the surrounding area. Still, Blaine didn't want to be out in the open with Isaac for too long. The police had seen them together once already. Boone wasn't a fool and he'd be on the lookout for individuals with their descriptions.

"Sure." Isaac slid over on the bench, allowing Blaine to take the seat. "Is there something I can do for you?"

Blaine stared off into the distance, silent for a few seconds. "I've been looking for you."

Isaac's brow furrowed with confusion. "Looking for me? Well, that's a bit strange."

"Alison was worried about you."

The man's perplexed expression didn't wane. "I haven't seen Alison in years. Why would she care about me?"

Blaine flipped open his wallet and withdrew the photo he'd kept of him and Alison as young adults and passed it to Isaac—an attempt to confirm that he was who he said he was.

Isaac looked at the photo but didn't speak, waiting for Blaine to answer his question.

"Alison sent me to find you," Blaine tried to explain, unsure how he would get this lost man to trust him.

"She disappeared years ago," Isaac said. "I can't imagine what she wants with me now."

"I can explain." Blaine stood. "But here isn't the right place to talk about it. Do you have anywhere to stay tonight? I have a motel room nearby if you want to crash for the night."

Isaac frowned. "Isn't there a rule about not going anywhere with strangers?"

Blaine chuckled. "Usually, that would be wise. But I think you know you can trust me." When Isaac only continued to stare at the picture in his hands, Blaine spoke again. "I'm sure you know you're in trouble?"

"Yeah." Isaac nodded. "I abandoned my daughter, so god knows my ex will kill me, if the cops or the alcohol doesn't do it." Then he shook his head. "The craziest part is that I don't remember doing it. I just woke up one day on the street. I can't remember touching a drink."

Blaine grimaced. Isaac had no knowledge of the complicated illness that swirled around inside him. No idea that the smallest trigger could manifest an entirely different persona.

"I think I can help you understand," Blaine said. "If you're willingly to trust me."

Isaac stared off into the darkened park before finding Blaine's face again. "Why would you help me? You don't know me."

"True," he agreed. "But Alison spoke highly of you and I have an affinity for helping those in need."

Isaac chuckled. "You sound just like your sister." Then he reached up and ran a hand through his messy, dirty hair. "Wouldn't happen to have a shower attached to that room, would you?"

Blaine smiled and took the photo from Isaac's outstretched hand. "You bet there is." He motioned for Isaac to follow him.

When Isaac emerged from the shower, Blaine was resting on one of the two queen-sized beds, flipping aimlessly through the TV channels. He'd hoped there would be news about what went down at the Parsons' mansion, but no one seemed to be reporting on it.

Whatever they'd done or found, the cops were keeping the media out of it. This only put Blaine more on edge. Boone had gotten too close and Blaine had to be sure they didn't get that close again.

"Feeling better?" Blaine asked Isaac as he settled into the opposite bed.

"Much." Isaac reached for the bottle of water Blaine had given him when they'd gotten to the room. "I honestly don't know how to thank you for helping me out."

Blaine grimaced. "I'm not sure you should thank me quite yet." He turned the laptop he had open on his bed towards Isaac. There, front and center of the page, was a photo of Isaac and a person who had been blurred out.

Isaac gaped at the photo for a moment before realizing what he was looking at. Then he shook his head. "I know I left my little girl behind, but I'm wanted by the police? This seems a bit extreme."

"This isn't about your child," Blaine said. "You're wanted in connection with a murder." Blaine's expression stayed taut so as not to alarm him. He wanted to make sure Isaac understood that Blaine wasn't afraid. Besides, Alison had told him the truth. Isaac wasn't the one who'd killed the girl—it had been the alter of that man, Rickie. The one that Isaac's alter appeared to be dating. It was a strange phenomenon, but Blaine had seen it more than once over the years since the drug's release. Somehow, these people found each other.

Mel had found Jackie, though their connection had been easy. Yet together they'd found Candy. The same thing had been true for previous people he'd helped. Alison shared a similar experience.

It was both amazing and dangerous. Blaine imagined it was this little detail that made the pharmaceutical company so deadly, as Alison implied. They could round up the afflicted in one fell swoop.

Isaac sat on the edge of the bed, clear confusion in his gaze. "How is this possible?" He looked up at Blaine. "And how are you so calm about this? Oh god, are you a bounty hunter?"

"No, far from it." Blaine glanced back towards the muted, flickering TV. "I'm calm because I know you didn't actually kill anyone."

Skepticism crossed Isaac's face. He didn't respond, instead reaching toward the computer to touch the photo. Tears formed in his eyes.

"Who is it?" Blaine asked of the blurred-out person in the photo.

"My daughter," Isaac said. "One of the few pictures we have together. How the police could have gotten their hands on it . . ." A look of realization crossed his face. "Cora." He reached for the phone. "I have to call her."

Before he could pick it up, Blaine blocked his way. "You can't call anyone. I'm sorry."

"She must be worried sick," Isaac said. "I have to make sure Lyssa's okay."

He shook his head. "I understand you're worried, but you are also in danger. If you call her and tell her anything, they'll come arrest you and I can't have the cops anywhere near me."

Isaac stiffened at his comment. "What do you mean?"

"I need you to trust me," Blaine said. He cracked a smile. "I know that's a weird thing to ask of you, since you don't know me. But if you call them, you will get arrested and I think before you do that, you need to figure out why they think you're tied to this case. You need to understand why you disappeared and can't remember anything."

Isaac didn't respond for a moment and Blaine didn't rush him. He didn't need to. The man wasn't unreasonable and no one wanted to get arrested for a crime they hadn't committed. Blaine understood the primal urge in him that wanted to see and protect his daughter. That he wanted to make sure she was safe. Now wasn't the time for that.

Isaac hesitated but eventually nodded. "Okay. Cora will keep her safe. I know that. What can you tell me about what's going on?"

Blaine frowned. He'd never really had the intention of spilling the truth to Isaac. Alison had left his alter breadcrumbs and Blaine wasn't certain the man would believe a single word he said. No, for now, they had to figure out their next steps, and Blaine needed to know if what Isaac's alter had said about Parsons being near death was true. Blaine couldn't risk him running.

"I'll tell you what I know about the murder," Blaine said. "Maybe then we can figure out how you were involved."

Blaine only hoped that Isaac's alter would surface soon and he could get the answers he needed. Then he could put himself far away from Isaac and the police who were searching for him.

Chapter Thirty-Eight

CORA PORTER

I t felt invasive, standing outside the office of Isaac's doctor. Had she come alone, that would have been one thing. A worried mother wondering about the stability of her child's father. Instead, she stood here with her lover as they tried to uncover Isaac's involvement in a murder.

Ryan only wanted to help, Cora knew that. He was hoping to find a clean connection to Isaac that would bring down his true target, Blaine. But there was also the question of how Isaac got tied into all this in the first place.

When Cora had first mentioned talking to Dr. Stephanie Kwon, she wasn't sure if Ryan would agree. When she'd asked to go with him, without involving Aidan, Cora was certain Ryan wouldn't approve. But the senior detective had been unfazed.

Instead, he found the address and together they made their way across the downtown core, to the prestigious office building where Kwon held her practice.

The woman had been unassuming and willing to speak with them. She'd cleared her schedule and met them in the entranceway before directing them into her office. She was petite, with shoulder-length, pin straight, black hair. She wore minimal makeup, which Cora had to admit wasn't necessary, as she had long, lush lashes that framed her dark, hooded eyes. She wore large, round glasses; Cora wondered if they were prescription or decorative. One could never really know these days.

Kwon motioned for Cora and Ryan to sit on the long couch in her office, then proceeded to take the solo armchair that Cora imagined she sat in for each session.

"I am sorry to hear about Isaac," Kwon began, her voice holding an edge of sadness. "I haven't seen him in several weeks, I'm afraid."

"That seems to be a trend," Ryan said, reaching up and rubbing at his collarbone and likely remembering just how recently he'd seen Isaac, or a part of him. "We're looking for a bit of clarity on his mental state." Ryan passed a piece of paper to Kwon. It contained the toxicology report of Rickie Hastings. "We picked up an individual whose state of mind was questionable. He'd been a steady user of Solydexran. Shortly after, we discovered a connection between Isaac and Rickie—they were both users of the drug."

Kwon's brow furrowed as she read over the reports. "Well, yes. I've treated Isaac for many years. We first met when I was new in the practice and he came in as a child. His father had passed and his mother had described some questionable behaviour. Through my sessions, I learned more about Isaac's relationship with his father and the abuse he suffered at his hands."

Cora drew a sharp breath, unable to stop herself. She knew of Isaac's father's death, when Isaac was only ten, but abuse? He'd never mentioned anything of the kind. Isaac didn't like to talk about his childhood, but a parent's death could be enough to put anyone off. Guilt swirled around inside her. Could his past trauma be why drugs and drinking came so easily to him?

"Isaac exhibited dangerous signs of uncontrollable anxiety after he stopped drinking," Kwon continued. "For a time, he'd turned to marijuana to try and quell the voices, but I'm afraid that may have made him worse. Solydexran had been successful in aiding his anxiety when it was first released, so I recommended he begin using it again."

Cora's shoulders shook, but she tried to keep her emotions reigned in. She hadn't realized that when Isaac had gotten clean, his anxiety had been too much. Had his memories of the abuse come back in full force? She looked down at her hands, willing the guilty tears to stay put. She'd been the one who pushed him to clean up his act. Was it her fault he'd turned to Solydexran? Was it her fault he'd become one of the statistics?

Ryan seemed to sense her discomfort and he reached out, gently giving her closest knee a quick squeeze.

"Solydexran has proven to have some devastating results," Ryan shared, passing another piece of paper to the doctor. This was a copy of the report Ryan had found in Calvin's house during his case. Cora had read it and still struggled to believe the words inside.

It was clear the doctor did too, as her shocked expression read disbelief. "This is not possible."

Ryan grimaced. "I'm afraid it is. All too possible. I've seen the effects myself."

"How was this not shared?" Kwon's voice rose an octave—it was clear that Ryan's report was causing her discomfort. "I have many clients that use this. Many that have no issues."

"It seems the evidence I presented wasn't conclusive enough for any movement against the drug," Ryan said, a bitterness in his tone. He'd told Cora how the evidence of the drug's wrongdoings had all disappeared when the women from his case went to trial.

"Many don't experience issues," Cora chimed in, regaining her composure. "The medication affects each individual differently. It seems to have more extreme effects in patients who have a history of trauma or mental health."

"That's all my patients." Kwon placed a hand on her chest, trying to calm her staggered breathing. Cora worried that the doctor may be having a panic attack.

"Are you okay?" she asked, leaning forward as if to get up and approach her.

Kwon's eyes met Cora's and for a moment Cora wasn't sure if she'd speak. Soon Kwon sucked in a long breath and breathed out loudly.

"I'm fine," Kwon said and turned her attention back to Ryan. "How can I help you? Because I assume you didn't come here just to tell me I've ruined all my clients' lives?"

"We're just looking for a timeline," Ryan said. "When did he start taking Solydexran? You also mentioned he'd stopped—when and why was that? When did he start again?"

Kwon stood and rounded her desk. She pulled open one of the drawers and withdrew a manilla folder. When she returned to her seat, she flipped it open.

"About five years ago, his alcoholism was at its worst," Kwon explained. "He came in telling me he'd been hearing voices. I attributed the latter issue to his alcohol abuse. It was something I'd seen before. I had a former patient who would drink and speak to her dead grandmother as if the woman was right in front of her. Originally, I prescribed Xanax in hopes that it would help him calm down. But when that proved to not work, I moved on to the newer drug, Solydexran. The results spoke for themselves. Within two weeks, Isaac was a different person."

Cora closed her eyes, thinking back to five years ago. She remembered a time when Isaac had seemed to improve. He'd showed up, he'd doted on Lyssa and for a moment Cora had believed things were getting better.

"But it didn't last," Cora said, remembering when her hope ran out. When he disappeared. When she found him drunk in his favourite pub across the city, when he was supposed to be picking up Lyssa.

Kwon nodded. "Isaac stopped taking his medication. He said he didn't need it, that he was fine. I can't force a patient to medicate themselves. Fast forward to just over six months ago. Isaac had been clean for three weeks and it was weighing on him. He confided in me that he was going to turn back to marijuana to tame his cravings, which I knew from his previous experience was a dangerous path. Marijuana use almost always sent him back alcohol. I asked him again to try Solydexran. He was hesitant but willing."

"Have you met his alter?" Ryan asked, as if reading Cora's mind.

Kwon's brow line furrowed again. "Alter?"

"His alternate personality," Ryan explained. "A common symptom of the drug use we've seen."

Kwon's face drained of colour. "What are you talking about?"

Cora couldn't believe her confusion. The doctor had literally read the report Ryan gave her only minutes before. Did she truly think they were lying about the consequences?

"He calls himself Noah," Ryan said.

A hint of recognition crossed the doctor's face and she flipped back in her notes. "That's a name he's mentioned before. That he'd spoken with someone named Noah. But that was years ago. When he was a child. He spoke about him often—I believed he was an imaginary friend, as one day he stopped talking about him and never mentioned him again."

Cora's stomach flip-flopped. So, Isaac had had contact with his alter before, in one way or another. Were those the voices he thought he heard? Did he think he was talking to someone else, rather than another version of himself? The idea made Cora's head spin. How could she have been so oblivious?

Ryan glanced sideways at her. "Well, I think that about covers it for now." He stood and Cora followed. She felt like she was in a trance, like she'd done everything wrong and should have known what Isaac was going through. He'd been trying, for her. For Lyssa. He was working to get better. He had demons buried that Cora knew nothing back. Had she known, would she have pushed him as hard? The guilt made her insides twist and turn. She'd been nothing but hard on Isaac and now, she worried she may have pushed him too far.

Chapter Thirty-Nine

NOAH BAKER

Noah's eyes shot open. Something was wrong. He sat up in the queen-sized bed and glanced around the tacky motel room. He stiffened when his eyes fell on his unknown roommate. There in the bed next to him, a man slept soundly, turned away from him.

Careful to keep quiet and not disturb the sleeping man, Noah crawled out of bed and reached for his coat, which had been flung over a nearby chair. He made his way to the door but hesitated. He didn't know where he was. He didn't have any money.

His eyes fell on the wallet that had been discarded on the tabletop. Noah glanced back at the sleeping man before reaching for it and flipping it open. He took the little amount of cash that was there, just a couple of twenties and went to place it back down when something else caught his eyes. Credit cards, IDs. More than one.

Noah glance again at the man who slept before slipping out the cards and reading them. The first read Blaine Roche, and Noah recognized the ID photo as the man from outside the CEO's house. After he'd learned that Dylan Parsons was as good as dead.

The next ID featured a similar though aged photo of the man, with the name Calvin Wright. Another beneath that one read Ross Bigly.

The credit cards in the wallet matched the aliases, though there wasn't one assigned to Calvin Wright. Who was this guy? Noah couldn't be sure if any of these IDs were real.

Noah was placing the cards back when he noticed a photo shoved into one of the holders. He slowly slipped it out, revealing the man who slept there standing side by side with a young woman. Noah couldn't believe it. It was Caroline.

The man groaned and rolled over. Noah froze, holding the wallet and photo in his hands. When no sound followed, he examined the photo closer. He could see the resemblance between the two now that they were side by side. The same nose, the same rounded eyes. Were they siblings? It seemed like an easy assumption.

But what was he doing here now? The last Noah remembered was hearing the cops and taking off. Had this man followed him?

The man stirred again and Noah didn't wait to find out. He dropped the wallet and the photo and dashed out the door.

It took him a moment to find his bearings, but eventually he realized where he was. The motel was in the west end of Ottawa, near the river. He began walking to the center of the city, unsure how to proceed. He'd been so intent on helping Caroline and on bringing the CEO to justice, but now with him on his death bed and cancer eating him from the inside out, Noah didn't know what to do.

Grace was in prison and would be convicted for murder; they had enough evidence. Caroline had vanished, and with her, the direction she gave him. He felt lost. More confused than ever.

With nowhere else to go, Noah made his way back to the rundown house Caroline had called home. Maybe, despite her disappearance, he could find some clue that would send him on the right path to find out the truth.

The house looked abandoned, which was no surprise to Noah. He'd known Caroline was leaving when she'd told him how worrisome his situation was. Further, he knew the police had already torn through the house. The remnants of police tape fluttering in the wind were enough of a tell-tale sign, even if he hadn't seen it himself over a week ago.

Noah combed through the house, finding nothing of value and grew dejected. Perhaps it had been a mistake coming here. All it did was remind him how grave the situation was and how badly he wished he had more guidance. In the short time that he'd known Caroline, she'd endeared herself to him. There was something about her that made him feel comfortable, like he'd met her before. It was an easy friendship.

He made his way down to the spare room where he'd stayed more than once and immediately something caught his eye. Despite all the personal possessions being removed from the house, there on the bedside table sat the dog figurine he'd asked Caroline about on his second night. He'd wondered then why she hadn't packed it up. Why would she have left behind something that had seemed so important to her?

Noah was across the room in a few short steps, lifting the figurine from its place. Why hadn't the police taken it? Perhaps they saw nothing of value in a decorative statue.

Noah wasn't sure he did either. He was moving to return the dog to its resting place when his thumb ran along a grooved edge. There was a break in the piece. He examined it closely. It looked like it could be two pieces. Carefully, he twisted the figurine in his hands and soon it broke apart, revealing a folded piece of paper inside.

Noah glanced around, feeling like he was invading Caroline's carefully kept secrets. Still, he couldn't deny himself any bit of advice or information his friend could give him, so he tossed the figurine aside and unfolded the short note.

He paused as he glanced over the text. It was addressed to him. Caroline had meant for him to find this.

Noah,

I am afraid that I have been lying to you. The truth is, you are not who you think you are. Unfortunately, you too have suffered from the devastating consequences of Solydexran. Two people live within you.

Your true name is Isaac Kirby. He is a confused but joyful man who has a young daughter to help care for. I had believed he'd only suffered minorly from his first use of the drug and I'd successfully encouraged him to remove it from his life.

I don't know why Isaac turned back to Solydexran. Perhaps he believed it had helped him, but whatever the case, his side effects have worsened and you, whoever you are to Isaac, have returned as the result of that.

I know this must be very confusing. Even impossible to believe. But I know if you truly consider your life, your problems and your memory loss, you will see reason in my words.

Be careful, Noah. You are wanted because you are the product of their failure. You must stay far away from them, as I do not know what they will do if they find you.

I am sorry I never told you the truth when I had the chance.
I fear I've lost my own way.
I wish you only good things, Noah. If you can, seek help.
Find a care facility you trust and do not mention the use of
Solydexran.
They will find a way to bring light to your situation. They
will help you return to the life you are meant to have.

Take care of yourself,
Caroline

Noah read and reread the note over and over until he couldn't process it any further. Could the words be true? Could he be one of the afflicted that Caroline had worried so desperately about?

He crumpled the note in his palm. How could she have lied to him and sent him on such a dangerous journey? He could have been taken. She didn't know the lengths these people would go to keep their secrets, yet she'd been willing to test them with him. Why? What did Caroline hope to achieve?

Noah stood and moved to her bedroom. He threw open the empty drawers and found nothing of value. When he moved to her closet, he found an empty passageway. Realizing there was nothing left for him in this house, he took the path, hopeful to find Caroline at the end and make her answer for her deceit.

Chapter Forty

BLAINE ROCHE

B laine awoke to find his motel room empty. The man who'd stayed with him the night before was gone and Blaine could only guess what had happened. After all, it had happened multiple times with Melanie over their years together. He'd wake up and find her gone, at some point in the night reverting to Patsy and returning to her marital home.

Blaine imagined it was what had happened with Isaac when he awoke and for a moment, he was annoyed to have missed that chance to interact with the man's alter. If only he wasn't such a heavy sleeper. These last few days had been exhausting. Trying.

Blaine moved to the table, where his things were strewn across it. The cash was gone, and Blaine almost laughed at the fact that Isaac's confused alter had robbed him. It wasn't much money, at least. The cards remained in their respective holders, but the photo of Alison from their younger years still rested on the table.

Had he recognized her? He must have, as it seemed he'd taken off in a hurry. Blaine took the photo and added it back to his wallet. He'd kept it close to him since they parted ways all those years ago. It was the only way he remained connected to her. Like holding a photo of her was holding a part of his past. It was foolish to keep something on him that tied them together, but he hadn't the heart to forget her face completely.

Blaine gathered his things and headed for the car that was parked at the back of the alleyway. Alison had confided in him about Isaac and all he had been through. In her desperation to help him, she'd left behind breadcrumbs at her old house for him to follow. She'd wanted to use him for their revenge, but she didn't have the heart to keep him completely in the dark. Blaine could only imagine how her attempt to use him was eating her from the inside. Alison had always been painfully empathetic. Blaine was surprised she'd been able to conjure up the strength to fool him in the first place.

Although unwilling to step foot anywhere close to where Boone and his cohorts would be searching for them, Blaine made his way back to Alison's home. He parked around the corner and checked his surroundings before stepping foot in the house. If they'd figured out that Alison and Caroline were one and the same, then this place wasn't safe. If they'd figured out the truth about who Alison and Blaine really were . . . then they'd know to keep an eye on the house, in hopes that he might resurface.

Blaine didn't find Isaac inside the home, but he did find the discarded figurine that Alison had described. It had been broken apart and tossed aside, indicating that someone had found the message she'd hidden.

Blaine returned to his car and drove to the closest place to where the tunnel would let out. When he left the car, he saw the man, sitting out in the open, an expressionless gaze staring at the setting sun.

"Isaac?" Blaine called to him softly, hoping not to frighten him.

The man turned his head towards the sound and gave Blaine the once-over. "I'm not Isaac."

The man held the note in his hands and Blaine was certain that whatever Alison had told him was either impossible to believe or too shocking to truly process.

"Are you Noah then?"

His eyes flashed with suspicion and then he quickly averted them. "Did you know the truth when you took me in?"

Blaine walked closer to him and sat down a comfortable distance away. "I had a suspicion. My sister never was great at sharing all the details, but I can put two and two together."

"To make four." Noah cracked a smile that faded almost instantly. He glanced down at the note. "I don't really know what I'm supposed to do with this information. Where I'm supposed to go."

Blaine nodded, understanding his predicament. "I think you know what you have to do." The decision was obvious. Isaac had to leave and hide. If he stayed, then he'd end up in prison or worse. He wasn't just an innocent man who suffered. He'd have a spotlight on him. Vivian would have said something to her handlers and Isaac had been seen by more than one person confronting her. It wouldn't be long until the Solydexran watchdogs closed in around them.

"Who is he?" Noah asked. "This man who is supposedly the real me."

Blaine shrugged. "I don't really know. He told me his name was Isaac. That he has a child."

The man's eyebrows rose at the implication. "Then running isn't the right choice."

Blaine agreed . . . and disagreed. But maybe going to the police, getting arrested and getting help was the best thing for this man. He had a life he could still live after all the treatment and after time had been served. There was more for him. He didn't have to be alone.

Besides, life on the run wasn't really a life. Blaine knew that better than anyone.

"What do you know about all this?" Noah asked. "This drug and the people behind it."

Blaine frowned and scratched at his neck before telling his story about what he knew and the girls he'd tried to save. When he finished, Noah didn't speak or ask any other questions and together they sat in silence for a moment.

Then Noah said, "He has cancer, the CEO. Stage four. Terminal." He shook his head. "I guess I thought him dying would be the thing that stopped all the bad. Or at least would offer me some justice for what was done to those I love. But I'm afraid I feel nothing. I don't think there is a real way out of this. At least not until the lies are exposed."

Blaine understood how he felt. They were the exact feelings that Blaine had been wrestling with for some time. Together, he and Melanie had agreed that killing Dylan Parsons was the only way out. But Blaine realized the company would live on without Parsons. Solydexran would live on without him. He no longer had the power to stop what had already been put in motion.

"The lies will be exposed," Blaine said. Sharing everything he'd been through and every way his family had been affected was always part of his plans. It wasn't enough to save a few when more and more problems kept arising. It was time for him to share the truth with whoever could help them get it out.

It was more than a conspiracy. It was a crime that someone had to answer for.

"Let's go back to the motel," Blaine said, standing and offering Isaac a hand.

The man stared at him for a moment before accepting the help up, then followed Blaine to where his car waited.

They rode silently back to the motel, both seeming unsure what to say or where to go next. For the first time since he set out on this journey, Blaine didn't know how to proceed.

Chapter Forty-One

CORA PORTER

The hustle and bustle of the police precinct told Cora something big had happened. She tried to flag down a rushing officer, but the man didn't even look her way. Cora rushed to Aidan's office, hopeful she'd catch him before he'd left for whatever it was he was doing.

She was surprised to find Ryan and Aidan together. The former looked ready to bolt, while Aidan was shrugging on his jacket.

"What's going on?" Cora glanced between the two detectives, her eyes wide.

"We got a call," Ryan said. "Someone spotted our two suspects together."

"Isaac?" Cora just wanted him found and safe. It was nerve-racking that he'd been MIA for so long. Worse, she was running out of ways to shield her daughter from it.

"Yeah," Aidan confirmed. "Him and Roche were spotted together entering a motel on the west side of the city. We're heading there now."

Cora straightened, hoping to be invited along, but Aidan didn't extend the invite. He just brushed past her. She looked expectantly to Ryan, who shrugged.

"Come with me."

Cora fell into step next to him as they hurried through the station to the parking lot. Aidan was waiting out front and he narrowed his gaze when he saw them exit together and Ryan gesture towards his own vehicle. Aidan didn't say another word before waving over his partner and ducking into the driver's seat of his car.

Aidan's partner seemed surprised by the invitation but quickly slid into the passenger seat before the car drove off.

Ryan chuckled. "I'm probably going to hear about this later."

"Same here." Cora didn't care, though and found no humour in Aidan's sour mood. She was desperate to confirm the sightings and needed to see Isaac. She needed to know he was okay.

As they drove in silence, Ryan reached out, placing his hand on her knee and giving it a gentle squeeze.

She turned from the road to look at his profile. He hadn't shaved in a while and a thick beard was growing in. She wondered if that was a normal practice for him, or if it had been brought on by the distress of the case. He'd taken it really hard when he'd lost Blaine Roche in their last encounter.

Cora had felt closer to Ryan since their last night spent together. He'd opened up more about the challenges of his former case and about his wife. She in turn, had trusted him with Isaac's story and how their college romance had blossomed until it ended in a baby and an angry alcoholic. Their stories were tragic in their own ways. The only difference was that Cora had a chance to still save the one she'd loved. Ryan had lost that chance long ago.

"Are you okay?" he asked, without looking away from the road. From his peripherals, he would be able to see her watching him.

"Yeah." Cora tore her eyes away from him, looking back down the highway as they raced along, following the other sirens and cars in pursuit of the motel. "Just hoping we find him."

Ryan nodded but didn't answer.

"Should we cut the sirens as we get closer?" Cora didn't want to alert Isaac to their arrival. "Hunter said to cut them once we got off the highway. I guess the motel is close by."

Cora couldn't help but wonder what had brought Blaine and Isaac together. It had been a question she'd posed to Ryan once already, but neither had a solid answer. Ryan still believed that Blaine, who was likely Calvin, was trying to help people who had suffered the results of his drug. Cora wasn't sure what to believe. Could it have been by chance that they'd come across one another, or had Alison played a role in bringing the alter in touch with her brother? Whatever the reason, Cora hoped they weren't too late.

They pulled off the highway and cut the sirens. Ryan rushed down the open side road, then slowed to a crawl as they approached the secluded motel. There were trees surrounding it, offering ample places to hide, but nothing seemed out of place.

Aidan was quick to jump out of his car, motioning for the other officers to gather around room five.

"Stay here," Ryan said as he climbed out to follow Aidan.

Cora fidgeted in her seat, watching as they approached the closed door. Aidan waved someone forward to slide a key in and open it. Then they all rushed the room.

She couldn't stop herself. Throwing open the passenger side door, she listened for any indication that Isaac might be there.

The shouting came first. Then gunshots rang through the heavy air. Cora sucked in a sharp breath and darted towards the motel room. An officer out front threw her arm out to stop Cora from entering.

She struggled in the officer's hold for a moment before realizing what she was doing. She stared wide-eyed, desperate to see if Isaac would come out alive.

Before she could begin to think the worst about his condition, Aidan emerged with a defeated-looking Isaac in cuffs.

"Oh my god," Cora cried out. Isaac looked ragged, run down. His hair had grown long, and he sported a thick, untamed beard. His eyes were cast downwards, but she could see the way his skin sagged and the heavy bags that made his expression dark and gaunt.

"Isaac?" she whispered.

He looked up at her. His eyes flashed with anger for a moment and then he tore his gaze away from her.

"Aidan, wait."

But Aidan didn't listen to her pleas. Instead, he moved right to his car and deposited Isaac in the back, rougher than he deserved. Then he slammed the door behind him and waved to his partner.

"Let's get him back to the station."

Cora looked at him desperately. "What happened?"

Where had Ryan gone? Would he emerge with Blaine in a moment? But he didn't. Cora looked around the officer blocking her from entering the motel room and couldn't see anyone inside.

When Aidan still didn't answer her, Cora ran to him and grabbed his arm. "Talk to me. What just happened?"

"You're not even supposed to be here," Aidan growled.

Cora stepped back, shocked by his anger and Aidan's face immediately softened.

"Sorry," he mumbled, looking away from her.

Cora stared at the man sitting in the back seat. It was certainly Isaac, yet he looked at her like she was a complete stranger. Had they found him in his altered state?

"Isaac was there and surrendered," Aidan explained. "We weren't so lucky with Mr. Roche."

Before Cora could ask about the gunshots, Ryan came jogging around the motel. Aidan looked towards him and Ryan shook his head, a defeated look on his face. Cora could only guess. He'd lost Blaine—again.

"I don't know how he did it," Ryan said. "But he got away."

"He was bleeding," Aidan protested. "What? You can't keep up with a wounded man?"

"It's the damnedest thing," Ryan said. "We pursued him on foot. He didn't have much of a head start. It should have been easy. But beyond the trees, there's another road. Someone picked him up."

Aidan shook his head. "Did you get a license plate?"

Ryan motioned over his shoulder to the other returning officers. "It's been recorded and sent to the station."

Aidan nodded his approval. "I'm going to get Isaac into questioning. Maybe he can shed some light on whoever was helping our fugitive." He glanced at Cora. "Call in your forensics team to collect the blood and the stray bullets. I have to go report my shots."

He turned on his heel and climbed into his car, then sped away with his partner.

Cora grabbed her phone and did as he'd said, calling in the team. They had to get whatever samples Aidan was referring to. When she hung up, she turned to Ryan with a wide gaze. "Bleeding? Shots? What happen in there?"

Ryan shook his head. "It happened so fast. Isaac was on the bed, then an officer was in and had him on the ground in a few seconds. We asked where Roche was and Isaac said he'd taken off through the back."

"The back?" Cora asked, following Ryan to his car.

"Yeah, there was a door back there leading to a covered patio. It would have been nice of them to mention that." Ryan scowled.

Cora didn't disagree. It was out of character for Aidan not to have all his entrances covered.

"It was amateur hour." Ryan.shook his head as he climbed into the driver's seat and Cora settled in next to him. "We saw him, standing at the edge of the trees. A gun in his hand. Hunter yelled for him to drop it, but barely gave him a chance. So he stopped and took aim. It was about three shots before he connected with him. His right arm, it looked like. But the guy barely flinched and just started running. We made ground, were getting close and then that car came out of nowhere."

Ryan shifted the car into drive.

"It sounds like we got a DNA sample," Cora said, thinking about the blood that had spilled.

He nodded. "And a way to confirm what we already know is true."

Cora didn't answer Ryan's hypothesis, because she still wasn't sure that Blaine and Calvin really were one and the same. While the idea sounded right, it just seemed so crazy that someone could go to the lengths he had to fake his own death, but as Cora had seen since the beginning of this case, nothing was as it seemed.

Chapter Forty-Two

NOAH BAKER

Noah stared at the table before him. After everything he'd learned from Blaine, his arrest was inevitable. It was clear, as Caroline had said, that not only the police were hunting him. Noah saw the arrest as the safest option. Maybe he would see Grace.

The detective who entered was tall and blond. He was the one from the papers. The one Cora had been close with. He reminded Noah of those asshole surfer guys from West Coast TV shows, that tried to paint the glamourous life of living on the beach. It only made Noah hate him more.

He pulled out the chair across from Noah and sat down, placing the folder he held in front of him.

"Hello, Isaac," the man said, a sneer on his face.

Noah frowned and shook his head.

The man rolled his eyes. "Okay, fine. I'll play your stupid game. I am Detective Aidan Hunter, although you know that. Who might you be?"

Still Noah didn't speak. Detective Hunter—why would Noah know him? Even as he considered it, he knew that in truth, Hunter knew Isaac and whatever his relationship with Isaac was, it didn't seem friendly.

Noah was still struggling to wrap his head around all the details Blaine and Caroline had shared. He struggled with the lies she'd told him and the intent behind her sending him after the creators of the drug. Since Julie's death, everything had spiraled out of control.

Hunter continued to look at him expectantly.

Noah shrugged. "Honestly, I don't really know anymore. But I've always gone by Noah."

Hunter nodded and withdrew a photo of a man and placed it in front of Noah.

"Do you know this man?"

He looked down at the photo and recognized Rickie immediately. He could still see Grace when he looked at him, but it was a strange familiarity.

"I guess," Noah said. "Probably not in the way you'd like."

Hunter withdrew another photo. This time, Noah reached for it and held it closer to him. This was the Grace he remembered. Her vibrant smile, her long blond hair, her dark manicured eyebrows. His Grace.

"And that one?"

Noah nodded. "That's Grace."

Hunter reached for the photos and took them away from him. The next picture he pulled out made Noah look away.

"I guess you recognize her."

Noah stared at the wall, unwilling to look at the photo of Julie's body. The tie was wrapped tightly around her neck and her dead eyes were vacant.

Noah leaned forward, pressing his forehead into his fists. Flashes of memory assaulted him. Watching Grace push her to the ground and grab the tie from the back of the chair. She was quick to wrap it around

Julie's neck and pull. Noah stood there, useless, unable to stop what was happening in front of him, until the sirens sounded and he abandoned Grace and Julie, the latter to her death.

He nodded but didn't look back at the picture.

Hunter pulled this one away, then placed another picture in front of him. This time it was a photo of the tie and the initials embroidered into the back.

Noah picked it up, unsure what to think. He recognized it, but not from the murder. From before. Why?

"That belongs to you," Hunter said. Then he cleared his throat. "Or to Isaac, I guess." Noah could hear the skepticism in his tone.

Noah didn't speak, as he didn't know what to say.

Hunter sighed and took the photo away. Next, he passed a photo of an orange pill bottle. A typical prescription. *Solydexran*, read the label. It was prescribed to Isaac Simon Kirby. Noah frowned, running his finger over the picture of the bottle. He knew about the drugs, of course, Caroline had told him all about Grace and her problems. He knew that people had been harmed by this and he knew that Julie had been working for them. It was a new realization that he too was an afflicted.

"This drug is bad," Noah said, sharing what Blaine had told him. "It was pushed to market with falsified trials. And the creators, they aim to harm people." Noah closed his eyes for a moment. "Dylan Parsons. He is the one who did this to me."

"Dylan Parsons is dead," Hunter said dryly. "And in terms of the creator . . . well, you were sharing a room with him." The detective dropped a photocopy of a news article in front of him.

The file was a bit blurry and the date indicated the article was several years old, but what Hunter had said was true. There in the center of the article was a photo featuring a man in a lab coat, meticulously measuring something in a test tube. To Noah, the photo looked staged, one taken for publicity, not actual work being done. It was definitely Blaine, though. The photo was undeniable, but the text was the strange part. They didn't call him Blaine, as the man had told him. They referred to him as Dr. Calvin Wright. Could Blaine have been one of the afflicted like himself, or just another liar? Noah couldn't be sure.

Before passing it back to the detective, Noah remembered the IDs he'd found on Blaine before trying to escape him the first time. There'd been one with a younger picture of Blaine with the name Calvin Wright, though he'd carried no other cards related to this person.

"I don't know anything about this," Noah said, pushing the file away.

Hunter grimaced. "Okay." He took out another photo and put it in front of him.

It was a candid shot of Blaine and Caroline side by side. Hunter pointed at the woman.

"Do you know her?"

Noah nodded.

Hunter raised an eyebrow but didn't respond.

"Caroline," Noah finally said.

Hunter shook his head. "You're looking at Alison Wright"—he pointed to Caroline—"and Calvin Wright." He pointed to Blaine. "Whoever these people are, they lied to you. Now, what can you tell me?"

Alison. Noah's shoulders slumped as he considered all the lies he'd heard over the past couple of weeks. The secrets they'd fed him. The way they'd manipulated him. But he couldn't bring himself to betray them. He didn't know enough even if he wanted to. This detective had it wrong. They couldn't have created the drug. They were trying everything to stop it.

Noah shook his head. "I don't know anything about them. I know they are tied to the drug in some way. They have an inner knowledge of this conspiracy and what's going on. But they're trying to stop it. Beyond that, I don't know anything about it."

Hunter's lips were pressed together in a firm line, but he simply nodded and took the photo. He tucked them all back into the folder and stood. He left the room without speaking again.

Noah was alone for only a moment before she came through the door. He recognized her, as he always did, though now she looked cautious, unsure.

"Isaac?" she asked, her voice quiet. "It's Cora."

He shook his head. "I'm sorry." He didn't know why he was apologizing, but it seemed like the right response to her tone.

Cora's face fell, and her shoulders slumped, but she still approached the table with careful steps.

Noah's gaze stayed fixed on her, though she didn't meet his eyes as she moved closer and pulled out the chair across from him. He'd never been this close to her and his skin prickled with excitement. She was even prettier up close. Not in the way that he would have expected to find attractive, but in a kind, conventional way. He didn't love the pixie cut she rocked, but he had to admit it suited her.

He glanced over her plain suit jacket and the way her eyes seemed to skirt around the room as if she was uneasy in his presence. But Noah was fascinated. What was her true relationship with Isaac? Were they friends, lovers, family? Envy boiled in the pit of Noah's stomach. He'd been obsessed with her for as long as he could remember. But was it truly Isaac's obsession he was play-acting? Noah wasn't sure he'd ever know.

"Can I speak to Isaac?" Cora asked, tilting her head slightly.

He clenched his fist, annoyed that he wasn't enough for her. Her sad eyes made his anger dissipate quickly. He looked away—he didn't know what to tell her. How was he supposed to summon the part of him he didn't even know was there?

"I don't think I can help with that."

Cora looked down at the table, then fished something out of her pocket. "Well, if you have any connection with him, can you tell him Lyssa is okay?"

Noah frowned again. Lyssa? Who was she referring to?

As if to answer his silent inquiry, Cora placed a photo on the table.

He picked it up, unable to believe what he saw. It was a photo of him, though he looked different, his hair styled in a way he'd never worn it, and beside him was a young girl who resembled Cora. Cora's daughter. Though her hair was much longer, it was the same jet black. But her eyes . . . well, she had Noah's eyes. Something about her was familiar. Like he'd held her in a dream.

He'd seen her before, on one of his many voyeur moments with Cora, but the feeling inside him was different. This familiarity was more than just a glance from a distance. He felt like he'd loved this child for much of her life. Like she truly belonged to him.

"How is this possible?" Noah asked, looking up from the photo.

Tears had formed in Cora's eyes, and she shook her head. "You never told me that your father hurt you. You never told me you were using and that when you got clean, the memories, the anxiety was too much."

Noah didn't know what she was talking about but didn't interrupt or stop her.

She reached across the table and touched his hand. Noah recoiled from the connection but still felt warmth where her fingers had grazed him.

"Sorry," she mumbled, looking away. Her cheeks flushed with embarrassment and a tear escaped the confines of her eye.

Noah leaned forward, for a moment wishing he could comfort her. He shook his head. Whatever relationship he had with her was a mystery, but Noah felt a connection, no matter how strange it was to him. And the daughter? Noah didn't know how to handle that. He felt for this family, torn apart by a faulty drug.

Soon Cora looked back at him, desperation in her tone. "Can I talk to Isaac? Please."

Noah shifted with discomfort. He wished he could give her what she wanted.

She continued to watch him for a moment, then sighed. "I'm sorry for everything you've been through."

Still, Noah didn't respond.

When Cora moved to stand, he gazed up at her. "How's Grace?"

For a moment, her expression faltered and confusion crossed her face, but as quickly as it was there, it disappeared.

Cora lowered herself back to the chair. "Grace was forthcoming. Confused in her own way, but also more aware."

"She knew what was wrong with her."

Cora nodded. "She told us all she could."

"How does this work?" Noah asked. "Now that you have us both on crimes that we weren't fully aware we committed." The idea was bewildering to Noah, but it was the only way to describe it. Could he be responsible for other things he was unaware of? He'd had moments of memory lapses but had never worried too much about it, as things seemed fine. Nothing out of place. But now . . .

It was clear that Noah's alter had a relationship with the woman before him. It was clear that he'd had a relationship with their young daughter. How often had Noah missed out on these parts of his life? How often had Isaac missed out on aspects of his? The consideration was too much; it made Noah's head spin.

"I can't really say," Cora said. "There will be a trial, as blame needs to be laid. A woman was murdered and no matter what the intentions or the reason, there will be consequences."

"Will they help us?" Noah asked.

"We will try," Cora said. "But the truth is, no one really knows the extent of the damage done by the drug. We don't know what getting better means yet."

Noah grimaced. The words did not fill him with much hope. He'd be tried and likely convicted of aiding and abetting a murder. Perhaps he'd cease to exist when Isaac returned, or perhaps Isaac would be the weaker personality and he would win out. Whatever the outcome, it wouldn't be the life he knew.

When he did not respond, Cora stood and headed for the door. Before pulling it open, she hesitated and glanced back at him.

"For what it is worth, she loved you," Cora said. "Grace, or whoever she is, really loved you."

Noah nodded his thanks, but he knew that already. Grace had committed an unforgivable act for him. For them. Noah had never known a deeper love than that.

Chapter Forty-Three

BLAINE ROCHE

The pain made Blaine come in and out of consciousness. Everything was blurry. His arm ached and sweat prickled on his forehead. The last several hours had been a blur.

The pain he'd felt when the bullet pierced him had barely registered until he made it to the road. When he saw the car Alison had promised, he ran over to it, all too aware of the cops pursuing him and the yells coming from behind him. He was lucky they hadn't hit anywhere too serious. Though, he could feel the blood running down his bicep.

Blaine flopped into the passenger seat, uncaring about who the driver really was or how he knew Alison. As soon as the door closed behind Blaine, the driver slammed the gas pedal, taking off down the open road.

Groaning, Blaine removed his shirt and ripped it in a way where he could tie it above the wound, using his mouth and free hand to do so. It he could stop the bleeding, then maybe it wouldn't be so bad. The last thing he would do was go to the hospital to get the bullet removed and the wound patched up. Alison would have to do it herself. He only hoped she hadn't forgotten how to mend a wound in her years away from her nursing degree.

The driver spoke to him, but Blaine didn't register what he was saying. He simply continued to work on the wounded arm. Once he had the shirt tied tightly around the wound, he leaned back in the seat and closed his eyes.

"You okay?" the driver asked. "Don't you die in this car."

Blaine almost shot him a cold look. He wouldn't succumb to a gunshot wound in his bicep. From what he could tell, the bullet hadn't gone very deep. He'd been able to move it, so the bone hadn't been hit and the hole was small, meaning impact hadn't been too hard. Blaine was lucky he'd gotten the head start that he had and that the cop seemed like a bad shot.

Even as Blaine thought that, he reasoned it might not have been as bad a shot as he thought. They definitely didn't want him dead. Or at least Boone didn't.

"I'll be fine." Blaine rolled his head and looked at the driver. He looked like a kid, or a young adult at the very least. His skin was smooth and his facial hair minimal. He looked worried and Blaine pitied him for a second. Alison was pulling all the wrong people into their problems.

"Is this your car?" Blaine asked.

The man shook his head. "A rental."

"Did you rent it?"

Again, the man shook his head.

Blaine looked away from him. "Good." He knew the police would track the vehicle as soon as they could. He didn't know this young man, but he also didn't want another person caught up in his problems.

Blaine didn't speak again until the man brought the car to a slow stop. Then he jumped out and rounded the car to pull Blaine from the passenger side.

Gripping the wound in his arm, Blaine hurried towards the lone wooden cabin. The door swung open to reveal Alison. Her normally calm face had been distorted into a look of worry.

"Get inside." Alison barely glanced at Blaine as she ushered him and the young man through the door and into the kitchen. "On the table," she instructed and Blaine got up on it, sitting and letting her examine his arm.

"Go get rid of the car and hide for a couple of days." Alison shoved an envelope into the man's hands and he retreated.

"Who was that?" Blaine asked.

Alison didn't answer. She stood in front of him, examining the wound. Then she turned and stepped out of the kitchen, coming back with what looked like a tool kit. Blaine couldn't be sure. He was starting to feel dizzy. The adrenaline of the chase had worn off and now the racing of his heart had been replaced with a dull ache throughout the right side of his body. The pain was beginning to grow.

"I need to lie down."

Alison didn't stop him from lowering himself to the surface of the table. Instead, she worked quickly, though Blaine couldn't force himself to watch. He cried out in pain when she dug into the wound and removed the bullet. He gritted his teeth as she carefully inspected the damage, then stitched up the opening. She discarded his torn shirt and dug through her kit to find a bottle of pills. Then she moved to his head, propped him up and shoved the pills into his mouth. Blaine choked them down.

He hoped they were painkillers.

He lay still on the table, unsure if he could find the energy to sit up or even move. At least the bullet was gone and Alison had stitched him up. But would they be safe here?

As he wondered, his mind started to drift. He forgot what he was doing and his eyelids grew heavy.

When he awoke, Blaine was acutely aware of the pain in his arm. His head felt clearer and despite the pain, he was able to sit up. He couldn't be sure how long he'd slept.

Carefully, he swung his legs over the side of the table and eased his way up, worried the blood loss would make him light-headed. When he was steady, he moved into the attached room.

Alison sat on the aged couch, staring aimlessly into the fireplace. She glanced up at him when he entered the room and her concerned expression broke into one of relief.

"You're okay." She said it as a statement not a question, as though she wasn't sure if he would be. "You've been out cold since last night."

Blaine nodded and sat next to her. "I'm alright thanks to you."

"You were lucky."

"It wasn't a bad shot," Blaine said, but he really didn't know. He was basing his assessment on his injured state. Perhaps it had been worse.

Alison nodded. "No, but it could have been. They got close."

"Someone must have tipped them off."

"You shouldn't have been with him," Alison said.

"I was trying to clean up *your* mess." Blaine resented his older sister in that moment. She'd been the one who put Isaac in harm's way. Who was he to allow that to happen?

Alison shook her head. "And did you?"

"Well, he didn't die," Blaine scoffed. "Or get taken."

"Only arrested."

Blaine frowned and looked away. Isaac's alter had known what was happening. He didn't want to run anymore. He wanted help. It was the right choice for him. It wasn't the right choice for Blaine.

"You're lucky we got a tip," Alison said. Though it hadn't been a tip so much as the police scanner announcing their pursuit.

"Keep telling me how lucky I am." Blaine sneered. "Because I don't feel very lucky."

Alison clamped her mouth closed and said nothing else.

"So, what now?" Blaine asked.

She turned to look at him. "There is something you should know."

He waited for her to tell him, but instead she stood and returned to the kitchen. When she came back, she was holding a newspaper in her hands. She dropped it on the table in front of him and Blaine realized what it was.

The obituary section. His eyes scanned the page until he saw it. The obituary for Dylan Parsons. The CEO had died.

Blaine felt nothing. He'd thought this was what they'd been fighting for. That this was the revenge they wanted to get. The man who'd started all of this, who had torn their family apart, was gone from the world. Shouldn't there be some joy?

Blaine shook his head. "He got off easy."

Alison seemed to be thinking the same thing as she lowered herself back to the couch next to him. Parsons would never know the lengths that Blaine and Alison had gone through to keep themselves safe. He would never know the way his actions had made so many suffer. He would never have to answer for the mistakes he'd made.

Even as Blaine considered all of this, he began to hope. Maybe with Parsons gone, they could finally let go. Maybe now they could move on. Despite the bad that had happened and the things that they'd both done, maybe his death was an open door for them to move on and forget. They could be a family again.

Alison continued to stare at the page and Blaine gently nudged her shoulder.

"What are you thinking?"

When she looked up at him, her eyes were watery and Blaine could see the guilt she carried. He opened his mouth to protest, to tell her that none of this was her fault and that the two of them had both made choices, but before he could speak, she put up her hand.

"I am so sorry, little mouse," Alison said. "I've been lying to you. But now, I have to tell you the truth."

Chapter Forty-Four

CORA PORTER

When Cora got the call the following day about the DNA results, she didn't know quite how to process it. She stood in the lab with her assistant, looking at the details.

"A 98 percent match?" Cora gaped at the results. The DNA they'd taken from Blaine was a close match to the information they had on file for Calvin Wright but not identical. Had the sample been compromised?

"That's what it says," the younger lab technician said, though the look on her face held the same disbelief Cora was certain showed on her own. "I ran two separate samples to be sure."

The blood they'd received from the scene hadn't been substantial, but it had been enough for her team to gather a few samples. The report told her all she needed to know. The DNA samples they'd collected weren't an exact match to the DNA that belonged to Calvin.

"There are some mutations in the sample compared to the one on file," the woman explained.

Cora frowned, not needing the woman to talk her through the details of the report. As she read over the concept again, she remembered a recent study that had tested the differences between identical twins. While some shared a 100 percent match in their DNA, they were few compared to the many who had mutations that showed up in one twin, but not the other. It was a recent development and still not widely researched, but it was the only thing Cora could attribute the results to.

The blood type was a match, but the DNA that floated around in it wasn't. Calvin Wright and Blaine Roche were not the same person at all. They were identical twins.

Cora placed the file down, her head spinning. She hadn't been sure what result she was expecting. She'd suspected that Blaine and Calvin were not one and the same a while back, but without concrete evidence, Ryan had been hard to persuade otherwise. They'd seen too many people pretending or thinking they were someone else. It was too strange to have someone like Blaine attached to a case revolving around dissociated identity disorder, without wondering if he too was a victim of the drug he fought against.

This file told the truth. He was Calvin's brother. Why was the brother out for revenge?

Cora turned and retreated from the room without another word to the associate. She found Ryan in Aidan's office, the two of them leaning over his desk, looking at his computer screen. Despite the relationship triangle they seemed to be entwined in, the detectives had proven to be formidable partners. For a moment, Cora wondered if Ryan would be open to requesting a transfer.

They both looked at her when she entered the room. Ryan's easy smile fell in place, while Aidan stiffened with discomfort.

"Any word on the DNA?" Ryan asked. He'd been asking her constantly since they submitted the sample for testing.

"You won't believe it."

The look on Ryan's face suggested otherwise.

"It wasn't a match," Cora said.

His confident expression faltered. "What?"

"The DNA, it wasn't a match," Cora said again, uncertain if he didn't hear her or didn't believe her. "The blood type coincides with Calvin's, but the physical DNA is only a 98 percent match."

"Then the sample was tainted," Aidan said firmly. "That's impossible."

Cora shook her head. "It's actually not. Identical twins can have almost identical DNA based on mutations within the womb or by their outward experiences. In fact, a 100 percent match on identical twins is rarer than not."

Ryan's brow furrowed with confusion. "Brothers?"

She nodded.

"How's there no record of twins?" he asked. "How's there no record of Blaine?"

Cora stared at him, lost for words. The adoption records of the Wrights had included only Alison and Calvin. Why was Blaine not with his family? Cora thought about that weird separated-at-birth scenarios that people liked to overplay in fiction. Stranger twins? Even odder.

"Could be a million reasons," Aidan said, rounding his desk. "Do you know much about the parents and why the kids were put into the system?"

Cora shook her head. They'd never looked too far into it because it didn't seem to matter. Was Blaine Roche his real name? Or was it the last name he adopted from wherever he came from?

There had to be a way to confirm the last names of Alison and Calvin before they'd entered the care of the Wrights. Further, there had to be a birth certificate for both, something to prove their existence.

Before they could explore the information further, a deputy pushed her way into the office. "Hunter, sorry to bother you but Isaac Kirby has surfaced." She looked at Cora. "He's asking for you."

Cora's heart leapt at the news. He'd been in holding for nearly thirty-six hours and charges would have to be laid soon. They'd been holding off, hoping Noah would give in to the dominant personality inside him.

Cora glanced at Hunter as he pushed by her.

"Where is he?"

"In room three," the deputy said, then turned and left.

Cora didn't wait for instruction before bounding down the hall to the interrogation room and seeing where Issac was seated through the one-way mirror. She stopped outside only when Aidan called her name.

"You have to let me in there," Cora said, turning back to him with a wide gaze. "I have to know how he is."

Aidan put a heavy hand on Cora's shoulder as Ryan drew closer. He gently moved her out of the way of the door. "You aren't a cop anymore. I have to handle this first."

He didn't wait for her response before pushed through the door to the interrogation room where Issac was.

Isaac's expression tightened when Aidan entered. "You're not who I asked for."

Aidan let out a stiff laugh. "Cora isn't a cop anymore. You get to deal with me first."

Isaac glanced toward the one-way mirror with a hopeful expression.

As if reading his thoughts, Aidan lowered himself to the chair. "She's listening and if you cooperate, maybe I'll let you talk to her."

Cora stiffened at the comment. Aidan had been even stingier with details and she didn't doubt that he'd withhold this from her. Then again, he had let her talk to Noah when they first brought him in, though Cora suspected that was in hopes of dragging out Isaac.

Isaac's brown eyes searched the mirror as if trying to make contact with her. Cora only stared back at the man she used to love, feeling her heart flutter.

"You okay?" Ryan asked, reaching out and catching her hand.

She tore her eyes away from Isaac and nodded. "I'm just glad he's okay."

"I know you were worried," Ryan said. "About Lyssa."

"I don't know what I would have done if I had to tell her she couldn't see her father anymore." Cora looked back at the window but didn't drop Ryan's hand. He'd be sentenced in some way or another, but convicted was better than dead.

"Why don't we start from the beginning," Aidan said.

Isaac tore his eyes away from the mirror and shook his head. "It's all a little blurry."

"That's to be expected." Aidan had seen one confused felon already and Ryan had experienced more. Nothing was a surprise anymore.

"Several weeks ago, I woke up in a shelter outside of the city," Isaac began. "I couldn't remember how I got there and my head pounded in a way I can't describe. As I lay there staring at the ceiling, I couldn't believe I messed up so bad."

"Why didn't you come back?" Aidan asked.

Isaac sighed. "I knew that waking up there, that my lack of memory, what day it was . . . I knew that meant I'd succumbed to my addiction once again and started drinking. Worse, I realized I'd been doing it when Lyssa was in my care. The damnedest thing is that I can't remember picking up a drink. My apartment has been dry since I went to AA and I was always so careful when I had Lyssa around."

"That doesn't explain why you stayed missing," Aidan interjected.

Isaac shot him a look that said he was getting to that part. He glanced up at the window. His eyes were round, sad, and full of regret. Cora knew he wanted to be telling this story to her directly, not to some cop who would relay it. Even worse, she knew he hated that he couldn't see her reaction.

"I was ashamed," Isaac said, turning back to Aidan. "I'd been clean before and failed miserably—and worse, I'd put the most important person in my life in danger."

"One would think you'd want to come back and confirm she was okay." Aidan raised an accusatory eyebrow.

Again, Isaac glanced towards the mirror and Cora knew the response before it came out of his mouth. He'd checked in. He'd known she was fine, but he'd still stayed away.

"I made sure Lyssa was okay," Isaac said. "I went by the apartment and saw she was gone. I went to Cora's house and saw her through the window. That was all I needed to know."

"What happened next?"

"I planned to check myself into rehab. I planned to get better." There was a desperation to his voice Cora had never heard before. "But that didn't happen. In fact, I lost days. I couldn't believe it. I knew then that I wasn't in my right mind."

"Why didn't you try to call?"

"I wanted to," Isaac said. "But before I could, he found me."

"Who is that?" Aidan asked.

"He called himself Blaine," Isaac explained. "A few years back, I had met his sister, Alison. She took an interest in me and started coaching me on my sobriety and anxiety. She started helping me ween myself off the use of any medication to stay healthy and sober. But then she vanished and when I was alone, it was a lot harder to think about sobriety. Without a coach, I fell deep. I started drinking again and my problems came back in full force, so I turned back to the medication to keep myself in check."

Aidan nodded along with Isaac's details, making notes as he did.

"I hadn't seen Alison in years," Isaac said. "When he approached me, it sounded like I'd seen her recently. Who knows at this point, maybe I had."

"Well, part of you had," Aidan said. "That much was confirmed when we brought you in."

"Right," Isaac said, shaking his head in disbelief. "Still hard to imagine a part of me that I don't know."

"You're not the first we've heard that from." Aidan looked back at his notes. "What did Blaine want from you?"

"He asked if I'd been at a house in Kanata. Some estate that he was concerned about. But I hadn't been there."

"Why did you go with him?"

Isaac reached up and scratched at the back of his neck. "Honestly? The offer of a shower. I felt so grungy. Who knows where I was sleeping."

"But a complete stranger."

"Yeah," Isaac said. "Something inside me said I could trust him. I can't really explain it."

"Were you together long?"

Isaac shrugged. "Who knows. He told me that I was wanted, though he didn't seem concerned. He told me that I shouldn't get arrested because he needed to avoid the police, so he wouldn't let me call or check in. By then, I just wanted to know that Lyssa was okay. That Cora hadn't gone frantic."

Cora frowned. He'd wanted to reach out, but he couldn't. She wished he'd been able to. To save her and Lyssa the heartache.

"I was going to call the moment I checked into rehab. The moment I could tell Cora I was fixing myself." Isaac looked at the table. "I've let her down so much."

Cora closed her eyes. Only this time, it wasn't his fault.

"When do you last remember being with Blaine?" Aidan asked.

"It was then," Isaac said. "The next thing I remember is waking up in holding. If I hadn't seen the search for me, then I probably would have panicked. Honestly, I figured you picked me up drunk somewhere, passed out."

Aidan smirked, but it slipped away quickly. "You came willingly."

"Well, that's good, I guess." Isaac's expression didn't give way to any feelings.

"Can you talk about the murder?" the detective asked. Cora could tell he was treading cautiously. If Isaac asked for a lawyer to be present, he wouldn't be able to ask anything further.

"Sure," Isaac shrugged. "But not sure what I can tell you."

Aidan produced a picture and put it on the table in front of him. "Your tie was the murder weapon."

Cora had since divulged the familiarity of the tie and the initials embroidered on it.

Isaac looked at the picture. "I guess whoever this person is inside me would have some of my things. From what I understand, I didn't do the actual murdering."

Aidan shook his head. "No, we have a confession about what happened."

Cora knew that confessions could be overturned. However, beyond the tie and Rickie taking the blame, they didn't have much to go on. The only ones who truly knew what had happened that night were the two jumbled personalities.

"Did you know the victim?" Aidan asked, producing another photo. "Julie Kanner?"

Isaac slid the photo towards him, but there was no recognition in his eyes. "I had a dream about an argument. Someone getting hurt. But it's all so blurry. I don't know that it was her or if it was even real."

"It was real alright," Aidan said, leaning back in his chair. He hadn't looked towards Cora once during the entire questioning process. He pushed another photo towards Isaac. "What about Rickie Hastings?"

Isaac scrutinized the photo. "He does look familiar, but I can't put my finger on it. Maybe a customer?" Isaac's carpentry business saw all sorts of people.

Aidan took the photos back and stood.

"Can I see her?" Isaac asked.

He exited the room without answering. Isaac looked desperately at the mirror.

"Well?" Cora asked, dropping Ryan's hand and stepping closer to Aidan as he appeared.

"Go see him." Aidan stepped aside.

Cora pushed through the door without a moment's pause.

"Cora," Isaac said breathlessly. "Lyssa?"

She crossed the room in a few short steps and threw her arms around his neck. "She's okay. Everything is going to be okay."

Isaac's hand touched Cora's arm and she allowed a few tears of relief to spill onto his shoulder.

Chapter Forty-Five

BLAINE ROCHE

The guilt on Alison's face made Blaine worry about what was about to follow. Had she sent more people on suicide missions? Had she denied what they both had agreed to do after the death of their brother?

She seemed to be fidgeting with the truth.

"Just tell me," Blaine finally said. The suspense was making his insides twists and the throbbing pain in his arm stronger.

"When the trials were falsified and Calvin's research was ignored, he did something drastic."

Blaine straightened. This was the first he'd heard of their younger brother doing something against the people who'd started this.

Alison closed her eyes for a moment, as if reliving the memory was painful. "He'd hoped that he could force their hand, make it so the drug failed."

"What does that mean?" Blaine leaned forward, ignoring the pain that followed the movement. When they were children, Calvin had been reclusive, leaving Blaine and Alison to their games. He was the youngest of the three, though only a few minutes behind Blaine and spent much of his days reading. But things changed as they grew. Calvin grew reckless, Blaine had learned that the moment they'd reconnected.

Their lives, though identical, had taken different directions. For years, Blaine had survived on his own, separate from Calvin and Alison. But Calvin had it all. He had parents who loved him and an older sister who watched his every step. When they'd first seen each other again, Blaine envied him. His younger brother was distant and uninterested in a new sibling. Blaine wanted nothing but family and wondered how Calvin had been the lucky one between the two of them. Then he died and Blaine regretted his feelings.

"Calvin didn't realize that his choices would have such disastrous results," Alison said, defending him as she always had. Even against Blaine in those early years.

"Stop it," Blaine snapped. "You've always made excuses for him. He's gone. Stop defending his every decision."

"You don't understand—"

"Enough!" Blaine cut her off. "I get it, you and Calvin had years together that I didn't have. But enough is enough. I am the only brother you have left. We've spent years trying to expose the people who took our brother from us and now you're telling me in reality, we've only been cleaning up yet another of Calvin's messes?"

As his anger grew, the pain in his arm intensified. Soon, he placed his head in his hand, trying to draw several steady breaths to ease the pain that clouded his mind.

When he looked at Alison once more, her eyes were damp with fresh tears. They were also wide, frightened. Blaine gritted his teeth and reached out, placing his hand on hers.

"Just tell me what he did," Blaine said softly, allowing his previous anger to evaporate.

Alison looked down at their intertwined hands. Then she drew a long breath. "He doubled the original dosage, believing that if he did, the results he'd seen in the trials would be exponentially increased and impossible to ignore."

Blaine tried to swallow the bile that rose in his throat. So, Calvin had made everything worse. Once again.

"Are you sure?" he asked. There were procedures in place and approvals that made this type of thing nearly impossible. Though if Blaine had learned anything over the years, nothing was truly impossible. After all, the original trials had been ignored, covered up and passed off as a success. The doctors who had been involved in the processes had been paid off in large sums and dismissed into retirement.

Calvin hadn't wanted the pay-off. Calvin only wanted to help people, as he'd always done. He wanted a true and effective solution to those who had suffered, as he'd seen Alison suffer. Blaine remembered those days well. Calvin had been hesitant about letting Blaine back into their lives. Maybe over time, it was easy to forget your twin. Maybe he began to think of himself as the only one, but Blaine, who'd been so alone for so many years, was desperate for the reunion with his family.

Alison had been high-strung and anxious over everything. It had been a driving factor for Calvin to get his doctorate in pharmaceutical science. It had been the reason he'd wanted a job at ACE. He'd wanted to help people like her.

Alison's anxiety had lessened over time. Xanax had worked wonders on her and soon she'd learned how to live and adapt. Soon the medication was no longer needed. Calvin had hoped Solydexran would be the thing to keep Alison stable forever, but he had been wrong.

"Yes, I'm sure," Alison said. "By the time he told me the truth, he'd been dismissed and the paranoia had become too much. He was convinced someone was following him. They were desperate to silence him—the company and those involved—as he would have ruined everything they'd done. Parsons was out of his mind."

Alison shook her head. "I tried to tell him to leave, to take what they offered and run. But Calvin refused to let his work be destroyed. He was sure that once the issues began arising in regular users, the public wouldn't be able to ignore the side effects. But he underestimated Parsons and just how far he'd go to keep his corruption hidden."

"Then people started disappearing?" Blaine asked.

"The first instance I heard of was when Calvin called me," Alison said. "He was frantic. He sounded like he'd been drinking and claimed that he'd seen people being taken. After they let him go, he followed the drug for a period of time and kept records of those who experienced side effects."

Alison looked away. Blaine knew what was coming, as she'd told him part of this story before.

"After that, I never heard from him again. The next thing I knew, I got a call from the police department saying Calvin had wrapped his car around a telephone pole."

Blaine remembered it well. He'd only reconnected with his siblings a few years before. He and Calvin had had a rocky start, whereas Alison had welcomed him with open arms. Calvin had been elusive and unwilling to accept Blaine into their life at first. He'd thawed over time when he realized Blaine's intentions were not vindictive. Blaine truly hadn't known the location of his family for years.

When Blaine had met Calvin, the man was a celebrated scientist. He didn't drink; in fact, Calvin had never touched a drop in his life. For him to end up in a drinking and driving accident—Alison and Blaine knew it was impossible. But no one would believe them. The level of alcohol in his body was too much to deny that he'd been consuming. Alison had tried to plead with the detectives, begged them to do a thorough investigation, but they wrapped it up and Calvin's death was ruled an accident.

A disgraced doctor who drank himself to death. What a legacy.

"When I found the formula, I couldn't believe what he'd done." Alison said. "Since Dylan wouldn't see reason, I knew I had to do something, so I tried to find those affected and work to get them off the drug. For some, that was all they needed. For others . . ."

Alison looked away from Blaine and he didn't rush her. This was more painful for her than he could imagine. He still remembered her panic after Calvin's mysterious death. The way her anxiety came full circle and she told Blaine she was being followed. She'd left Toronto quickly, and Blaine had found himself inheriting a house from his dead brother. With his ID and identical looks, Blaine had taken it over and never bothered to transfer ownership. He never did get asked about the supposed death certificate that was tied to the name he was using, but perhaps they didn't bother to look. Money had never stopped coming, so questions didn't get asked.

"Some would get better, then return to the drug, like you saw with Isaac," Alison explained when she'd regained her composure. "Some were too far gone."

For a moment, Blaine imagined a life with Melanie. One made possible by this small little pill. They'd live in the old farmland he'd inherited from the couple who took him in. She could be at peace, free from her demons and the life that Fraser had cursed her with.

He shook his head to clear the images of them drinking wine and watching the sun go down, laughing together while they cooked dinner, making love late into the night.

"Somewhere along the way, I got tired." Alison looked at him with wide, sad eyes. "I thought I'd lost both my brothers—I thought I was alone. I didn't want to keep fixing Calvin's mistakes and I got angry at the people who made our lives this way. I wanted revenge and I thought the best way to get it was with the help of those who had been unknowingly afflicted. I sent more than one after Parsons," Alison explained. "But each time, they never got close enough. Each time, they were discovered and taken." Her shoulders slumped at this mention. "I knew it was happening, but I couldn't stop. I was so desperate to get revenge. To feel something, some type of control. I was a fool."

"You were angry," Blaine said. "No one could blame you for that."

Alison grimaced. "If only that were true. Anger isn't reason enough to put some of the people I met in danger. I don't even know what happened to the ones they took away."

Blaine didn't answer, as he wasn't sure what he could say to ease his sister's troubled soul. They'd been put in an unthinkable situation. It was unfair to both of them. To Calvin.

"When I met Grace," Alison said, "I couldn't bring myself to put her in harm's way. She was so kind, vibrant, and she knew she was a part of Rickie for a reason. She knew more about her dominant personality than any of the others I'd met. Her insight fascinated me. Of course, I learned about his childhood over time and how Grace had protected him when he was young. She was so loving. A caregiver. But it seems her love was ultimately her downfall."

Alison spoke about the murder that had started the chain of events leading them here. The murder that had gotten Boone into this city, hot on his trail, and gotten Blaine shot. All because Grace had murdered a woman out of jealousy. Blaine knew the truth, of course—that while Grace acted out of a jealous rage, Julie was working for the ones who would put her in harm's way.

"When I told Grace who Julie worked for and what would ultimately happen to her and Noah if Julie found out the truth, Grace ran out." Alison shook her head. "The worst part of it all was that I was truly trying to protect her. I couldn't imagine that she would kill Julie out of anger. I couldn't imagine that she would think that was the only way to protect herself."

The phone rang shrilly on the wall and they both glanced towards it. Slowly, Alison stood from the couch and approached it. Her steps were hesitant, cautious.

"Hello?"

Blaine couldn't hear the other end of the call, but it unnerved him to think his sister was possibly divulging her location to anyone. He'd never asked her much about the woman who owned the cabin or why she'd allowed her use of it. Greta made herself scarce whenever Blaine was around.

"Why would you do that?" Alison's tone was accusatory. "You have no idea what we have been through."

Blaine straightened. Who could she be talking to? But Alison didn't give anything away. She wouldn't even look him in the eye.

Her stiff posture told him that the conversation made her uneasy and the way her brow line crinkled revealed her concern. But there was something in her eyes. Hope, maybe?

"Okay," Alison said, and then she hung up the phone.

A tension clung to the air as she moved from the phone to the couch without a word. She looked stunned.

"What was that about?" Blaine asked.

Alison turned her torso towards him. "Vivian Parsons."

"The poster child?" Blaine asked. "Who was asking about her?"

"Vivian Parsons," Alison said again.

Blaine frowned. "What are you talking about?"

"Vivian Parsons just called to tell me she knows everything about what happened," Alison explained. "She's about to make the story public."

"What story?" Blaine's head was spinning.

"About everything. About the false drug results, about the unexplained disappearances, about Calvin's death." Disbelief was written on Alison's face. "When Dylan died, she found everything he'd kept hidden away. Everything he'd tried to bury. He kept it, for some reason."

Blaine frowned. Why would Parsons have kept all the evidence that incriminated him, his company and everything he'd worked for? Could it have been a decision borne of conscience? One made because he regretted all that he'd done, all the harm he had caused? Blaine couldn't be sure, but at least a credible source with documented evidence was behind their drive to pull the drug from market. Maybe things would slowly get better.

Chapter Forty-Six

CORA PORTER

C ora gripped her purse tightly to her chest as she waited for Isaac to be led into the visitation room. She'd left Lyssa with her mom for a few hours, desperate to get a chance to talk to him on her own. Other than their brief moment in holding, she hadn't gotten a chance to see him before he was charged and moved to general population. Now he, along with Rickie, were waiting for their trial. Though, Isaac still had a chance to make bail.

Soon, a prison guard entered the room, holding Isaac's right arm tight as he led him through the double doors into the general visitation room.

His long hair had been washed and pulled back from his face. Heavy bags under his eyes gave evidence of his exhaustion.

Yet when Isaac sat at the table across from her, his easy, familiar smile fell in place.

"Cora." He breathed her name as if it gave him life. "I'm so glad you're here."

"You have no idea how glad I am to see you, safe." Cora lowered herself to the bench, never taking her eyes off him.

"How's Lyssa?" There was a desperation in his tone as he searched her eyes for an answer.

"She's good," Cora said. "Missing you, but good. No harm done." She wasn't sure how accurate her assessment was. She could only imagine the harm that might come to Lyssa due to Isaac's actions, but it didn't do to dwell on that right now.

Isaac's smile faded and he looked at the table between them. "We both know that's probably not true."

Cora swallowed the words that wanted to follow, that wanted to reassure him. Instead, she reached into her purse and pulled out the drawing Lyssa had made for her father.

"Lyssa wanted you to have this," Cora said. "I'm not sure if you can keep it."

Isaac took the drawing in his hands. It was of him and Lyssa at the park. Lyssa had used a new set of markers and meticulously drawn each detail she could think of. The red slide in the park where she and Danny had spent many afternoons. The rusting swing set and even the bench off to the side. Cora had been impressed with her level of detail, but she understood it. Lyssa had wanted to make something special for Isaac, something that would remind him of her when he looked at it. Though Cora had no doubt Lyssa was often all Isaac considered.

Isaac smiled as his eyes danced over the details of the picture, though they lacked the same light and joyfulness they once had. She couldn't imagine the pain and heartache he'd been through. Or the past he'd hidden from her. She couldn't imagine the anxious feelings or conflicting personalities. How exhausting it must be to have another living inside you.

"Cora, I'm so sorry," Isaac said, tears filling his eyes as he placed the drawing down. "I've messed up everything."

"No, you didn't," Cora said. She wished she could reach out and hold him. Take Isaac in her arms and rub his back like she used to when they were together. When she was certain the worst thing that they'd ever face was a bad exam or a wicked hangover. "This is my fault. I pushed you to get clean. I pushed you to be better." She swallowed hard, trying to keep the tears at bay. "I didn't know about your father. Your past. Why wouldn't you tell me?"

Isaac looked away from her. "My past has nothing to do with this."

"It has everything to do with it," Cora said. Isaac still wouldn't meet her gaze. "Your trauma is part of what caused this. Did you know Noah?"

Isaac shook his head. "I remember a Noah. An imaginary friend, I think. But another personality inside me? I never knew that."

Cora nodded, remembering what his psychiatrist had said about Noah. She suspected they'd never really know how much of an impact Noah has had on Isaac and his growth.

"I didn't know you turned to medication in place of your addictions. I wish I'd been there to help you," she said when neither had spoken for a moment.

Isaac shook his head. "I still don't really know what's wrong with me. I don't know if I can get better."

Cora didn't know either. They didn't know enough about this drug and what it had done. They didn't know how deep the damage went.

"None of that matters right now," she said. "For now, we are going to do whatever we can to make sure you get there."

It broke her heart to know how desperate Lyssa was to see her father. It broke her heart further to see how lost Isaac was without his child. It was a cruel world that had put Solydexran and whoever Noah was, in the way of their relationship.

"I wish I could have been better, for both of you." Isaac met her eyes and Cora once again saw the twenty-year-old she'd fallen in love with during their second year of university. The man she'd thought then would be her forever. No one could ever really predict love and life.

Cora gave him a sad smile. She'd been desperate to have Isaac back and now with an impending trial on the horizon and the severe psychiatric work Isaac would have to do, she didn't know how often Lyssa would get to see him. It scared her to know that the single-parent life she'd accepted when Isaac first disappeared was here to stay, at least for the immediate future.

"But I promise," Isaac continued, "when I am better, when all this gets figured out, I will never let you or Lyssa down again."

Cora tried not to cringe at his words. Isaac had broken so many promises over the years and Lyssa constantly forgave him. It was Cora's fault, really, never allowing her daughter to be exposed to the fact that Isaac had failed. Cora always covered up his messes and his lies, but she wouldn't be able to do it forever. As Lyssa grew each year, so would her doubt and her understanding. One day, the girl would realize the man her dad was. Cora only hoped he'd truly be changed and better by then.

"Hey, you okay?" Isaac asked, drawing Cora back to him.

She nodded. "Yeah, sorry. Just thinking about all of it, you know?"

"That I definitely get." Isaac leaned back, putting distance between them. "I keep wondering how I got here."

"I wish I could have helped before it was too late."

When Isaac spoke again, his tone was harder. "Don't you dare take on any of this blame. This is my mess, Cora. You have to stop cleaning up after me."

Though she knew it was true, she reached into her purse again, unable to deny him one last lifeline.

"I've contacted the best defence lawyer I can afford." She slid the business card across the table towards him. "She will come meet you tomorrow and talk you through your bail hearing. If we're lucky, you can be out on bail soon to await your trial." Cora didn't mention that Rickie had been denied bail due to his confession and his complicated mental state.

Isaac picked up the card and fingered the edges. "I don't deserve this."

"You do," Cora said. Then she stood. "Just get back, okay? For Lyssa."

"For Lyssa," Isaac agreed.

Then she bid him goodbye and exited the visitation room the way she'd come.

Outside the correctional centre, she let her shoulders fall and her body crumple forward. The strain of being strong had worn her down. She wished they'd found Isaac intoxicated or high. She wished it had been anything but what it was. As long as Noah lived inside Isaac, with the threat of surfacing, he wasn't a fit guardian for Lyssa's busy life. At least if he'd been abusing drugs or alcohol again, then rehab would've been an option, but now . . .

Cora forced her shoulders back and tried to clear the distressed look off her face as she made her way towards her car. As she slipped inside and looked back at the grey, plain walls of the prison, Cora couldn't stop the blame from creeping in. If only she'd known. If only she could have done something more. If only.

Chapter Forty-Seven

NOAH BAKER

T he woman they'd brought in was plain and unassuming. She wore an oversized grey suit and had black, cropped hair that rested just above her shoulders. The spectacles that donned her face were round and skinny, a style that hadn't been popular for the past several years, or so Noah guessed. As he looked her over, he realized he never really knew what was in style, especially not these days. It made him feel dated and out of touch.

Everything about this situation made him uncomfortable. He hated being scrutinized and judged. He hated the invasive questioning that the cops had performed, then his lawyer, and now the psych evaluation. He was beginning to feel like a test subject, being poked and prodded, but with questions instead of needles.

None of them could properly grasp what was wrong with him. Not that he could. Still, they'd call him by the wrong name, recount events he couldn't remember, making him feel more disjointed and confused than ever. He wondered if Grace had felt the same when they first brought her in. He often thought of Grace.

"You seem frustrated," Dr. Kwon said. The psychiatric doctor had introduced herself with her full name, though Noah quickly forgot her given one. She claimed she was Isaac's doctor, someone who knew him well. She claimed Isaac had spoken about Noah before. None of this meant anything to him.

Noah didn't care who she was or how she'd helped Isaac. He was frustrated, distracted, and tired. It was all too much for him to process. Part of him was angry at Caroline—no, Alison—for all she had done to him and how she'd put him in harm's way, but he was also grateful. She was the only one who'd provided him with the truth, no matter how wicked it really was.

"I don't think that should be a surprise." Noah crossed his arms over his chest and looked away. The room they'd been left in was windowless and Noah was keenly aware of the damage he could do to this petite woman without intervention. The cameras positioned high on the walls told him someone was watching and they were likely close by, possibly right outside the door.

"No, you're right." Kwon cracked a smile. It was neither pleasant nor condescending. Noah had a hard time getting a read on this woman. "What in particular is frustrating you?"

Noah paused to consider the question. "I guess I don't really know. I'm frustrated that there is someone inside me I don't know. I'm worried that I may not truly exist and I'm just a part of someone else. I don't know what to expect. Will Isaac get better, as everyone keeps saying and will I cease to be a part of him? Or am I always someone that will be around?"

Noah had been running through the scenarios since they picked him up at the motel. Since he learned the truth, since Isaac had emerged and spoken with the police. He wasn't the only person inhabiting this body. He couldn't control the switches. He didn't decide how Isaac came and went.

Kwon nodded along with his thoughts as she jotted down the details. "Why don't we talk a bit more about Isaac and what you remember?"

Noah looked away. Kwon hadn't answered any of his questions.

"Isaac began to use Solydexran around five years ago. He used it for about four months before he opted to stop." Kwon referred to her notes as she read the facts to Noah. He'd heard them once before from Cora. She'd tearfully pleaded with him to let Isaac speak to her, but Noah had no way of appeasing her wishes, though he'd have been lying if he said he didn't want to. She'd been so kind and hopeful. It made Noah feel like scum, denying her what she needed.

"He went back on the medication just over six months ago," Kwon said. "It seems you resurfaced after that."

Six months still caught him off guard. He'd only been living for such a short period of time. It didn't feel that way to Noah. He felt like a real person, with a real past. He'd been an engineer once, before he'd lost his practice and things went downhill and he began drinking. He'd met Julie at a bar and they'd dated for only a few short weeks before he met Grace and fell head over heels for her.

"When did you meet the victim?" Kwon asked.

Noah grimaced at the word. They'd been referring to Julie this way since he was brought in. They never called her by name, like she wasn't a person anymore, just a statistic in their database. Like the person she was didn't really matter. Though Noah supposed, after death, perhaps it didn't. She was now a clue that needed to be solved. A murder that someone needed to be responsible for. He and Grace.

"Julie and I met probably around six months ago," Noah said. The more he'd learned about Isaac and his double life, the more he wondered if he'd met Julie the first night he'd resurfaced. To Noah, it had felt like any other night out. How could it be that he'd come into this body a full-fledged person with memories of a life that never existed?

"We dated for a time," Noah said. "It was a rocky relationship. One I wasn't fully committed to. I liked her a lot, don't get me wrong, but it never felt right. She also thought I was flaky, claimed I dodged her calls and disappeared for days at a time. But we were so new and that's how new relationships work. Sometimes people don't call. Sometimes they go away for a while."

Kwon nodded. "And do you remember these times that you were avoiding her?"

Noah shrugged. "Not really, but I'd been a heavy drinker for some time. I fell into the sauce when my career went down the tubes. I struggled to find work after that, odd jobs. Yet surviving had never been a real problem."

"You never questioned why that was?" Kwon asked.

"I had a good career," Noah said, frustration rising in his voice. "I had saved money. I knew how to survive." This had been brought up more than once. Questions about how he possibly couldn't have known the truth. What about his ID, didn't it reflect Isaac's information? What about the apartment Isaac owned, that clearly belonged to him and not Noah? But Noah honestly couldn't say he'd noticed any of the strangeness people expected him to. He never thought he was someone else. He didn't have reason to.

Kwon nodded again. "And what about Rickie Hastings; how do you know him?"

Noah's eyes narrowed at the doctor. "I don't know him."

"And Grace?"

"Grace was the light of my life," Noah said. He'd recounted the story of their meeting more than once in the past few weeks. With Alison and again with Blaine. With the police and with Cora. He'd been over this story time and time again. Not once had he ever suspected her to be anything other than what she told him.

"It was maybe four months back," Noah said. "A chance meeting. A meet-cute, as Grace used to say. She loved old classic films that featured unlikely duos meeting in everyday places. She loved that our story began the same way."

"What drew you to her?" Kwon asked.

"Nothing and everything. She was such a vibrant person. Anyone who met her just loved her instantly. She could turn heads and encourage laughter. She was unlike anyone I'd ever had in my life. I don't think I ever saw anyone sad around her." Noah paused. "Except Julie."

"How did Julie find out about you?"

"It was an afternoon in the park. Grace and I had just finished a picnic lunch, something I thought would be stupid and lame but ended up being sweet and fun. Like everything Grace made me do. Julie happened to be walking by and spotted us. By then, I'd barely spoken to her. I'd stopped returning her calls and basically ghosted, which I know was a poor choice."

"When she saw us, her eyes grew so wide, with surprise and anger maybe. She walked right up to us and demanded to know why I stopped calling, why I had just disappeared." Noah shook his head. "I wanted so badly to tell her it wasn't her fault, but I couldn't form the words and Grace was quick to my defense. She could be so incredibly kind, but she could bite back as well . . . she did just that with Julie and sent her away.

I won't repeat the hurtful things Grace said. They caught me off guard and made me question her for the first time since we met."

He took a deep breath. "Several days later, I got a call from Julie. I didn't pick it up, because I felt terrible about everything that had happened in the park previously. I was a coward and I didn't want to face her. But her message was desperate. She warned me against Grace and wanted to tell me something important. I only wish Grace hadn't heard the message—then maybe Julie would still be alive."

"What did Grace do when she heard Julie's voicemail?" Kwon asked.

"She flew off the handle," Noah said. "Into a fit of rage, like I'd never seen before. Her eyes went wild and she called Julie awful names. She said if Julie wanted to speak about her, then she could do it to her face. She stormed out of the house and I followed her. That was when it all went down."

Noah clamped his mouth shut when it came to the murder. He didn't want to relive the memories that seemed foggy, distant. Now he wondered how lucid he'd even been for the whole ordeal, or if the trauma had made Isaac try to surface.

Thankfully, Kwon didn't ask him about the incident or to describe how Grace had tackled Julie and wrapped the tie she'd grabbed around her neck, pulling until Julie went limp. He didn't have to talk about what it was like watching Julie struggle. How she stared at him and the realization dawned that he was going to let her go. That he had picked Grace over her and that Julie would die for it.

That look had haunted Noah since that day. He would never forget the decision he'd made, but he also couldn't regret it. When he discovered the truth about Julie and what she wanted to do to Grace, Noah realized that he would have always been in a place where he had to pick one over the other. He only wished Julie had never entered his life in the first place.

Noah still struggled to wrap his head around it all. How did these pieces fall so perfectly in place? Julie entering the bar the same night Noah reappeared, if that was how it really had happened. Because beyond the memories he'd made with Julie, everything before felt less real. As if he'd been dropped into a life and told what his life was beforehand.

It was strange to consider it now, with the lens that he might not be a real person. How did one process that detail? That he only existed because he was a creation of childhood PTSD? How did one come to terms with the fact that they truly didn't exist? Noah struggled with the idea of it all and hoped his treatments would offer some clarity. Though as he hoped for these things, he knew that clarity could mean that he ceased to exist entirely and how could one really hope for that?

Chapter Forty-Eight

CORA PORTER

The call came through Ryan's cell phone when he and Cora were out having a drink. They immediately dashed to the station and along with Aidan, heard the news.

Vivian Parsons, heir to the Parsons's fortune was coming forward with damning evidence. A series of arrest warrants were being put forward, for higher-ups in the company who had long been retired. Members whose signatures accompanied the false documents. Had they known the trials were forged? If they didn't, they'd have to prove it.

"I can't believe this," Ryan muttered under his breath. Cora felt the same. Had this woman known all along? Had she lied when Ryan and Aidan questioned her?

The breaking news story was still unraveling when Ryan returned to Cora's house that evening. Together, they sat and watched Vivian's address to the public about the confusing drug.

She appeared doe-like with her wide, frightened eyes that glistened in the lighting from the surrounding press. Though they couldn't see it, Cora imagined hundreds of reporters around her podium, eagerly awaiting the juicy gossip.

Ryan gripped Cora's hand and leaned forward in his seat. She knew what this meant to him. The discovery of the drug in his case that had led to the arrest of the girls. He'd been worried his evidence had been brushed aside, but now it would prove useful.

She also knew his fears. The truth was out. The CEO was dead. What did Blaine need to do now other than run? Had Ryan lost his chance at finding the man he'd hunted for months?

"I am here to apologize for the wrongdoings of my father and his company," Vivian said. Her voice was strong despite the fear written on her face. "In recent days, since his passing, many things about Solydexran and its production have come to light. A drug that I have fought tirelessly to give troubled people access to is not all it seems, and for that, I feel ashamed and embarrassed that I am the face of this scandal."

Vivian looked down and drew a breath before continuing. "I have learned that not all benefit from the great effects of Solydexran. In fact, many have suffered horrendous side effects, that have left their lives crippled and destitute. It has turned lost individuals into science experiments and has ripped loved ones from their families.

"Solydexran was created to help people. Instead, it has preyed on the weak and brought those who are suffering to more pain." Her eyes welled with tears. "I cannot believe that I have been sharing the greatness of this drug, when so many have been lost to it."

Vivian spoke about the trials and how there was evidence about falsified claims, how they were still working to uncover the whole truth.

Cora looked at Ryan, who still stared at the screen.

"Are you okay?" She gave his hand a gentle squeeze.

When he looked at her, she could see how exhausted he was. The bags under his eyes were more prominent in the lit living room and there was a clear defeat that hadn't been there before.

"I don't know what this means," Ryan said. "The truth had to come out. Someone has to answer for the mistakes of the past, but now he has no reason to stay."

Blaine. Cora didn't need Ryan to clarify to know who he was talking about. He wasn't wrong. Blaine's mission had been tied to the truth coming out and getting justice for the woman he had loved. Would he go back to her?

Ryan would keep a watch on Patsy Morrison's whereabouts and treatment for as long as they'd allow. Even Cora questioned if Blaine would risk such a visit. He'd loved the alter, not the woman whose body it truly was. Perhaps he was no longer interested in Patsy without the rough alter she'd fabricated.

"I'm sorry," Cora said, unsure what else she could offer.

"Let's go to bed." Ryan stood. "I'm sure there will be more details for us in the morning."

Cora flicked off the TV and led Ryan up the twisting staircase to her primary bedroom. She'd dropped Lyssa off at her parents' after school, after her young daughter had asked about another sleepover with Nana. Cora had been hesitant at first, unable to ignore the trauma of the past few days. But the feel of her mother's arms wrapped around her and the excited grin on Lyssa's face as she skipped through the front door, made Cora relax and have hope that maybe Lyssa could get through all of this and end up okay on the other side.

It was a good reprieve, giving her a moment of Ryan's private time. She still wondered what the finality of this case meant for the bond they'd built over their few weeks of work.

Still, she found that she missed her daughter. She wanted to hug her and tell her how much she loved her. Big truths like these tended to bring out the worried, protective mother that Cora had buried deep within her.

The next morning, Cora and Ryan arrived at the police station to find Aidan talking to a polished woman in a pressed suit. He motioned for Ryan to come over and the woman looked in their direction.

"This is Detective Boone," Aidan said. "The one I was telling you about."

The woman nodded. "Agent Simcoe, with the Special Investigative Unit." She reached for Boone's hand but didn't acknowledge Cora. Cora stepped away from the group, sensing she wasn't welcome. Remaining in earshot, she listened to their conversation.

"I have to thank you," Simcoe said. "Your thorough work back in Toronto put us hot on the trail of this conspiracy. We've been waiting for an egg like this to drop since you first uncovered the truth."

Ryan had been sure no one had even acknowledged his case, or so he had told Cora. His case seemed to have been swept under the rug, details disappeared, and he was never invited to testify at any trial. Ryan had been sure it was just another cover-up, but now it seemed it had made more waves than he thought.

"There have been reports of disappearances," Simcoe said, her voice low. "We sent a man undercover to follow Ms. Parsons. He was able to gain her confidence and has been helping her uncover the truth about the drug, without her knowledge of his assignment. And now, with Ms.

Parsons's discoveries, we may be on the right route to finding out what happened to these people. People like the sex workers of your case." She nodded to Aidan. "And the criminals in yours."

Cora flinched at the word "criminals."

"Disappearances?" Ryan asked and Cora was thankful he did. It was the first she'd heard about it.

Simcoe nodded. "Some users of Solydexran were reported missing and never found. Their trails cold. No bodies, no trace. It was the strangest thing. But there was always a lead-up. Every person who reported someone would collaborate that they'd been acting strangely, so when nothing turned up, it was generally believed they'd relapsed, gone off their medication, and vanished. Some seemed to vanish under the guise of requiring further treatment, though not one report could firmly say which hospital or doctor they were being treated by."

Cora frowned. For a time, this was what she'd believed was happening with Isaac.

"But that isn't what happened?" Ryan asked, skepticism in his voice.

"According to the reports and claims of Ms. Parsons," Simcoe said, "no. It appears they were relocating those who had adverse effects. We have yet to find out where or what they did with them at this time."

Ryan shook his head. "What about the doctor, Calvin Wright?"

Simcoe frowned. "There have been some whisperings that his death may not have been an accident. That perhaps he is more tied into this trouble than once believed."

"This is insanity," Aidan chimed in. "How could something like this go undiscovered for so long?"

Simcoe cleared her throat. "With a team dedicated to covering their tracks. The biggest question we have now, is how such a drug slipped through the system to approval?"

Cora had her suspicions. Ryan had mentioned a doctor in his past case, one who was paid by a supplier to distribute Solydexran. It hadn't been a large sum, but large enough to entice her into complying. Who knew how many others had been bribed the same way? It was not unlike the historic release of opioids and the payoffs that had doctors prescribing the addictive drugs.

"Do you have a moment to discuss some of the finer details of your case?" Simcoe asked, stepping aside for Ryan to enter the conference room.

He glanced back at Cora for only a moment before nodding and entering the room.

She watched him go, leaving her alone with Aidan in the hallway.

"What a case," Aidan said, running a hand through his hair.

"I can't believe that there have been unsolved disappearances," Cora said. "This drug has been in the market for only five years or so—how many people have been affected in this time?"

Aidan shrugged in response. He was only focused on the case he had to close.

"What are you going to do?" Cora asked, hoping he'd honour her wishes to go easy on Isaac. He needed psychiatric help, not a jail cell. He needed to get better and pay for his crimes somewhere that wouldn't harden him into the criminal he wasn't. Cora needed him to be able to emerge a better person, a better dad for Lyssa.

"What we discussed," Aidan said simply. "Someone's dead and there will have to be penance for that. I can't guarantee there won't be jail time, but with the mix of the alters, we don't truly have a motive for the death. I'm not even sure how to classify this. A crime of passion, I suppose?"

Aidan cracked a half smile, but Cora couldn't return it.

"I'll make my recommendations to the prosecution," Aidan continued. "They'll both stand trial, as they were both there for the murder, but it's likely they will grant leniency for Isaac. He doesn't know the victim and Rickie's alter has laid the blame on herself."

When Cora didn't answer him, Aidan turned for his office.

She followed his steps and hovered around his office door.

"What did you need now?" he asked as he sank into his chair.

"How did it end up this way?" Cora asked, though she knew Aidan couldn't provide an answer. Isaac had always been smiling in the face of trouble. Now she knew it was the way he coped. That his past had a darkness in it he chose to keep quiet about. That Noah had been a part of his life before and he carried his own demons, ones that Solydexran had reawakened.

When Aidan didn't answer, Cora turned to leave.

"Hey," Aidan called her back, his tone soft. "Don't beat yourself up over this. I know you're gonna blame yourself. It's what you do. But none of this is the result of anything you did. Nothing you could have done would have changed it."

Cora nodded her thanks and left. While she knew Aidan's words were true, they didn't take away the guilt that swirled around inside, that maybe if she'd been more aware, maybe if she'd noticed him faking it, then maybe it could have been different.

Chapter Forty-Nine

BLAINE ROCHE

B laine watched Vivian's entire address with his eyes fixated on the TV. She was tearful and guilt-ridden. She took the blame for the years of hardship, for the pain her father had caused, and for the people she influenced to try the drug.

It was being pulled from the market immediately, but the damage was already too great. Too many had already suffered and now users across the country would start to question if they were truly the only person inhabiting their bodies.

Alison emerged from the kitchen holding a tray with tea and set it down on the table in front of Blaine. The aroma of steaming peppermint brought a smile to his face.

"Can I take a look?" she asked, sitting down next to him and reaching for the bandage wrapped around his arm.

Blaine didn't answer or make a move to stop her from unraveling the wrap and examining the wound beneath.

"It looks okay," Alison said of the gunshot wound, discarding the soiled bandage and retrieving a fresh one. "How's the pain?"

"It's fine," Blaine said. The pain was less intense, a dull ache that was only worse when he made sudden movements. Her treatment had been quick and clean. Blaine was lucky.

Alison didn't answer as she busied herself rewrapping his wound. When she finished, she offered him a cup of tea. "You've watched this three times already." She glanced to the TV. The news had cycled some portion of Vivian's address over and over again throughout the day.

"I keep hoping for more," he said, reaching for the cup she passed him. He brought the cup to his lips and enjoyed the sinus-clearing scent before taking a hesitant first sip. The tea was scorching, so he placed it down.

"There is more," Alison said. "But nothing more she can give you. She did the right thing, coming forward."

"How did she know to reach you?" Blaine asked. The past two days had brought about too many changes and too many questions—Blaine hadn't had a chance to clarify his sister's relationship with the Parsons family.

Alison looked away. "Just know that any lie I told you was for your own good. Or at least that's what I believed."

Blaine frowned. He didn't like the sound of that. Since he'd found Alison, it felt like she'd been coming clean about lie after lie. Yet still, secrets clung to the air around them.

"Years ago," Alison explained, "when I fell in love with that married man. It was stupid, but I was so desperate not to end up like our family that I sought out someone who could take care of me. When I met him, I didn't know he was married. It wasn't until I tried calling his house and his wife answered that I found out. I masqueraded as a nanny looking for a job. I went to their home and I met her. The joke was on me, because even when he confronted me about it, I was so desperately in love with him, I was willing to share."

Alison looked away. "For a time, I worked as a nanny on the side and we kept up our quiet affair going. Until his wife became suspicious. I thought maybe he'd leave her for me. I loved him. I was so blinded. He didn't feel the same."

"What does this have to do with Vivian?" Blaine asked.

"The man was named Dylan Parsons."

"What?" Blaine remembered the relationship well, but he hadn't known the culprit. It had been a sore point between Alison and Calvin. She'd tried hard to keep Blaine in the dark.

Alison drew a breath. "I made a deal with him. If he gave Calvin work, good work, then I would leave them alone. I wouldn't ask him for anything else. I left him behind and Calvin got an amazing job, creating and testing a new drug. He made great money and it was stable. Everything was going perfectly and I was getting over my obsession, when Calvin told me what he'd discovered."

"When the trials failed." Blaine remembered the fallout from Calvin's confrontation with Dylan Parsons. Only a few months later, his brother was dead.

"I tried to reason with Dylan. I tried to tell him that it would come out," Alison explained. "That there was no way he was going to be able to cover up the results that Calvin had found. But Dylan didn't agree."

Blaine nodded. The CEO had claimed the issues were negligible. That the results spoke for themselves and the side effects were typical. He brushed Calvin's worries aside.

"He stopped taking my calls after a few days," Alison said. "I began trying him from different numbers. Including this one."

Blaine straightened in his seat. "Why hasn't anyone come to look for you?" If they had a way to reach her, why didn't they take her down like they had their brother?

Alison shook her head. "They looked for me here ages ago. Dylan was always keeping an eye out for me. When I realized he would do to me what he did to Calvin, I ran and didn't look back."

"But he must have kept a record of you, of numbers you used, places you'd been," Blaine reasoned. A man who'd been threatened would be foolish not to.

"All Vivian told me was that she found my name and number in Dylan's things," Alison said. "She may not know the whole truth about Solydexran and the evils around it, but she knows us, me and Calvin. She met Calvin as a child and I was her nanny for a time."

"Why didn't you ever tell me this?"

"I've been trying to protect you your whole life," Alison said. "Since we were kids. When social services took Calvin and me and had us documented, he wailed for his twin brother. But I convinced them there were only the two of us. I convinced them that you didn't exist."

Blaine frowned, unsure if he should be thanking his sister for that treatment. The years he'd spent alone as a child had shaped and haunted him. He'd had to grow up too fast, slept in shelters, under bridges, until his early teens, when the Roche couple took him in. All the while, Alison and Calvin had been adopted together by loving mothers and had full lives. Something Blaine had been denied.

"I don't know if that was really protecting me," Blaine said. "I never wanted to be without you both. Without Calvin."

Alison grimaced. "I know that now. I often wonder how different things would have been if Mom and Dad had survived or if you hadn't run off that afternoon they came for us. But we can't ever go back and I can't apologize for what I thought was the right thing."

"I do often wonder how a lot of things could have been different," Blaine said. For the thousandth time since they separated, Blaine thought about Melanie and about the life he'd imagined. A world where things were different and they weren't burdened by the mistakes of others. A world where they could love each other freely and openly. It had been a long-time dream of his, one that he imagined would come to light. But he'd been a fool. He couldn't change her fate and he couldn't change his.

Alison reached out and squeezed his hand. "Now we can make things different. With the drug off the market, we can find those who have been hurt or are suffering and we can help them seek the help they need." Alison looked at Blaine with hopeful eyes. "We can find them. We've already found so many and together we can help them."

Blaine gave her a half smile. "You know I'm still a wanted convict, right?"

"Well, you'll stay out of Toronto," Alison said with a laugh. "The truth is out there and now we owe it to Calvin to overturn his mistake and help who we can."

Blaine looked away from his sister and towards the TV, which flashed with obnoxious commercials. "Okay, let's do it."

Chapter Fifty

CORA PORTER

Cora sat on the bench at the edge of the playground. Lyssa raced around the obstacles, directing some of the younger children on proper play or which swing to use next. She was beginning to outgrow the small playground by their house and Cora was thinking about her next steps. She'd always dreamed of putting a pool in their yard. A place for Lyssa to have her friends over.

It had been years since Cora had full custody of her daughter, but with Isaac's impending conviction, it was something she'd have to get used to. Working full time and juggling a seven-year-old would have its challenges, but it didn't compare to when Lyssa was only two and Isaac was nowhere to be found. The stress of the unknown, the busy schedule, and the unpredictable work calls were the biggest challenge.

Cora's parents were ever supportive and her best friend Hadley had taken Lyssa more than once. It helped that she had Danny. A built-in playmate, or so Cora's mom used to joke. That was the curse of an only child, no siblings to distract them.

She worried about Ryan and his return to Toronto. What would it mean for their relationship to end up five hours apart? Long-distance was hard in an uncomplicated relationship, but for them, the barriers that would keep them separated would probably prove too difficult to overcome.

Hadley had scolded Cora for being so negative, encouraging her to live in the moment with him and enjoy the time they spent together. For Cora, it was different. Their relationship had been built around the mysteries of this case and the fallout of the drug. She didn't know how they would be with one another when there wasn't a shared investment. Maybe it wasn't meant to be.

"Hey." Ryan's gentle voice came from behind her, pulling her from her doomed thoughts.

Cora's looked over her shoulder at him. "Hey." She gave him a small smile, which he returned. The genuine warmth in his gaze made her doubt melt away. Whatever the two of them had, it was something she'd fight for. She'd never met anyone who made her feel as stable and heard as Ryan did.

He settled on to the bench next to her. "You okay?"

"I am now." She rested her head on his shoulder and continued to watch Lyssa dash around the playground.

"Why did you want to meet here?" Ryan asked, glancing around like he expected something to pop out of the surrounding bushes.

Cora lifted her head and nodded towards the playing children. "I think it's time for you to meet someone rather important to me."

"Lyssa?" Ryan asked, following Cora's gaze to the little girl with long, dark hair and bright pink leggings.

"Yeah." Cora stood and took Ryan's hand. "Lyssa, baby, come here please."

The little girl's head turned in the direction of her mother. Then she bounded across the sandy playground.

"Yes, Mommy?"

Cora released her hold on Ryan's hand and placed a hand on her daughter's shoulder. "I wanted you to meet someone special. Lyssa, this is Ryan."

Lyssa blinked up at him, surveying him as if trying to decide what was so special about him.

Ryan smiled warmly and bent down to Lyssa's level. "Hi Lyssa, it's nice to meet you." He offered her his hand and the girl eyed it for a moment before slipping her hand into his.

"Hi," she said, though so softly that Cora could tell her daughter was uncertain.

"Ryan's a good friend of mine," Cora explained. "He's been working with me for a few weeks now."

"With Daddy?"

Cora nodded. "Yes, Ryan helped us figure out what was wrong with your dad. Ryan made sure your dad got help, to get better."

Ryan seemed to grimace at the suggestion, but it disappeared so quickly, Cora wasn't sure what she'd seen.

"Your daddy is very brave," Ryan explained, looking directly at Lyssa as he said it. "We are making sure he gets the best help possible, so that he can come back and spend time with you again. You are the most important thing to your daddy."

Lyssa didn't respond, but she nodded, which Cora knew meant she heard but wanted to get back to playing.

"Okay, Lyssa," Cora said. "You can go back to your friends. Maybe we can have Ryan over for dinner one night."

"Okay, Mommy," Lyssa said. "Nice to meet you." Then she turned and dashed back to the playground.

"She's sweet," Ryan said, straightening and reaching for Cora. "She looks just like her mother."

Cora offered a half smile, because while Lyssa was a spitting image of her, she had Isaac's eyes. That defining feature made it impossible to forget the father who, though absent, loved his daughter beyond measure.

"Thank you for trusting me," Ryan said. He leaned closer to Cora and planted a gentle kiss on her temple. "I know how important she is to you and what this meeting means."

Cora nodded and lowered herself back to the bench. "We haven't really talked about it."

He sat down beside her.

"What this all really means," Cora continued. "You're heading back to Toronto soon. Then what?"

"I get it," Ryan said. "This isn't what I expected to happen when I came to Ottawa for a consult. I didn't know who I would meet." He turned towards her. "I know long-distance is hard, but I'm not ready to let you go. If you want to try. I want to."

Cora thought for a moment. "There will be a lot of challenges."

"Has Lyssa ever been to Toronto?" Ryan asked with a smile.

She shook her head.

"I think she might like the change." Ryan looked toward the playground, where Lyssa was gathering the kids and beginning a game of tag. "There's the CN Tower, the aquarium. I bet we could even take off to Niagara Falls one day."

Cora smiled at the idea of playing tourist with her daughter and Ryan. The image was appealing. Their own little family. Every family had complications they handled, so why couldn't theirs?

"I think she would like that," Cora said. "I think we both would."

Ryan smiled and leaned in, giving Cora a gentle kiss. When he pulled away, he leaned back on the bench and draped his arm over her shoulder. Cora watched him for a moment, admiring the easy grin on his face. He truly seemed at peace.

"How are you, after everything?" Cora asked.

Ryan released a long breath. "Totally honest?"

Cora nodded.

"It's been hard. We found a cabin in the woods, close to where the tunnel in Alison's house let out and it's clear she and possibly Blaine, were living there for a time." Ryan shook his head. "I don't know how we missed it the first time. I guess we never expected her to venture that way. If it wasn't for the phone number from Vivian Parsons, we may have never even thought to look there."

"Any idea where they could have gone?" Cora asked.

Ryan shook his head. "No, not a trace. And no reports of gunshot wounds being treated at the hospital, though from the looks of it, Blaine was treated at the cabin. We found traces of his blood. Their DNA was all over the place. The elderly woman who owns it has nothing of use. She claims she didn't even know they were wanted."

"Someone must be able to tell you where they went," Cora said. "Traffic cameras, anything."

"We're trying. But I'm not getting my hopes up."

Cora reached over and placed her hand on Ryan's leg. "You'll find him."

"The craziest thing at this point is that I'm almost willing to just let him go." Ryan shook his head as if he couldn't believe what he was saying. "Sure, he aided and abetted a crime and harboured fugitives, but with everything coming to the surface about Solydexran and the drug trials, those crimes seem insignificant now."

"But the law is the law," Cora said. "Even for a minor crime, he has to be charged and properly tried."

"Of course," Ryan agreed. "But I'm beginning to care less and less about that now."

She didn't comment, surprised that he'd so willingly brush off his obligation as an officer of the law.

"All I want now is to know the whole truth." Ryan stared off into the distance. "What really happened with Alison, Blaine, and Calvin? How did Blaine remain under the radar so long and what happened to cause this whole drug scenario to spiral out of control?"

Again, Cora didn't answer. The relationship between the three mysterious siblings was beyond anything she understood. There was a mystery to them and their past and no real way to discover the truth. Before the foster care, there was no record of Alison or Calvin, and Blaine being on his own was an enigma. The farm where Ryan had found the girls, had come up a dead end. Patsy had claimed it belonged to Blaine's father. It was now in Blaine Roche's name, but finding any additional details on him was difficult. The last name he bore belonged to a family without children. Had he stolen the farm? Had they taken him in? Only Blaine could share the whole story.

"Maybe I'll be able to track him down and get him in a room," Ryan said. "But until then, I think I have to let the case die."

Cora gave his leg another gentle squeeze.

"I just hope that one day, I'll learn the real story that got this family so tied up in a drug conspiracy." Ryan offered her a small smile.

"I think you'll be lucky," Cora said. "You never know. Besides, one day Blaine may want to tell his story and who better to share it with than the man who helped bring all the troubles to light?"

Ryan chuckled. "You mean the one who's trying to arrest him."

"It's more than that," Cora said. "You always just wanted to help."

Ryan hummed his response but didn't answer. He was hard on himself, but Cora knew the truth. Ryan wanted Blaine not only to answer for the disappearance and the crimes he'd committed, but also to better understand the circumstances that had gotten him where he was.

One day, Cora hoped, Ryan would get his answers.

Acknowledgments

What do you say about your third book? That there are too many people to thank. I swear with each book, the list grows longer and longer.

When Alex first asked me to keep writing *Wicked* because Rising Action was interested in signing *Twisted*, I wasn't sure where to go. While I knew how I wanted *Wicked* to end, I had only written the beginning and still had a huge story to tell. So, THANK YOU.

To Alex and Tina, you are a shining light that takes my stories from the darkest drawer I shove them into and spin my words into gold. Without your guidance, insight, expertise and dedication, my career and writing wouldn't be where it is today. Here's to the years to come and the words to flow.

To Dylan for his detailed copyedits and ability to pull exactly what I'm trying to say out of some of my wordier paragraphs.

To the fabulous Nat Mack, for another amazing cover that will wow the masses, especially when pictured next to its predecessor, *Twisted*. Watch out Bookstagram!

To my dear friend Tash, for all her expertise in the police world and fielding my endless questions about procedure and process. I'm so grateful someone I love went through that rigorous training, so I don't have to

To Rebecca Hodge for talking me through some of my early drafts and providing the expertise to properly understand the ins and outs of drug development.

To Brooke Dorsch for being my favourite Beta Reader and always willing to check out my next draft. I'm so glad we found one another in this wild writing world.

To my writing friends, you are plentiful and you know who you are, but in particular, Denise, Kristen, Jess, Sam, Kathy, Brianne, Arden, Marie, Dave, Patricia, Kelly, Bianca, Jenell, Nicole, Gloria, Sayword, Barb, Lynn, Beth, Sarah, Sarah, Sandy, Renita, Julia, Tara, Stuart, TC, Lydia, Eden, Suz, Jessica, and so many more. You each keep my writing alive with your endless support, love and passion. Your willingness to discuss books, to read pages and to just enjoy each other's bookish company is something I will never forget.

I'd be nowhere without my author groups. The Ladies of the Sexy Train. The Toronto Area Women Writers and the Hot Authors of Summer. And a special thanks to my newest crew, The Eleventh Chapter: Jen, Jenn, Kerry, Caitlin, Tanya, Colleen, and Sharon. I love the community we've built and can't wait to see where we go!

To the online Bookstagram Community and the Bookstagrammers of Toronto/Ontario area, you guys are a light in the bookish world, making our events too fun and our writing worthwhile. This is one of the most supportive communities I have been so blessed to be a part of and will continue to follow and keep up with each of your posts (even if my TBR hates me for it.)

To my sisters, who are always behind me no matter what, I've always loved been the littlest of us.

To my parents. You are literally the most wonderful people to ever exist and to think that I am even half of either of you is something I will forever be grateful for.

To my Collingwood Book Club and friends, thank you for always picking my book as one of our monthly reads and supporting me at the (hopefully!) annual book launches.

To my forever besties, no words are ever enough to describe my love for you.

To my partner, your patience and enthusiam about a world that is so beyond your scope is never under appreciated. I know I wouldn't be where I am today without your constant support and encouragement.

And last but most definitely not least, to all my wonderful readers. I am so grateful you continue to pick up my work and enjoy my stories. I was so excited to bring Blaine's story to you and share another side of Twisted. Thank you for sticking with me. I hope you enjoy the books I have on the horizon, and who knows... maybe Ryan and Blaine's story isn't quite over!

About the Author

Maggie Giles is a Canadian author who writes suspenseful women's fiction and thrillers. Her debut novel, *The Things We Lost*, was named a 2023 distinguished favourite in Women's Fiction by the Independent Press Awards. She is a member of the International Thriller Writers and currently works in marketing. Maggie dove into writing a novel head first despite having aphantasia, a condition where one lacks a visual imagination. She lives in Ontario with her mastiff-mix, Jolene, and spends most of her days enjoying the outdoors, from swimming to hiking to skiing in the winter.

Looking for more suspense? Check out Rising Action's other thrillers on the next page!

And don't forget to follow us on our socials for cover reveals, giveaways, and announcements:
X: @RAPubCollective
Instagram: @risingactionpublishingco
TikTok: @risingactionpublishingco
Website: http://www.risingactionpublishingco.com

RISING ACTION

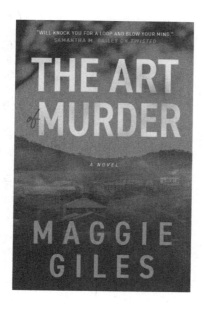

THE ART of MURDER

A NOVEL

MAGGIE GILES

In the tranquil town of Cedar Plains, where safety and community are sacred, Courtney Faith's ideal life is upended by a body found on a local farm, shattering her peaceful existence. Her friend, Alexa Huston, intimately familiar with chaos, gets entangled in an accidental murder that escalates her spiraling life into deeper darkness. Alexa wrestles with a disturbing question: Is murder justifiable if it targets the deserving?

As bodies accumulate, the local police scramble for answers. Torn between loyalty and justice, Courtney discovers evidence linking Alexa to the crimes. Their friendship frays as Courtney grapples with a dire choice: expose Alexa and risk her own darkest secret, or protect a friend and possibly destroy everything she cherishes.

Caught in a deadly dance of secrets and lies, Courtney must decide whether to confront the monster behind a familiar face or let their secrets stay hidden, buried within the town's heart. Their darkest deeds are cloaked in silence, and no one truly knows anything.

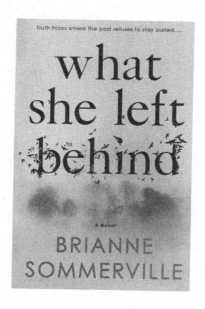

Truth hides where the past refuses to stay buried....

what she left behind

A Novel

BRIANNE SOMMERVILLE

Recently fired and adrift, Charlotte Boyd agrees to oversee renovations on her parents' small-town summer home that holds a tragic past. After discovering an enthralling diary hidden amidst junk the previous owners left behind, Charlotte connects with the author—a troubled teen named Lark Peters who died by suicide at the house sixteen years ago.

When an unsettling incident forces Charlotte to seek refuge at the local pub, regulars, including the police, warn her of Lark's older brother, Darryl, who has become a recluse since Lark's death, and may know more than he's letting on. But Charlotte sees a side of Darryl others don't, being an outsider herself.

In a search to uncover the truth, Charlotte must question those closest to Lark and reconcile her own past trauma. Because if Lark was actually murdered, then whoever is responsible might be lurking in Charlotte's own backyard.

No one was supposed to know. I've always been so careful. My Darlings, how did
we get here?

Evil lurks behind the perfectly manicured lawns, ornate iron gates, and long wind-
ing driveways of affluent DC–but not for long.

Stay-at-home mom Eloise Williams is PTO president and a respected local phil-
anthropist who sits on the boards of many distinguished charities. In addition to
being a doting wife and mother, she is also a serial killer.

But Eloise isn't the only lady of society playing a part. As the hidden lives of Eloise's
inner circle are exposed, the body count rises. When stalker becomes prey, Eloise
desperately clings to control.

Money and power can only buy influence and safety for so long. Eventually, the
curtains lift, exposing the chilling reality hiding in plain sight.

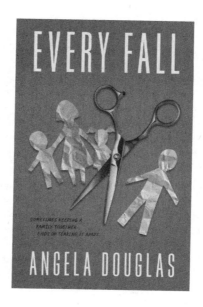

EVERY FALL

SOMETIMES KEEPING A
FAMILY TOGETHER
ENDS UP TEARING IT APART.

ANGELA DOUGLAS

Bree knew that life married to a beat cop would be tough, especially in the crime-infested city of East Bernheim, but she believes they will be fine living in "the Burner" even after she has their first child. Family life is manageable until one day crime follows them home, threatening their safety.

At a loss of how to keep his family safe and keep his job, Jake agrees to stretch their finances and move an hour away, to a bigger house in a somewhat better neighborhood. Their life seems to improve until Bree, heavily pregnant with their second child, begins to hear voices and suffer strange dreams. And then when tragedy strikes on the job, Jake enters a spiral of guilt and grief that degrades his grip on reality.

Bree, isolated and struggling, must protect her children from the one person she thought would always keep them safe. She and Jake are haunted in every way, and not just by whatever is lurking inside the house. A thriller that tackles toxic masculinity in police culture and trauma, Every Fall will have you on the edge of your seat.

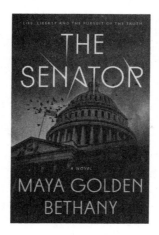

US Senator Oliver Michaels of Maine campaigned on the hopes of changing Washington. One year after becoming the youngest senator in Congress, Oliver finds himself disheartened by systemic bureaucracy, partisan finger-pointing, the power of lobbyists, and the collapse of his marriage.

When New York Times reporter Alex Broussard shows up at his office, Oliver is presented with a shocking corruption scheme involving two congressmen, the head of the Environmental Protection Agency, and a chemical manufacturer. With this real opportunity to clean up dirty DC politics, Alex reignites Oliver's pledge to help people lost in messy legislative battles and abandoned by government in sacrifice zones. Yet, lofty political aspirations aren't the only things burning with passion. Working side by side, Alex and Oliver, once an item in college, realize feelings still linger for one another.

Alex and Oliver's efforts to expose the unlawful plot also uncovers the fact that they are pawns in a rigged game hosted by those who will do anything to keep their positions of power and their wallets padded - even kill. The stakes continuously rise, putting Alex, Oliver, and their family and friends in grave danger. Each must decide what's more important; the safety of their loved ones or the health of the public.